CW00554023

The Taste of Proof

Also by Bill Knox

THE TASTE OF PROOF

Bill Knox

Constable · London

First published in Great Britain 1965
Copyright © 1965 Bill Knox
This edition published in Great Britain 1999
by Constable & Company Ltd, 3 The Lanchesters,
162 Fulham Palace Road, London W6 9ER
The right of Bill Knox to be identified
as the author of this work has been
asserted by him in accordance with
the Copyright, Designs and Patents Act 1988

ISBN 0 094 79920 2

Printed and bound in Great Britain by
MPG Books Ltd, Bodmin, Cornwall

A CIP catalogue record for this book
is available from the British Library

For Bill Munns
An expert witness

1

THE interview room was on the ground floor of Barlinnie Prison's C Hall, the untried prisoners' wing. It was a small, bare room where the harsh scent of disinfectant clashed sharply with the stale odours built up over the prison's long years of use.

Detective Chief Inspector Colin Thane, head of Glasgow's Millside Division C.I.D., stood over by the window and watched a work party of prisoners stroll unhurriedly across the courtyard outside, one of them pushing a handcart. He glanced at his watch as the procession passed round the corner of the block. He'd come to Barlinnie, that grey, antiquated, fortress-like jail on the outskirts of the city, to talk to two Millside prisoners whose cases and backgrounds were poles apart.

The first had just left to return to his cell—a chain store sales manager used to the expense account life and now waiting trial for fraud and embezzlement. A week in C Hall, where untried sheep were segregated from the convicted goats, had aged and broken the man almost beyond recognition.

Thane shrugged aside a flash of pity. The next interview, at any rate, would be on different terms. Frank Humbie, five previous convictions, remanded in custody for further inquiry, could be relied upon to move as easily through the Barlinnie routine as another man would have negotiated the hazards of a holiday camp.

Humbie had made a formal sixty-second appearance before the Sheriff Court that morning. The charge had been 'having on June fourth, along with a person or persons unknown, broken into premises occupied by the Glen Ault Whisky Liqueur Company Ltd., at 392 Wood Street, Millside, forced open a lock-fast safe, and stolen therefrom three thousand pounds belonging to the said Company'.

7

The Millside night-shift team had enough evidence to convict Humbie twice over—but there were other reasons why Thane had decided to see him.

The interview room door opened, and he turned.

'Humbie, sir.' The prison officer waited expectantly as the man in the buff corduroy garb of an untried prisoner moved past him into the room.

'I'll give you a shout when I'm ready,' nodded Thane. He waited until the prison officer had gone out, closing the door. Then he gave Humbie a brief nod of recognition. 'Sit down, Frank.'

The man took the chair on the far side of the table, accepted the cigarette Thane offered, and lit it with one of his own matches. 'Thanks.' He relaxed a little. 'Well, it's been a few years since I saw you, Mr Thane.'

'Nearly four,' agreed Thane. The last time Humbie had drawn eighteen months for theft and assault. 'I was beginning to think you'd learned some sense.'

'Me?' Humbie was a small, bulky man. His age, according to the C.R.O. file, was forty-six. He had receding fair hair, broad, blunt hands and a plump, small-eyed face. When he smiled, the face assumed a cynical twist. 'I haven't admitted doin' anything yet.'

Thane read the signs, sighed, helped himself to a cigarette, and stood silent for a moment. A flicker of impatience crossed his face. He'd been planning to finish work in time to join the rest of the Millside Division golf team for a meal before the half-yearly challenge match against the Headquarters select. But now it looked as though Humbie was going to be stubborn.

'All right.' He drew out the other chair and sat opposite the man. 'Frank, you've grown careless. With a record like yours, robbing your employers is just damn' stupid.'

The facts were comparatively simple. At one o'clock that Thursday morning, with the rain a gentle drizzle, a beat constable patrolling Wood Street had seen a car drive past him. There were two men aboard, and cars were rare in that backstreet area after midnight. Trained reaction made him note the car's registration number and then go on, expecting trouble. Minutes later he spotted an opened window on the middle floor of the Glen Ault company's three-storey office block. Next door, at the firm's blending ware-

8

house, the night watchman knew nothing. But the beat man checked by telephone with the duty officer at Millside Division, was told the car he'd seen had been reported stolen earlier that night . . . and the next stage was smooth routine.

The night-shift C.I.D. team who checked the office block found the back ripped from the Glen Ault safe. The Scientific team who arrived a little later refused to be surprised that the jemmy marks on the wooden frame of the 'forced' window didn't quite coincide with the same jemmy's marks on the outside sill. The safe, an old model, had been opened by using a drill to bore through the weak sheet metal at the rear then tearing it open by sheer brute force leverage. There were no fingerprints on the safe—they'd hardly expected any. But they cast further around. Most neds got careless once they'd finished a job. . . .

A small cupboard in the same room, the managing director's office, had been forced open. Inside were bottles and glasses, and an opened, part-used bottle of whisky sat on the floor nearby. The bottle had been wiped clean, but the bottle cap, tossed into a wastepaper basket, bore a clear thumb- and fingerprint. At Headquarters, the Fingerprint Bureau shuffled through their filing system, made a fast match, and produced Frank Humbie's card.

While they worked, the stolen car was found abandoned in the Northern Division. The steering wheel and controls had been wiped clean. So had the forced and empty cashbox lying on the front seat. But there was a pen-knife halfway down the back of the seat, the broken tip of its main blade matching the forcing mark beside the cashbox lock. The knife's grip was in black horn, with a little silver insert bearing the initials 'D.D.'.

'Douglas Dalziel,' mused Thane. 'You know him, don't you?'

'Young Dougie—the clerk in the main office?' Frank Humbie gave a cautious nod. 'He lives not far from me. Why?'

'He didn't show up for work this morning. He wasn't home at all last night.' Thane's fingers rapped a brief, impatient tattoo on the table. 'Let's save time, Frank. You drive a van for the Glen Ault company. Last night you were almost two hours late on your last delivery run—so

9

late that the night watchman was the only one still around to let you into the warehouse parking lot.'

'The van broke down,' grunted Humbie. 'Can I help it if the feed pump seized? It took time to fix.'

'So you said,' snapped Thane. 'The pump and fuel lines are covered in road dirt, haven't been touched for weeks. No, you had somebody hidden aboard the van when you drove into the warehouse yard last night, somebody who had a key to the door that leads from the yard into the office block. He got there, then once it was dark he opened that window and helped you in from the street.'

Frank Humbie gave a cheerful, almost insolent grin. 'You make it sound convincin' enough. Only thing is, I've got a wife who'll swear I was at home from before eleven last night.'

'She usually does,' agreed Thane comfortably. 'No, I'm not worried on your account—the fingerprint evidence is enough on its own. But I want Dalziel, I want that money recovered, and the sooner the better.'

'Want me to wish you luck?' queried Humbie.

'Always the funny man, eh?' Thane shrugged. 'Well, you made a botch of last night's job. But you got the best part of three thousand pounds from the safe, and I don't like neds pulling things like that—not in my division.' He rubbed one thumb thoughtfully across his chin. 'Still, the only cash my lads found at your place was the housekeeping money. That means either the stuff is well hidden or Dalziel has it.'

'Better find Dalziel and ask him, then.' Humbie avoided the Millside detective's gaze and concentrated on the room's bare, whitewashed ceiling.

'We're planning to do that.' Thane gave a suspicion of a smile and delicately trailed his bait. 'A pity, isn't it, the way Dalziel hopped off?' He gave a frown of mocking anxiety. 'I don't blame you, Frank. It probably seemed a good idea having him keep the cash until later. He hasn't a record—he wasn't liable to go straight on the suspect list, especially if your little trick with the window had come off. Chances are he only decided to bolt when he realized he'd left the knife behind. No'—he shook his head—'surely he couldn't have planned this disappearing act in advance. But it's your hard luck, Frank. He gets three thousand in

10

spending money—and you get landed with a possible three to five years inside.'

'Except if I helped you it might be different?' Humbie's fat face twisted. 'I'll take my chance. Write it down if you want—"nothing to say".' He scraped back his chair and shuffled to his feet, carefully nipping the half-smoked cigarette and stowing it in a pocket. 'Finished?'

'For now.'

Frank Humbie thumped on the door. It opened, he gave a quick, sardonic salute, and went out.

·   ·   ·   ·   ·

Detective Inspector Phil Moss, Thane's second-in-command, was having a hard day. In itself, that was nothing unusual. Phil Moss sometimes wondered if he'd been destined by nature to act as an unwilling whetting stone for other people's indignation. His stomach rumbled, and he frowned across his desk in the main Millside C.I.D. office.

'Frank's been remanded by the court, Mrs Humbie. Even if I wanted I couldn't change the fact.'

'Then where's your boss? Where's Mr Thane?' Jean Humbie, a thin, belligerent redhead in her late thirties, sat stiffly on the chair opposite and gripped tight on the handbag in her lap. Her neat but dated navy-blue suit was the best item in her wardrobe. The pert white hat perched on her head had been bought at a Sauchiehall Street store's Summer Bargain sale the previous week. She was angry, and she didn't bother to hide it.

'Chief Inspector Thane is out.' Moss eyed her warily, conscious of the barely suppressed grins coming his way from the two duty detective constables at the far end of the room. 'But he'd say the same—we've a case against your husband and the rest is for the courts to decide.'

'A case!' She brushed the fact aside. 'Frank hasn't been in any kind of trouble for years. He promised he'd pack in that sort of nonsense after the last time—I told him he had to, or we were finished. I couldn't take any more. And he's done it . . . a steady job, steady wages coming in. He's been with this Glen Ault place for more than a year now.'

'And before that?'

'Well, it—it's difficult for a man like Frank at first.

11

Plenty of casual work, but the steady jobs are hard to find at his age.' She bit her lip. 'Look, you say this car drove away from the Glen Ault office about one this morning, don't you?'

'That's when the constable saw it.'

Her head came up. 'Frank was home half an hour before then. I can vouch for it.'

'He was home at twelve-thirty?' Moss gave a weak smile. 'When Detective Sergeant MacLeod arrested him this morning you said Frank had been home since about eleven last night. You'd better make up your mind, Mrs Humbie.'

She flushed. 'Well—all right, I was lying. I thought—I thought maybe Frank really had done something. I'm his wife, and——'

'And wives usually try to protect their menfolk,' Moss finished for her.

'Wouldn't your wife?'

He shook his head. 'I'm not married.'

'I see.' She didn't seem to find the fact surprising. 'But this is the honest truth. Frank came home at twelve-thirty, half an hour before he's supposed to have been driving away from that robbery. Doesn't that make a difference?'

Moss picked up a pencil and doodled awkwardly on the corner of his desk-pad. 'Anyone else in the house at the time—anyone who could back this up?'

She gave a slow, reluctant shake of her head.

'We know Frank didn't get back to the warehouse from his last delivery run until about eight last night. Did he come home after that for a meal?'

'No. He always goes straight to the Newton dog racing on a Wednesday night.'

'The Newton track closes before ten,' reminded Moss.

'Let me finish.' She didn't like the interruption. 'That's half the trouble today, the way folk are never allowed to finish what they're saying. When Frank came in he said he'd won a couple of pounds betting on some dog, and then he met up by accident with a lad he knew. They had a few drinks somewhere and with the money he won it became a few drinks too many.' Jean Humbie gave a faint, twitching smile. 'Frank knows I don't like to see him that way, so he walked most of the way home to sober up a bit.'

'Did he say who he met?'

She nodded. 'A lad called Dalziel. He works in the Glen Ault office.'

Moss cleared his throat. 'We've heard of him already, Mrs Humbie.'

'Then you'll ask him about Frank?'

'We're already looking for Dalziel.' Moss laid the pencil down. 'Nobody's seen him since last night. I'm sorry.'

'I see.' She paled, and her fingers gripped tighter on the handbag. Then, half-hopefully, she suggested, 'Maybe it was this lad Dalziel and somebody else, and they just made things look like Frank did it.' She read the expression on his face. 'But my Frank's got a record, hasn't he?'

'That's not what matters——'

'Isn't it?' She cut him short. 'Frank didn't do it. I'll show you—I'll come back here and prove it.'

'How?' Moss spread his hands appealingly. 'Mrs Humbie, you don't know all the facts——'

'I know Frank.' She got up from the chair, something close to hatred in her eyes. Then she had turned and was sweeping out of the office.

Phil Moss watched her go. As the office door slammed shut behind her he heard a chuckle from the other end of the room. He swung round on the two d.c.s.

'What's wrong? Nothing to do?'

'Eh, well . . .' the nearer of the men swallowed awkwardly.

'Then get on with it.' He scowled at their suddenly bent heads for a moment, then opened the top drawer of his desk, rummaged among the selection of pillboxes inside, and chose a white, lozenge-shaped tablet from one of the largest.

The last peppermint-flavoured fragments of the aluminium glycinate soother were dissolving in his mouth when the main door swung open again. He glanced up and brightened a little.

'Cutting it pretty neat for time, Colin, aren't you?'

'I'm lucky to make the game at all.' Thane gave the two d.c.s. a cheerful nod in passing, raised an eyebrow at Moss's appearance, and grinned. 'Come on through, Phil. Let's hear about it, whatever it is.'

Moss followed him to the Chief Inspector's room, a small, sparsely furnished office with a window which

13

looked out over the tenement buildings of the older part of Millside Division and the crane-spangled skyline of Glasgow's dockland.

'Close the door, Phil.' Thane tossed his grey soft hat on the coat-stand in one corner and headed for the cupboard-like private washroom which, with a camp bed and the worn leather chair behind his desk, represented the status symbols of a divisional C.I.D. chief. 'I'll get ready while we talk.'

Moss obeyed, while water began to splash into the hand-basin. 'How'd you get on at Barlinnie?'

'So-so.' Thane had his jacket and tie off, and began rolling up his shirt-sleeves. 'I saw Kinhorn, your fraud and embezzlement. He says you're right. The extra cheques in that last book weren't used. He burned them.'

'Fine.' Moss crossed over to the window and looked out. 'What about Humbie?'

'Our Frank?' Thane's muffled voice held a chuckle. 'Sometimes I wish we were like the army and could charge a man with dumb insolence. He's saying nothing—but I tried the line about young Dalziel taking off with the proceeds, and he didn't like it.' The splashing increased. 'Give him another couple of days mouldering in C Hall with nothing to do but think about it and he'll start talking.'

'Mrs Humbie was here.'

'Oh?' The splashing stopped for a moment. 'What did she have to say about it?'

'Plenty.' Moss compressed the interview into a short, clipped, hundred-word recital.

'What did you make of it?' asked Thane above the noise of the washbasin draining.

'Just the usual. She's tried hard enough in the past to keep him out of jail.'

'Not that—I meant about Humbie mentioning he'd been with young Dalziel.'

'The first stage in cooking up a stand-by alibi,' suggested Moss with a dry laugh. 'Clumsy, but maybe they were hoping that making it look as though the window'd been forced would leave us thinking it was an outside job.'

'Could be. Frank Humbie's never been the brightest of characters. Did anyone at Glen Ault identify that whisky bottle?'

14

'Bottle and cap,' agreed Moss. 'Seems the managing director's been noticing evaporation from his private stock —somebody having the odd nip when he wasn't around. He kept a level mark on the bottle, and his initials were scratched on the cap.'

'What about the night watchman, Phil?'

'We checked him out first go. He's a harmless old fellow. Hardly knows what year it is, but as honest as they come. You know the type—all he wants out of life now is a little money for beer and 'baccy.'

'Then that's it.' Colin Thane came back into the room. He'd changed from his workaday grey suit to fawn slacks and a heavyweight tartan shirt. He pulled on a hairy, shapeless brown tweed sports jacket and patted the pockets. 'Got a cigarette handy?'

'Uh-huh.' Moss obliged from a battered pack and shared a light with him. 'Well, we still need Dalziel.'

'Dalziel—and the money.'

To be both friends and a highly effective team they were an oddly contrasting pair. Thane was the younger man. Married, with two children and a home in a bungalow suburb, he was in his early forties, just over the six-foot mark and dark-haired with a cheerfully rugged face and a powerful build. He carried his weight—now a few pounds over what it used to be—with the supple ease of a one-time athlete. Moss, on the other hand, looked more like a book-burdened bank clerk than a policeman. He was a small, grey man, wiry, thin-faced, his exact age hidden in the Headquarters files but probably in his mid-fifties. His juniors swore he must have bribed his way past the minimum height specification at his entrance medical. His outlook on life depended much on the daily reckoning of his state of health—and his stomach ulcer, guarded with an unshakable, almost hypochondriacal, devotion against any suggestion of surgery, had become a cherished legend in every division in the city.

'I had a bottle of that Glen Ault stuff once,' mused Thane. 'Got it as a Christmas present. Mary liked it—most of the liqueurs are too sweet for her taste. But the Glen Ault liqueur's different, drier.' He chuckled, remembering that the bottle was to have been the base for a lampshade

15

until he dropped and broke it. 'Still, it's an expensive drink, even by the thimbleful.'

'I've tried it,' grunted Moss. 'Nearly burned a hole in me.'

Thane gave a nod of appropriate sympathy. There were times when Phil Moss, with his sparse, sandy hair, his baggy suits and crumpled collars, could be a trial. But the same Moss could plod and sift and absorb the detail of a job until he was satisfied—and then go out and hold his own in the dirtiest of back-street battles.

Against that, Thane was a thruster—a thruster with a predilection for backing a hunch. He forcibly disciplined himself to tolerate the need for refinements, he would rely to the limit on every scientific aid he could find, but when circumstances dictated he would willingly act first and sweat out the result later. Phil Moss maintained the balance—and when opinions clashed that dry reproachful face could often make Thane curse, think again, and take a less explosive course.

Still, the Glen Ault robbery was little different from a thousand others. . . . Thane crossed to his filing cabinet, opened the bottom drawer and took out the box of half a dozen golf balls he'd bought first thing that morning.

'How much have we got on Dalziel, Phil?'

Moss ruminated over a puff of smoke. 'He's twenty-six, he's been six months with the Glen Ault company as an invoice clerk, and he rents a room with a family over in Shannon Street—you know, over in the Fortrose scheme.'

Thane nodded. The Fortrose development, the latest of Glasgow's vast city-owned rehousing areas, had already added some ten thousand people to the population of Millside Division. Before it was finished the figure would be nearer twenty thousand. 'What about background?'

'His folks live up Aberdeen way—I've teleprinted the county force to keep an eye open in case he turns up there. The local station says he was pretty wild as a teenager, then settled down. His family are solid enough—want me to find out more?'

'There's no rush.' Douglas Dalziel was already a name and a description being circulated to every force. 'Still, we could use a photograph.'

'We've found one,' said Moss. 'I put a plain-clothes man

16

on the job this afternoon. He got it from one of the girls in the Glen Ault office—Dalziel dated her a couple of times. It's strictly a holiday snapshot, but Headquarters are blowing it up.'

'Fine.' Thane glanced at his watch. 'Well, I'd better get moving. Haven't changed your mind about coming along?'

'To trudge round some grass watching a bunch of alleged adults trying to hit a wee ball with a stick?' Moss found the notion ridiculous. 'I've more sense. Anyway, I knew a fellow once . . . collapsed and died on the last green. Too much for him.'

'Did he miss his putt?' Thane felt tempted to launch into the other old one, about the golfer who stopped in mid-swing to raise his cap as his wife's funeral drove past. But—no, Phil wouldn't have appreciated it.

. . . . .

With eight players to a side, opponents drawn from a hat, the Headquarters versus Millside match was always something of a needle vendetta. Depending on outlook, it was a chance to show the chair-borne Headquarters mob where they got off or a further opportunity to show the peasants in the Divisions how brain can beat brawn.

The match had been arranged over the Highrigg course, there was a small but noisy support group for both factions, and it was Thane's doubly bad luck that he was last off the tee and that his opponent was Headquarters' latest discovery—a twenty-year-old probationary constable who casually admitted he'd made the West of Scotland amateur semi-finals two years back.

By the turn, Thane was three down, had lost one of his new balls, most of his temper, and any shred of appreciation for the diabolically contrived ingenuity of the Highrigg bunkers. Having an opponent who called him 'sir' and treated him with all the respectful deference due to a maiden aunt didn't improve matters. Another lost ball, hooked wildly into a small wood at the fourteenth, signalled the end. Beaten five and four, he treated it as a merciful relief and retired to the clubhouse where the Headquarters team had already begun celebrating.

'A ruddy massacre.' Inspector Campbell of the Millside

uniformed branch, heavily disguised in antique plus-fours, gave him a gloomy nod as he entered the lounge. 'Henderson and Wilson won their games, Barland halved his. The rest . . .' he shrugged. 'What are you for, Colin?'

Thane ran his eye along the bar's well-stocked shelves, considered his thirst, and settled for a special-brew lager. Over by the door, Chief Superintendent William 'Bhudda' Ilford, head of the city's C.I.D., a massive, red-faced figure, was chairing his side's celebrations. The noise and tobacco smoke in the room were growing proportionately. Thane gave a rueful wave towards Ilford, then picked up his drink and began to talk to Campbell, a quiet man whose life was mainly bound up with duty rosters and a mystic cult named divisional statistics.

He'd decided it was time to leave for home and had just refused Campbell's offer of a refill when he heard his name shouted and saw the white-coated barman coming towards him.

'There's an Inspector Moss on the 'phone, sir—he says it's urgent.'

Thane swallowed the dregs in his glass and followed the man back to the bar counter, conscious of the professional curiosity around him. The buzz of conversation died down as he lifted the receiver.

'Well, Phil?'

Moss's voice came over low and earnest. 'Trouble, Colin. Better forget whatever you're doing.'

'Where are you?' Thane half-turned his head. Bhudda Ilford was standing inches from his side, one eyebrow raised in interrogation.

'At Frank Humbie's place. His wife's dead. A relative found her about half an hour back. I've just arrived.'

'Dead? What happened?' Thane could sense the now complete hush around him. He eased the receiver from his ear to allow Ilford to eavesdrop.

'Hard to tell, but it looks like suffocation. And the house has been turned upside down. I've got the Forensic mob on their way, and Doc Williams should be here any moment. The address is 160 Gradient Terrace. Have you got transport?'

'Yes. Hold on.' Thane grabbed the pencil Ilford slid in front of him and scribbled on the face of a handy beermat.

18

'Right, Phil, it'll take me—oh, fifteen minutes. Keep things warming till I arrive.' He hung up, his face grim, and turned to face Ilford. 'Jean Humbie, sir—the wife of the ex-con we picked up for last night's safebreaking.'

'You put out a "detain and hold" for his partner. Name of . . . Dalziel, wasn't it?' The fat, red-faced, almost comical figure was suddenly grimly official, his mind dredging through the small mountain of divisional reports he'd read that day. 'And you were still looking for the money.'

Thane nodded.

'Right.' Ilford swept his gaze towards the clustered golfers. 'Party's over, lads. Dan——'

Superintendent Dan Laurence, head of the Forensic Branch, an untidy, white-haired figure in a loose double-knit wool sweater, put down his glass and took a step forward.

'Your mob are on their way, Dan.'

'Then I'd better go and keep an eye on them,' rumbled Laurence.

'Need anyone else?' asked Ilford.

'Not till I find out more.' Thane checked his cigarettes, beckoned the barman, and slapped some loose change on the counter for the two fresh packs he received.

'You'll keep in touch.' Coming from Bhudda Ilford, there was no request involved. 'I'll be on call at home.'

Thane gave a brief nod. For a moment his attention had wandered. On the bar shelf nearest the serving gantry was a distinctive flagon-shaped bottle made of dark amber glass. He didn't need to read the label to identify it. Glen Ault whisky liqueur was already well enough known. Now it looked like getting some additional free publicity— thanks to murder.

.   .   .   .   .

The fifteen minutes he'd suggested had lengthened to nearer twenty before Colin Thane braked the small second-hand Austin saloon which was his family transport and parked among the cluster of police cars outside the high block of council flats in Gradient Terrace. He got out, a borrowed raincoat buttoned over his golfing outfit, and waited until Dan Laurence had scrambled round to join him.

19

Gradient Terrace was well named. It was built on the side of the long, steep hill which dominated the middle of the Fortrose development. Darkness had fallen, and all around and below them the lights of Glasgow winked a vast multiple tracery against the night. A gusting wind was blowing, and the small crowd of rubber-necking locals gathered nearby were displaying a shivering hardihood.

There was a uniformed constable on duty at the entrance to the block. He saluted as Thane approached.

'Twelfth floor, sir—the elevators are down the hall. I think the Fingerprint boys are finished with them.'

'They'd better be,' snarled Laurence as they walked along the bare corridor with its glaring rooflights and yellow painted walls. 'I'm no ruddy mountain goat.'

There were two elevators, with a central button control. Laurence pressed, the indicator panel flickered, and a moment later the right-hand lift's door sighed open to give a rear view of one of Laurence's squad, busily concentrating on using a powder spray against the rear wall. The man looked over his shoulder and gave a cheerful nod.

'All clear to come in, Super . . . the button panel's impossible. Half a million people seem to have used it, and that's being conservative.'

They stepped in, and as the lift began to rise Laurence glanced around. 'What about the rest?'

'Prints all over the walls, and the other lift's the same.' The detective constable sighed. 'What do we do about it, Super?'

Laurence shrugged. 'Rig some polythene sheeting to protect them. In a place this size we can't knock both elevators out of action. Keep one running while the prints on the other are being photographed, then change round.'

'You want all the prints?' The man swallowed at the thought. 'There'll be hundreds!'

'Then you'd better get on with it,' growled the Scientific Bureau boss. 'Otherwise you're going to have a long night.'

The elevator door opened. The detective constable watched them leave, and swore to himself as he got back to work.

There was another uniformed constable on duty at the door of Humbie's flat. The small hallway inside was a litter of Scientific Bureau equipment, and a murmur of voices came from the nearest room. Thane went through first, into the intense glare of a photo-flood lamp.

'Hold on!' Phil Moss sang a warning from over by the window. They stopped short, heard the click of a camera shutter, then the lanky police photographer standing on a chair stepped down and signalled he was finished for the moment.

Counting Moss and the photographer, there were already five people in the room—the others were one of Laurence's men, a Millside detective constable and, immaculate as ever in dark suit, white stiff collar and a plain silk tie, Doc Williams the police surgeon. The room itself was simply but adequately furnished. At one end was a sideboard, a gateleg table and chairs. At the other, near the big picture-glass window with its undrawn curtains, a three-seater couch covered in sagging moquette was placed opposite the room's most expensive fitment—a twenty-one-inch console television set, angled out from the wall and its back-plate lying to one side.

Jean Humbie's body lay in front of the console set. Her thin face seemed unmarked, her red hair was only slightly ruffled, and she rested half on her back and half on her left side, her left arm bent beneath her.

'Same clothes as she was wearing this afternoon,' said Phil Moss conversationally as Thane reached him. 'She's been dead for not much more than an hour.'

'That's a rough estimate,' warned Doc Williams, bent once more beside the woman. 'There's no sign of rigor yet —well, Thane, who won?'

'Headquarters.' Thane looked around, his mind registering each detail. The room was a mess. Drawers had been emptied from the sideboard on to the carpet. The couch had been used as a discard pile for books, crockery and even a rifled sewing basket, its skeins of wool and reels of thread scattered around.

'The rest of the place is the same,' commented his second-in-command. 'Somebody really did a job of work on it.'

Thane nodded. 'No prizes for guessing what he was after. Did he find it?'

'Seems that way,' said Moss slowly. 'Want to have a look at her first?'

21

'You'll find it interesting,' promised Doc Williams, squatting back on his heels. 'You too, Dan . . .' He gave a bleak smack of his lips. 'I've never seen one quite like this before. Suffocation, of course, but that's only half the story.' He cleared his throat in lecture-room style as Laurence and the two Millside men bent beside him. 'Most suffocations I get are standard pattern. Livid face, staring eyes, protruding tongue, blood froth at the mouth.'

Behind them, the young detective constable swallowed and stared hard out of the window.

'But this one?' The police surgeon shook his head. 'All we've got, at a first glance, is that bluish tinge around the lips—though her fingertips and toes have the same signs.'

'It happens,' agreed Thane, scratching his chin. 'What's so special?' He looked again at the dead woman. The tinge around the lips was plainly noticeable—a red-smeared paper tissue on the floor showed that Doc Williams had already wiped away most of her lipstick.

'She seems peaceful enough,' murmured Moss. Relaxed in death, Jean Humbie's face was oddly youthful, the anxious, bitter lines smoothed.

'Aye.' Superintendent Laurence peered closer, frowning. 'Well, what are we supposed to be looking for anyway?'

'There's a scratch, a small one—just to one side of the nose,' mused Thane, inwardly cursing the police surgeon's guessing game. 'And one or two marks around the chin. Bruises?' He looked around, puzzled. There was no cushion, no obvious wadding lying around.

'Bruises and tiny skin haemorrhages—and you'll find a larger bruise on the back of her head,' declared Doc Williams. 'It's a "Burking"—beautifully done. Pressure applied to the mouth and nostrils, fixation of the lower jaw and chest.'

Phil Moss groaned. 'Like to put it in English?'

'Burking—Burke and Hare, the old-time body-snatchers!' Thane snapped finger and thumb. 'That's how they operated when they gave up digging in graveyards. One held their victim down, sitting on her chest. The partner squeezed his left hand over the mouth and nostrils and used the right to keep the chin jammed up.'

'That's it. Three minutes or so and they'd another corpse for sale.' Doc Williams rose to his feet. 'We've a slight refinement here, with the woman coshed and probably unconscious. Makes it a one-man job.' He smoothed down his jacket. 'Well, I'll have first crack at the p.m.—even though old MacMaster will come steaming along the moment he hears about it.'

The two Millside men exchanged a brief, cynical glance. Professor MacMaster, the chief forensic authority at Glasgow University, was no glory-hunter—but an off-beat medico-legal item was pure meat and drink to his insatiable interest in the ways of violent death.

'It'll make a good paper,' mused Doc Williams. 'Hasn't been a Burking around here this century——'

'Huh.' Superintendent Laurence got to his feet with a heavy sniff. 'Well, I've still got to get some work done. I'll see how the lads are getting on.'

As he went off and Doc Williams began repacking his medical bag, Thane guided Phil Moss over to the window. 'What's the score at our end?'

'Precious little,' confessed his second-in-command. 'An uncle named O'Brien found her. He's waiting in the flat next door—I phoned you from there. Oh, and I've had young Beech go door-knocking around the neighbours.'

'Beech?' The Millside chief raised a questioning eyebrow towards the waiting detective constable.

'Not much luck, sir,' admitted Beech. 'Nobody heard anything out of the usual or saw strangers around. The woman next door came nearest to helping. She says she heard the elevator stop on this floor about ten o'clock . . . she remembers because she was waiting on her daughter getting home. The girl turned up about quarter of an hour later, and she didn't bother after that.'

'Right.' Thane looked at his wristwatch. It was eleven-thirty now—a ten o'clock arrival for the murderer fitted with Doc Williams' estimate. 'What else, Phil?'

'Over here.' Moss steered a path to the rear of the television console. Removing the set's fibre back-plate had exposed a box-like space below the picture tube's wires and valving. 'Might have been made for the job.'

His mouth a tight line, Thane crouched down to see for himself. Lying at the front of the space was a small and empty blue canvas bag. He'd seen plenty like it before—the Bank of Central Scotland always used the type for issues of silver coin. To clinch matters there was something else lying at the far rear of the space—a book of bank withdrawal slips with 'Glen Ault Ltd' ink-stamped on the cover.

'Well, she was wrong about Frank,' said Moss softly.

Thane grinned. 'She wasn't alone. All right, he had the money—but why wasn't it found when this place was searched this morning?' His voice boded ill for Detective Sergeant MacLeod, who'd been in charge of that little detail. 'Come on, let's take a look around the rest of the place.'

The flat was compact. The living room, two bedrooms, a small kitchen and an even smaller bathroom constituted its total accommodation and the furnishings were neat, plain, sometimes shabby and always inexpensive. The same trail of disorder was everywhere. One bedroom had obviously been that used by Frank Humbie and his wife. The other had a single bed, gay wallpaper, bright curtains and a small, chintz-draped dressing table.

'As I remember, there's a daughter—she was at the schoolgirl stage last time Humbie was in trouble.' Thane opened the door of a wall cupboard and looked in at a tangle of feminine clothing.

'She's eighteen now and working in a hotel up north,' Moss told him. 'That's according to Uncle Joe next door. Where now?'

'The kitchen again.' Thane strode off, brushing past the photographer in the hall, a burly, angry figure, still cursing his own miscalculations. Why hadn't he slapped a watch on Humbie's home? It was easy enough to remind himself that it was almost impossible on a medium-sized robbery case, that like every other divisional C.I.D. chief in the city his men were under-strength and overworked. Glasgow's burglary statistics were running around the 12,000 a year mark—about one crime in three ending with an arrest. Statistically, it was disappointing. Yet even maintaining the ratio was a strain, and the city's record was better than most.

But Jean Humbie was dead. He felt part of the blame on his shoulders, whatever the background.

Dan Laurence was in the kitchen, poking around the cupboards. He turned as they entered, his manner rueful.

'You're not going to have much luck wi' fingerprints, Colin. This joker wore gloves. We've got one or two wee traces of them here and there and nothing more. Still, we'll keep trying. You never know.'

A tray on the kitchen countertop was set with two cups and saucers, sugar, milk and a plate of small iced cakes. Thane crossed to the stove. The electric kettle, plugged in ready to be switched on, was full. There was a can of instant coffee lying beside it.

'She knew this uncle was coming?'

Moss nodded.

'Which means she opened the door expecting to find him there.' Thane gnawed his lip for a moment. 'Let's say it was Douglas Dalziel—would she have invited him in when she knew we were looking for him, when she thought he was the character who'd railroaded Frank to Barlinnie?'

'Would she have any choice?' asked Moss bleakly.

Thane shrugged. 'You know what the sound-proofing's like in a flat like this, Phil. Most times the folk next door can hear when you change your shirt. Any kind of scuffle, a shout——'

'With television sets and radios going all around? It might not register.' Another thought struck Moss, one he didn't like. 'Who's going to tell Humbie?'

'I'll do it.' Thane pondered for a moment. 'But before that I'll have a talk with Uncle Joe. All right, Phil, let's do the obvious. Get on the blower. Special search for Dalziel . . . airports, docks, the lot. If he did this to get the money then he's going to be running, running hard. Let's trip him up before he gets too far.'

'It's not my worry, but'—Dan Laurence edged his way between them, frankly curious—'just what do you do when you get him, eh?'

'I know what I'd like to do,' said Thane savagely. 'Let Frank Humbie have him to himself for half an hour.'

.   .   .   .   .

Joe O'Brien was an elderly little gnome of a man—a gnome with a two-day growth of beard, bald, with wide blue eyes and a set of loose false teeth which occasionally clattered when he spoke. He sat back in the armchair, an

25

emptied whisky glass still clutched hopefully in his left hand, and gave a nervous grin.

'Aye, that's right, son. I got here about half-ten an' rang the bell at Jean's place. Rang it two or three times in fact.'

They were in the main room of the flat next door. The tenant, Mrs Cador, a plump, garrulous widow, had reluctantly departed for the kitchen with her daughter Sheena, a busty platinum blonde with a beehive hairdo who looked about twenty-five but was probably nearer sixteen.

Thane shifted himself gingerly in his own chair, a contemporary-style wickerwork saucer which threatened to swallow him at any moment.

'But you got in. Did you have a key?'

'I'd a feelin' you'd ask that.' Uncle Joe got up, stole a quick glance towards the closed door, then waddled quickly across to the table and poured himself a substantial nip from the waiting bottle. 'Ella Cador's a decent soul . . . she's no' likely to mind,' he excused himself, taking a quick drink. 'Aye, about the door now. It was locked, but it's—it was my own sister's daughter's house, wasn't it? She never minded me doin' it—and this time it turned out for the best, didn't it?'

'It was an emergency,' agreed Thane wearily. 'How did you do it?'

'Wi' a wee bit celluloid strip,' confessed O'Brien. 'Ach, it was easy enough.' For a moment his eyes twinkled. 'I used to be pretty good at that sort o' thing. But the last time I was in the jail would be while you were still in your pram, son. I've led the upright life for long enough.'

'Right.' Thane prompted the little man on. 'So you opened the door, went in, and found your niece dead. Was the television set on?'

'No.'

'Did you touch anything?'

'Eh? Touch or steal—is that what you mean?' O'Brien bristled at the thought. 'The place was in a mess. But I left it. What do you take me for anyway? It would ha' been worse than robbin' a grave!' His face flushed with anger.

'Simmer down,' advised Thane. 'I said "touch" and that's what I meant. What did you do once you'd found her?'

26

'I nipped through to Mrs Cador's here, knowin' she had a telephone.' O'Brien finished the rest of his drink in one gulp. 'After I'd called the police I just waited at Jean's door until the first o' your blokes got here.'

Thane took out his cigarettes, gave O'Brien one, lit it for him with a match, then heaved himself out of the basketwork saucer. 'Why did you come here tonight?'

The bright blue eyes narrowed perceptibly. O'Brien took a long, deep draw on his cigarette before replying. 'You know Jean reckoned you blokes had porridged the wrong fella when you pulled in Frank for the Glen Ault job?' He took Thane's nod in his stride. 'Well, I run a wee billiard hall off High Street—manage it, anyway. Jean came straight there to see me after she'd been at Millside station an' had got the polite goodbye from Inspector Moss. She wanted me to help her.'

'Help her?' Thane frowned. 'To try to prove Frank innocent?'

'That's the way of it.' O'Brien shrugged. 'Ach, I told her Frank's story was a bit feeble—winnin' at the dogs, this bloke he went drinkin' with after, then that business about how he walked home to get the booze off his breath. But——'

'But you said you'd help?'

O'Brien nodded and drew on his cigarette again. 'I've got one or two pals, like. An' I know the bunch Frank usually rubs around wi' at the dog-racing. They're reasonably straight. Anyway, I said I'd try around. Jean had her own ideas—something to do with this lad Dalziel.'

'Dalziel?' Thane pounced on the name. 'What about him?'

'She didn't say—apart from that she'd remembered something Frank once told her about this Dalziel, an' that if it meant what she thought it did she'd have half the Millside cops drawing unemployment money before she was done.' He blinked apologetically. 'Jean was always a bit strong in her opinions.'

'So you arranged to meet at the flat tonight and pool what you'd managed to find out.' Thane's mind dwelt for a moment on the thought of the thin, red-haired woman so resolutely chasing shadows.

'No, we didn't.' O'Brien shook his head emphatically.

27

'Not at first, anyway. But she 'phoned me at the billiard hall just before ten—she'd tried earlier, but I'd still been out, chattin' up some of the lads. She said she was goin' back to the flat, an' wanted me to come right over.'

'Did she say why?'

'Well . . .' O'Brien massaged the skin on his head with one set of stubby, blunt-nailed fingers. 'Ach, it didn't make sense. She said she'd a good mind to let Frank rot where he was, but that she'd got what she wanted.'

'Nothing more?'

'That was all she'd say,' shrugged O'Brien. 'You know what 'phones can be like. You never know who's listenin' in along the way.'

'You've no idea what she meant?

'I've just said so, haven't I?' The little man gave a scowl and puffed hard on his cigarette.

'And what about you, Joe?' asked Thane, his face expressionless. 'Did you have any luck?'

'Me?' O'Brien dodged his gaze. 'No.'

'You're sure?' The Millside detective put a needle-like stab into the words. 'This isn't a robbery job now—remember that.'

'I was her uncle, wasn't I?' The gloom in his voice was genuine enough. 'Here then . . . here it is for what it's worth. I couldn't find anyone who saw Frank at the Newton dogs. But he was wi' this lad Dalziel all right. They were in the lounge bar o' a pub in Dumbarton Road earlier on.'

'Which pub—and when?'

'The Wyvern—that new place wi' the wee fish tanks round the walls. The fish swimmin' around are supposed to be good for the nerves, but they'd put me right off for a start.' O'Brien's nose twitched at the thought. 'It was Bonce Page who saw them—he's one of the regulars there.'

'He knew Dalziel?'

'No. But he said Frank was wi' a younger bloke who looked like an office clerk—you know, collar an' tie stuff. He said it was a bit before six o'clock.'

'Did he talk to them?'

O'Brien shook his head. 'The Wyvern's pretty busy about that time, and Bonce had a girl on his hands.' His lips twitched unhappily. 'I suppose that lot lands Frank in trouble up to his neck, him spinnin' this line about his truck breaking down.'

Thane shook his head. 'No more trouble than he was in before. Joe, I'll get somebody to take a full statement from you. We'll need Bonce Page's address——'

'He won't like it,' warned O'Brien. 'He's got a finger in the used-car game, an' this sort o' thing could be bad for trade.'

A thin grin crossed Thane's face. 'That's his hard luck.'

2

LIGHTS out at Barlinnie is at 9 p.m.—and it was considerably after midnight when Colin Thane drove up the narrow, winding private road to the massive main gate of the prison. The deputy governor was waiting for him, and together they walked through the maze of silent, darkened buildings to C Hall. There, the night officer was expecting them—he led the way up an iron stairway to second gallery level, switched on Frank Humbie's cell light from the outside switch panel, then unlocked the door.

Humbie was still asleep. He lay on his back, snoring gently, and came awake with a protesting groan as the deputy governor shook him by the shoulder.

'Hell, no . . .' He scowled a sleep-dulled protest as he recognized his visitors. 'What kind o' jail is this anyway? Can't a bloke get a night's kip without the cops burstin' in?'

The deputy governor glanced at Thane and said nothing. This wasn't his task, and he was glad of the fact. Over at the door, the duty officer studiously turned away.

'Sit up, Frank.' Thane stood with his hands in his raincoat pockets, his voice quietly grave.

Humbie looked at him, muttered an oath, then threw back the blankets and swung his legs over the edge of the bed.

'Well?' he demanded. 'What is it this time?'

'Bad news, Frank—about your wife.'

'Jean?' Humbie's manner changed immediately. 'Is she —is she ill or somethin'?'

Thane shook his head. 'I'm sorry, Frank. She's dead.'

'Dead?' Humbie looked as though he'd been kicked. The colour drained from his face and he rose slowly to his feet. 'How? What's happened?'

'Better sit down, Humbie.' The deputy governor eyed

30

his charge awkwardly. 'Try and take it easy.'

'Easy?' The man looked at him in a daze.

'Her uncle found her. He went to the flat about ten-thirty this evening.' Thane could taste the man's shock and gathering grief, but it was best to get it over with. 'She was murdered, Frank. All I can say is that—well, we know it was quick. Here . . .' He gave Humbie a cigarette and held his lighter steady while the man's trembling hands cupped round the flame.

'Thanks.' Humbie whispered the word then slumped back on the bed.

Thane waited a full minute. 'You want to hear about it?'

Humbie looked up, took the cigarette from his mouth, and nodded.

'She was knocked unconscious, suffocated, and then the house was searched.' Thane told the rest as briefly and sparingly as he could.

How much of it all Humbie was taking in they couldn't be sure. Only once did he show he was really listening—when Thane told of the finds behind the television set. The man's head jerked up, his mouth opened, and then he seemed to shrink down again, his eyes closed, head shaking from side to side.

Thane finished, turned to the deputy governor, and gave a shrug. He'd done his best.

'Mr Thane . . .' The plea came as a hoarse, broken whisper. 'Will . . . can I get out of here? To see her, I mean?'

'For the funeral at any rate,' nodded Thane. 'We'll fix it. But I'll also have you brought out to the flat in the morning. The reason why Jean was killed seems pretty plain. But we've also got to know whether anything else is missing.'

'Anything else?'

'The money's gone,' emphasized Thane. 'Dalziel was your partner on the Glen Ault job, wasn't he?'

Humbie stared down at the floor of his cell for a long moment. Then he stubbed out what was left of his cigarette and gave a sigh. 'He was.'

'Did he know you'd have the money hidden at home?'

'Yes.'

'Did you split it at all? Or did you keep the lot?'

31

'Can't you wait a bit?' Humbie rose unsteadily to his feet, reached up to the shelf, and found his cigarette packet. It was empty, and he gave a trembling, close to hysterical grimace. 'Ten a day in here—I'm a forty man outside.' He gnawed his lip. 'Look, let it wait, Mr Thane. Please.'

'All right, Frank.' Thane quietly took out the unbroken pack of cigarettes from the two he'd bought at the High-rigg clubhouse and laid it on the bed. He looked at Humbie again, then felt in his other pocket, found the pack he'd been using, and placed it beside the other. He went out, the two prison officers followed, and, as the key grated in the cell lock, the deputy governor joined him for the walk back to the outside world.

The duty officer for C Hall left Frank Humbie's cell light on for the rest of the night—for practical as well as sympathetic reasons. The first time he checked through the cell door spyhole Humbie was sitting on the bed, his head in his hands.

He returned twenty minutes later. Frank Humbie had dragged the table across his cell to the faraway wall. He was standing on the table, just able to look out through the high, barred window into the night. His hands were clenched on the bars and he was weeping with low, strangled sobs which racked his body.

The prison officer shook his head. He'd heard grown men weep many a time in the night. He'd heard them shout and curse, sing hymns, groan. But he'd never heard such despairing grief.

Quietly, he slid the spyhole back to the closed position. One thing, at least, was certain. Whatever else he'd done, Frank Humbie had loved his wife.

．　　　．　　　．　　　．　　　．

After the first couple of hours in any murder hunt there is either an arrest or what, to the outsider, is anti-climax. If it is the latter, the Scientific squad are plodding their methodical way, there are statements to be taken, post-mortem arrangements to be put in hand, the inevitable press conference to be faced, the preliminary report to be drafted for the Chief Constable's conference. No fireworks, no car chases, just a solid grind of work.

It was close on 4 a.m. before Colin Thane decided he could leave his office in Millside Division. Phil Moss had departed twenty minutes earlier, but Thane used the extra time to telephone Bhudda Ilford and bring him up to date, then to have a last quick word with the three night-shift C.I.D. men who'd been left to cope with the rest of the Division's cares.

He arrived home at four-thirty, to be greeted by a half-hearted yelp from the Thane family's boxer dog in its kitchen basket. When he got to bed, the sky was already beginning to grow light and the first birds were chirping.

Mary Thane stifled the bedside alarm when it rang at seven, got up, and waited exactly half an hour before she wakened him with tea and a cigarette. She would have let him sleep longer, but she knew the drill when the pressure was on—and Thane's wife had long had her own private arrangement with Peggy, the night operator at the Millside Division switchboard. Most C.I.D. wives were in the switchboard grapevine, for better or worse.

By eight, Thane had washed, shaved, dressed and was finishing a quick breakfast. He'd seen the morning paper headlines. The stories of Jean Humbie's murder were thin on fact and heavily padded—but a woman murdered and her house ransacked while her husband lay in jail was a gift to the city's crime reporters. Picture coverage ranged from old stock blocks of the Gradient Terrace flats to a couple of snapshot reproductions of a much younger Jean Humbie than the woman he'd known.

Where had they come from? Thane thought of Uncle Joe, wondered how much the old gnome had made from the deal, and listened for a moment to the sounds coming from upstairs as his wife roused their two youngsters for another day's school.

The black shape of the duty C.I.D. car drew up outside the house with a brief hoot of its horn before either Tommy or Kate had put in an appearance. He got his hat, shouted a goodbye, heard the answering chorus from upstairs, and gave the dog a pat on the way out. Phil Moss eased open the rear door of the car as Thane came down the short garden path, and he swung into the back seat of the car with a weary grin.

''Morning, Colin.' Moss spoke briefly to the uniformed

33

driver in front, and the Jaguar drew away, heading for Millside. 'How'd you feel?'

'Rough.' Thane yawned in spite of himself. 'What I saw in the papers didn't help. Anything fresh?'

Moss shook his head. 'No. I checked in by 'phone before I left. Humbie's daughter is flying down from the north this afternoon. That's the first plane she can get. And MacLeod's picked up Bonce Page—he's got him waiting for us.'

'Good.' Bonce Page might or might not matter. Thane was thinking more of Detective Sergeant MacLeod. 'You take Page, Phil. I'll see MacLeod alone.'

'Mac doesn't often slip up,' murmured Moss. 'He's heard about the television set——'

'From you?'

Moss gave him a sideways glance but said nothing. There were times when being number two in the Division office involved the need to act as a shock absorber—for everybody's sake.

Bonce Page was sitting in the main C.I.D. room when they arrived. A lanky, long-haired ned of about thirty with nicotine-stained teeth and dirty fingernails, he wore a grey gaberdine jerkin over a pair of sharply creased navy slacks. But his white shirt was overdue at the laundry.

'Here, I want to complain . . .' He sprang to his feet as they approached.

'Do you?' Thane looked past him to Detective Sergeant MacLeod. 'Where'd you find him?'

'On his way to the airport, sir. He was booked on the morning flight to London, using the name Harry Blake.'

'It was a pal's booking,' protested Page uneasily. 'He said I could take it—I've got business down there, urgent stuff.'

'Tell it to Inspector Moss.' Thane brushed the man aside. 'Mac, better come through.'

Detective Sergeant MacLeod trailed him through to the inner office, closed the door once they were in, and waited unhappily.

'Who was with you when you arrested Humbie at his place yesterday?'

'Gunn and Edwards, sir. Edwards took Humbie down to the car.' MacLeod was terse and formal.

34

'Leaving two of you to search the place,' snapped Thane brusquely. 'Yet neither of you checked that television set.'

'No, we didn't, sir.' MacLeod shifted his weight from one foot to the other, trying to choose his words. 'I'm sorry. Mrs Humbie was being difficult, and it made things pretty awkward. That's—well, that's all I can say about it, sir.'

'So you missed it.' Thane suddenly remembered his hat. He took it off and rammed it on the peg behind the door. 'Well, you were in charge, Sergeant. Chief Superintendent Ilford's going to want to know what went wrong. What do I tell him? That Mrs Humbie was being difficult?' He slumped his weight down on the big leather chair and scowled. 'Not that that's what matters. Look, Mac, if we'd found that money yesterday . . .' He stopped and shook his head.

MacLeod flushed and finished it for him. 'Then the word might have got around and she wouldn't have been killed, sir? I've thought of that—quite a lot.'

'As long as you have.' Thane looked at him for a moment then nodded. 'All right, that's all for now.'

'Sir.' MacLeod turned to leave. As he did, an edge of white bandage showed for a moment below the shirt cuff on his right arm.

'Wait a minute,' growled Thane. 'What's wrong with your arm?'

'Nothing much,' said MacLeod slowly. 'She took a swipe at me with a milk bottle. It got me on the wrist.'

'Jean Humbie? Yesterday morning?'

MacLeod nodded. 'I said she was a bit difficult, sir. But there didn't seem any sense in charging her—it's mainly bruising.'

'I see.' It made a difference. Thane could picture the kind of party it must have been, arresting Humbie, controlling his wife and trying to give the place a proper going-over all at the same time. 'Well, you got Page anyway. That's more than we could do last night.' He refrained from asking how MacLeod had done it. But it couldn't have been easy. 'All right, Mac. Ask Phil Moss to come through if he's finished with Page.'

'Yes, sir.' MacLeod hesitated. 'I'm—am I still on full duty?'

'What the hell else?' Thane blinked. 'Mac, you'll maybe end up on the carpet before Ilford—but the odds are you'll have to wait behind me in the queue. I've made my own mistakes.' He gave a faint, reconciliatory twinkle. 'Here's one you can help me on. Who's the boss at Glen Ault?'

'The managing director, George Greenlaw—he's pretty helpful.' MacLeod relaxed a little. 'I . . . I'd like to get involved in this, sir.'

Thane pondered the point. 'You can. But it's mostly a shoe-leather job. Jean Humbie left here and saw her uncle. After that—well, we don't know and we've got to find out. That means checking taxi ranks, bus terminals, the lot— you know the drill. Take Gunn with you.'

Detective Sergeant MacLeod swallowed, nodded, and went out. Thane took a moment to glance through the collection of mail and reports lying on his 'In' tray. He dumped most of them into the one marked 'Pending' but opened a large envelope which had the Headquarters 'Urgent' stamp on its front. Out fell a photograph—the enlarged holiday snapshot was coarse and heavily grained, but at least he now knew what Douglas Dalziel looked like. The picture showed a tall, slightly built youngster in his early twenties, with thick dark hair, a broad forehead and a wide grin.

He sat back, studying the face. Then he shrugged. Faces never told much on their own.

When Phil Moss came in a few moments later, followed by an orderly balancing two mugs of tea on a tin tray, Thane was standing by the divisional map which occupied most of one wall.

'Thanks, son.' Thane took one mug from the young constable, sipped it, and was satisfied. Moss took the other and settled himself on the edge of the desk as the orderly went out.

'Page doesn't add much,' said Moss, slightly disappointed. 'From the description he gives it sounds pretty positive Dalziel was with Frank Humbie in the Wyvern Bar. They seemed excited about something—and Page noticed a Glen Ault van parked in a side street just before he went into the Wyvern. The time fits. Humbie could have driven Dalziel around for a little then gone on to the warehouse yard.'

'Old stuff,' grumbled Thane. 'We'll get all the robbery detail we want from Humbie. What about Page himself? Why was he baling out?'

'Joe O'Brien.' Moss took a gulp of tea and grimaced. 'Ach, this stuff tastes like tar. Still—Uncle Joe got the word to Page late last night that we'd be looking for him. Page didn't want to get involved—he's behind in maintenance payments to a wife somewhere. So he decided to take a trip. About the only other thing I got out of him is that he had a few drinks with Humbie about a week back, and Humbie began hinting that he wouldn't be driving a van much longer.'

'Well, that's come true.' Thane gave a brief, cold twist of a grin. 'But it leaves us still having to scratch around for better than we've got. Phil, I'm going out to the Glen Ault place. You look in at Joe O'Brien's billiard hall and tell him we want him here for another talk. Try young Dalziel's lodgings after that—give his room a real going over.' He sniffed deliberately. 'Let's make sure we've missed nothing there. Last thing on the list, head out to Barlinnie and collect Humbie—I've fixed an inquiry release into our custody. Bring him out to Gradient Terrace and I'll meet you there.'

'When?'

'I want to look in at Headquarters first—let's say around ten.'

Moss took a last swallow of tea, abandoned the rest, and nodded. 'Right.' He drew a hand across his mouth. 'I wonder where he is, Colin . . . how he feels, what he's doing?'

'Dalziel?' Thane shrugged. 'He's probably buried himself somewhere, and has the jitters every time a floorboard squeaks. But we'll dig him out, Phil—and soon.'

.   .   .   .   .

The Glen Ault whisky liqueur company was one of half a dozen small Scottish firms which quite happily shared the residue market once the two main trade-names in the business had taken their very considerable slices of the

37

cake. But some shrewd low-budget advertising, combined with a produce which cut through with a tang to even the most jaded of after-dinner palates, had established Glen Ault as the best known of the liqueur lilliputians.

Their warehouse and office in Wood Street was near enough to the dirty, oil-slicked water of the Clyde dockland area for an occasional squad of seagulls to occupy a rooftop perch. Wood Street was by far from the best part of town—its soot-stained buildings formed a rambling complex of industry and commerce, garment factories and scrap metal yards side by side with storage depots and derelict huts. But the Glen Ault premises were well maintained. The paintwork was fresh, the windows had glass, and the high wire fence surrounding the yard area had its base neatly weeded.

The C.I.D. duty car pulled into the kerb outside the office and beside a couple of grimy toddlers playing a determined game of pavement hop-scotch. Thane left his driver on radio watch, avoided colliding with one of the youngsters, and pushed through the building's glass doorway.

'Can I help you?' The girl at the inquiry counter was in her mid-twenties, quietly dressed, with a well-boned face and shoulder-length chestnut hair. She had a typewriter at her desk and the office switchboard, a small private branch exchange unit, was just to one side.

'Chief Inspector Thane from Millside police,' he told her mildly. 'Mr Greenlaw in yet?'

She gave a sober nod. 'He got here a few minutes ago, Chief Inspector. He said the police might be round—about Mrs Humbie, I mean. Just a moment.' The girl stepped over to the switchboard, plugged into an extension, spoke for a few seconds, and then returned. 'Mr Greenlaw's in his office. I'll take you up.'

'Fine.' Thane followed her down a short corridor, past a couple of doors from which came the muted clack of typewriters, and then on up the flight of stairs beyond.

'Chief Inspector,' the girl stopped and turned at the top of the stairway, 'do you mind if I ask a question?'

'Depends what it is, I suppose.' He gave her a brief smile of encouragement.

'It's about Dougie—Douglas Dalziel.' She moistened

38

her lips. 'Is there—have you found him yet?'

'You're the girl who gave us the photograph?'

She nodded. 'I'm Barbara MacPhail. I'm—well, a friend of his.'

'A close friend.'

'We went out together a few times.' She gave a slight shrug. 'Nothing more, if that's what you're wondering. But I like him. This morning . . . well, everybody's seen the papers. You can guess how people here are putting two and two together.' Her eyes were steady and serious. 'He's just not the type, Chief Inspector—not the type who would do anything as horrible as this.'

'Types don't come into it,' he told her gently. 'If they did, life would be a lot easier for people like me. But—no, there's no news of him yet.'

'I see.' She bit her lip. 'Thank you.'

The last door in the corridor above had 'Managing Director' printed in red lettering on the reeded glass of its upper panel. Barbara MacPhail knocked, and a loud, hearty voice shouted an indistinguishable reply. She looked at Thane, gave a quick nod and a half-smile, and left him to it. He opened the door and went in.

'You're even earlier than I expected,' boomed George Greenlaw, striding across the room with his hand outstretched. The man's grip was strong and firm. 'We've met before, Chief Inspector—just over a year ago.'

Thane combed his memory. The head of the Glen Ault company was a tall man, almost as tall as Thane. His age, at a guess, was around fifty. His dark, naturally curly hair had a few streaks of grey around the temples and his slim build was emphasized by the cut of his dark hand-tailored suiting. But it was Greenlaw's face which held attention by the sheer tragedy of what had occurred. His features had been youthful and clean-cut. But while the right side twisted in a bright grin the left hung slack and limp in the grip of a local paralysis. Only the eyes balanced, keen and intelligent.

'You were preaching improved office security to the local business club,' reminded Greenlaw. 'That was before this happened.' He stroked a forefinger casually over his left cheek.

'I remember,' agreed Thane. 'At least, I remember the

39

meeting.' His talk had been one of a series they'd tried on orders from the Chief Constable. The results had been far from wonderful.

'We only spoke for a moment or two,' mused Greenlaw. 'And this face business makes quite a difference.'

'An accident? '

'No. Went to bed one night feeling fine, woke up like this next morning. Nerve damage, according to the doctors—could have been a chill, an infection.' He shrugged. 'It happened a few months back. Come and sit down.'

They crossed towards Greenlaw's desk, a massive glass-topped piece of furniture which was bare of papers. To one side, the ripped safe still lay empty and open. The rest of the room was austere and simple, the walls painted a dull cream and the plaster ceiling veined with hairline cracks.

'You've heard about Humbie's wife?' asked Thane as he settled in a chair.

'I've seen the papers, but that's all.' Greenlaw sighed. 'You know, I took on Humbie despite his record because he seemed to deserve a break. But if I'd guessed anything like this would happen . . .' He flipped open the lid of a small, gun-metal cigarette box. 'Like a caramel? I'm trying not to use the other things.'

'No, thanks.'

'Can't say I blame you,' sighed Greenlaw, helping himself. 'I suppose you're here about Dalziel—though if he killed the woman he must be a madman.' The half-slack mouth gave a twist of curiosity. 'I'm taking it he is your number one suspect?'

'He's certainly on the list.' Thane felt in his inside pocket and took out the book of bank withdrawal slips they'd found at the flat. 'For the record, can you identify these?'

Greenlaw glanced at them and nodded. 'They were in the safe. Where'd you get them?'

'At Humbie's place.' Thane pocketed the book again. 'I'd like to hear anything you can tell me about Dalziel.'

'That's not much. Still . . .' Greenlaw sucked the caramel for a moment. 'Dalziel started here about four months ago —the men who spoke to me after the robbery probably told you that. He was our invoice clerk on the export side of

40

the business, and any time that was left over he spent helping out the cashier.'

'The export business is fairly considerable?'

'Pretty good,' agreed Greenlaw. 'The North American
market's going steady, and the European trade's building
up. You know our product?'

'I've tried it.'

'And enjoyed it?' Greenlaw chuckled. 'Well, let's hope
so anyway. We're compounders. In other words, we buy
bulk stock of straight, ordinary whisky from the distillers
and blenders. Then we add our own syrups, extracts from
herbs distillable with alcohol. Things like citronella and
aniseed, mint, juniper, wormwood—there's a long list to
choose from.'

'You make it sound easy,' murmured Thane politely.

'It is and it isn't,' mused Greenlaw. He took the caramel
from his mouth, looked at it in disgust, and dropped it
from finger and thumb into the wastebasket. 'Hate the
things. Still, they help . . . no, there's nothing complicated
about the whisky liqueur business provided you've got the
right recipe, a different recipe. And once you've got that
recipe you guard it every way you know.'

Thane nodded. He'd heard this part before—how the
boss of one liqueur firm was said to lock himself alone in
a room while he personally mixed secret ingredients into a
fresh batch of essence for the next week's production. 'But
your liqueur whisky recipe wasn't in the safe?'

Greenlaw winced. 'You've got the term wrong for a
start. We make a whisky liqueur, Chief Inspector. A
whisky liqueur. This term liqueur whisky is just a trade term
some of the distillers use. It means a very old, very mature
blend of whisky which has had nothing, absolutely nothing
added. It might be—well, up to twenty years old. Not
much more, though. After that, whisky usually begins to
lose quality. I've tasted a bottle of hundred-year-old stuff
—it was like high-grade paint thinner.' He shook his head.
'Well, never mind the lecture. The recipe wasn't in the
safe. And all I can really say about Dalziel was that he was
a good worker. I keep my nose out of what my staff do
after office hours.'

'Let's stick to office hours then,' urged Thane. 'Would
Dalziel have had a key to the door between the office and
the warehouse area?'

'Yes. Part of his job involved checking export shipments as they left the warehouse.' The Glen Ault man's eyes twinkled briefly. 'When you gave your talk to the business club you suggested compartmentizing warehouse areas— that's what gave me the idea of keeping that door locked all the time. It's the only door between warehouse and office, as you know—and since I did it there's been a fall in pilferage. The only people who have keys are those who've got to work between the two places.'

'And the money?' Thane sensed the man's gathering impatience. 'I know you've told this all before. But I want a first-hand version. This was a particularly large sum, wasn't it?'

'Correct. Dalziel went along with Miss Rodell, our cashier, to collect it from the bank the afternoon before we were robbed. Maybe it sounds funny now, but I sent him as an escort. The money—well, part of it was for wages, but we only employ about forty people altogether. The bulk of it was for a cash transaction.' He stroked the dead side of his face. 'I was planning to buy some fresh stock of—well, an ingredient. The man concerned prefers cash.'

'And has an easier time with his income tax?' Thane shrugged. 'Well, that doesn't concern us. Had Dalziel money troubles?'

Greenlaw gave a sigh of half-concealed exasperation. 'I don't know. He was reasonably well paid, he seemed happy enough, and I don't pry into my employees' affairs. Try Greta Rodell, if you like. She may know more.' The telephone rang and he scooped it up, listened, and gave a grunt. 'Right, send him up, Barbara.' He replaced the receiver and rose from his chair. 'Sorry about this, Chief Inspector. But I've a Customs and Excise man due to see me. Is there anything else?'

'I'd appreciate a look over your warehouse,' said Thane rising.

'No trouble there. Greta Rodell can take you over.' Greenlaw had a question of his own. 'How does any of this help?'

'The more we know about Dalziel the better chance we have of finding him.'

'If he hasn't skipped abroad by now,' said the Glen Ault

42

man pointedly. There was a sharp double knock on the door and he went over to open it. 'John . . . come on in.'

'Company?' The man who peered in seemed reluctant to enter.

'It's all right, Chief Inspector Thane, this is our local Excise watchdog, John Kelso. Surveyor of Customs and Excise, to give him his Sunday title.'

Thane shook hands with the Excise officer, a plump, weather-beaten barrel of a man with mild brown eyes half-hidden behind the thick lenses of his horn-rimmed spectacles.

'I can come back——' began Kelso.

'No need,' Thane assured him. 'I'm just going.'

'The cashier's office is the door on the right at the top of the stairway,' directed Greenlaw hastily. 'Sorry, Chief Inspector, but this is a busy day.'

Thane found himself more or less piloted out into the corridor. He had a last glimpse of the exciseman's embarrassed expression, and then the door closed.

.   .   .   .   .

Greta Rodell, the Glen Ault cashier, was a surprise—a petite, handsome woman in a neat black dress with a narrow white Peter Pan collar, her hair, a natural pale gold, cut in a short, almost boyish style. She smiled in a flash of large white teeth and then swept a bundle of ledgers and papers off the only spare chair in the room.

'Sorry about the mess, Mr Thane—but the end of the month's always a busy time for statements and returns.'

'And being without Dalziel won't have helped.' He gave a nod of understanding and tried to guess her age. It was difficult—she wasn't young, yet she was one of those women who by their very carriage and personality made calculation dangerous. She wore a heavy bloodstone ring on her wedding finger, but no other jewellery.

'That's true enough.' She sat back, smoothing the wrinkles which had gathered in the lap of her dress. 'Well, how can I help you?'

'Dalziel went with you to the bank on Wednesday. At any time that day did he seem nervous or excited?'

'No—at least not more than usual,' she said crisply.

43

'Something had been bothering him for a good few days. I'd wondered whether it was money or a girl, but he wasn't the communicative type.'

'What about his work?'

'I'd no complaints there.' She took the cigarette he offered and accepted a light. 'He coped with a lot of the routine stuff—I'm landed with the lot now, and it's pretty heavy going.'

'How much warning did you get that there'd be more money than usual to be collected?'

'Several days.' She curled sideways in the chair, her arm resting against the back. 'George Greenlaw mentioned it to me.'

'And you mentioned it to Dalziel?'

Greta Rodell permitted herself a rueful shadow of a smile. 'Yes. Pretty silly, wasn't it? What do you want, Chief Inspector—a spot of good old-fashioned Chinese self-criticism?'

'No. An idea of how long Dalziel had to make plans, plans that might include his own private escape tunnel. Still, his friendship with Frank Humbie is also a puzzle.'

'Why?' She flicked the ash from her cigarette. 'They worked for the same firm, and they lived fairly close to one another.'

'You knew that?'

'Of course. We're a small firm, Chief Inspector. Anyway, I'd seen them together quite a few times.'

'Humbie came here to see him?'

'No. But I've seen them talking in the warehouse, arriving for work on the same bus, that sort of thing.'

'Did Mrs Humbie ever come here?'

'Just once.' She frowned again. 'Let's see—it would be about four months back. Her husband was off sick for a few days. She brought in a doctor's certificate and collected Humbie's wages for the week. She seemed a pleasant enough woman.'

'In her own way she was,' said Thane quietly. 'Thanks, Miss Rodell. Just before I go I'd like a quick look over your warehouse area.'

'Well . . .' She got up, stubbed her cigarette on the desk ashtray, and contemplated the papers spread around. 'I'll show you it provided you won't take too long. I just wish

44

I could see what all this has to do with Mrs Humbie's murder. . . .'

'The safe-breaking and the killing were linked,' reminded Thane patiently. 'We've got to check both ends to be sure of what we're up against.'

'That makes sense,' admitted Greta Rodell picking up her handbag. She led the way. They went down to the ground floor, along another corridor, and stopped at a heavy wooden door while she located the key in her handbag and turned the lock. Once through the door, she carefully locked it again.

About thirty yards of open ground separated the Glen Ault office from the warehouse, which was a big, high-roofed building with heavy wire-mesh screens guarding every window. Greta Rodell guided him to a small side door and they went in, walking through a storage bay piled high with cases of whisky liqueur sealed and banded ready for delivery. A ceiling-high partition separated the storage bay from the next section, where a squad of girls in white caps and overalls worked in a large room lined with piping and valves.

Thane stopped for a moment to watch the clacking machine they tended, feeding empty bottles into one end of a moving rack and then packing the filled, capped and labelled flagons as they emerged from the other end of the complex process.

The woman at his elbow stirred impatiently and he followed on again, through another cavern-like area almost filled by the vast bulk of two massive vats surrounded by the apparently inevitable piping.

'The compounding's done here,' she explained briefly, nodding a greeting to two men using a block and tackle to manœuvre a heavy hundred-gallon cask of bulk whisky into position. 'The vats are metal, lined with fibre glass. The one producing just now is on the left—the other one is being prepared for new stock.'

Thane guessed each of the vats would be close to the thousand-gallon category. Another two casks of whisky, still unbroached, were waiting on a low, iron-wheeled trolley.

'What's a week's normal production?' he asked.

'About five hundred cases—multiply by twelve if you want the number of bottles.' She shrugged. 'By some standards it's not a particularly big operation, but it's steady, and there's a good market.'

'You've a foreman?'

'Yes. His name's Ed Yuill—over here.'

Greta Rodell set a brisk pace through the rest of the warehouse building to a glass-walled cubbyhole of an office beside a large vehicle doorway.

Yuill came out to meet them—a thin, pale-faced man with stooped shoulders and a crumpled brown work-jacket. He gave a surly nod as Greta Rodell handled the introductions.

'I can tell you this much about Humbie,' he grunted. 'He was a stubborn, surly cuss to have to work wi'.'

'Did you know he had a record?' asked Thane.

'Mr Greenlaw only told me after your mob arrested the bloke.' Yuill took the stub of pencil stuck behind one ear and used it to scratch his scalp for a moment. 'Well, at least I didn't hire him.'

'I knew he'd been in trouble,' volunteered the woman. 'Mr Greenlaw told me. But we felt it better for Humbie's sake that nobody else was told.'

'I'd ha' kept a closer eye on him, that's for sure,' scowled the foreman.

'But you knew Humbie and Dalziel were fairly friendly?' probed Thane.

'Depends on what you mean by friendly. Humbie's job kept him out o' here most of the day. We've only three drivers—two now, I suppose. Ach, I saw Dalziel talkin' to him now an' again, but I was too damned busy to bother.' His eyes narrowed. 'Mind you, just the last few days Dalziel kept pokin' his nose around the warehouse. An' I saw him talkin' to Humbie one lunch-break. They were bein' thick as thieves about something.' The humour of the remark pleased him. 'Ach, well, one's in jail now an' the other shouldn't be long in joinin' him, eh?'

Thane ignored the man's grin. 'What was Humbie's scheduled run on his last trip?'

'He'd a load o' a hundred cases to deliver through at Leith docks. It was a consignment for Hamburg.'

'And he completed the delivery?'

Ed Yuill used the pencil again. 'He did. I double-checked on it as soon as I heard you'd nabbed him.'

46

3

EVERYTHING has its drawbacks, decided Phil Moss. It was another fine, warmy, sunny morning—which meant that the seat leather of the patrol car was already baked hot, the whole interior of the car felt like an oven, and the glare of sunlight was pulling at his eyes. He found an irrational anger at the way the burly uniformed driver sat so comfortably in front, even something wrong with the way the man's red neck bulged against the tight blue collar of his shirt.

Worse was to come. The Eagle Sporting Centre, Joe O'Brien's billiard hall, had an imposing enough title. But the Centre, a grimy hall in Jack Lane, behind the High Street shopping area, was a faded, dim-lit basement where the air was eighty per cent stale cigarette smoke.

'Joe's out,' shrugged the young table attendant whom he found swamping out the floor with a bucket and mop.

'When will he be back?'

The attendant didn't know. 'Somebody telephoned 'im, and he just took off.'

Moss gave a dyspeptic scowl. 'Then when he comes back tell him we want another talk—and that he's to stay put until I see him.'

The next call was at Dalziel's lodgings in Shannon Street. It was a small four-roomed flat, two up, occupied by an elderly couple named Grey.

'We only let the one room,' said Mrs Grey awkwardly, shuffling through the flat on slow, carpet-slippered feet. 'My man's retired from the railways and when you're on a pension things can be a wee bit tight—so the extra money comes in handy.'

'The usual bed and breakfast arrangement?' asked Moss.

'Och, Mr Dalziel could have an evening meal too when

47

he wanted,' she explained. 'And he was no trouble, no trouble at all. He had his own key, as we're early bedders —and he never disturbed us.' She opened the door of a small bedroom which had the added comforts of an armchair and writing table. 'This was his—still is, I suppose. His rent's paid for another week.'

She watched with interest while he began a methodical search. 'There was a policeman here already doing this. Eh—do you think maybe he missed something?'

Moss hoped not. At the end of twenty minutes he was satisfied. Douglas Dalziel appeared to have abandoned what few personal possessions he had, from spare suit to toothbrush, but there was nothing in the room which seemed of interest.

Another thought struck him. 'Mrs Grey, did anyone call here last night asking about Dalziel?'

She gave a quick sniff. 'Aye, there was a woman—and a real cheeky one she was.'

'Thin, red-haired, in a navy-blue costume?'

The old woman rubbed one carpet slipper against the other. 'That's her all right.'

'What did she want?' Moss waited anxiously, wondering why Jean Humbie had chosen to come to Dalziel's lodgings.

Mrs Grey shook her head. 'She wanted me to tell her something that was none o' her business. She wanted to know if Mr Dalziel ever had any women visitors.' She sniffed. 'I told her this isn't that kind o' a house, and slammed the door in her face.'

'That was all she asked?'

'That was all I let her ask, Inspector,' said Mrs Grey indignantly. 'It's bad enough him runnin' away like this, leaving me with the police popping in an' out of here like jack-rabbits. But I'm not standing for strangers annoying me!'

'And even if Dalziel had visitors there'd be nothing wrong in it,' said Moss soothingly. 'Was there a—you know, a rather special visitor?'

'No women—not the way she meant,' snorted Mrs Grey. 'But a young lady was here twice—somebody from his office. Barbara her name was. A nice, dark-haired girl.'

That left only Barlinnie on his list . . . and at the prison, at least, they were ready for him. He had a quick cup of tea with one of the gatehouse officers while Humbie was brought from C Hall.

'He's taking it pretty badly,' mused the prison officer. 'The night-shift man on C Hall told me about it before he went off duty. They ended up giving Humbie a sedative about three o'clock this morning.' He shrugged. 'Well, you never can tell. I'd have labelled Humbie a hard-case. You know how it is—when you're a screw, you don't mind the hard-cases. They come in here an' they've sense enough to settle down an' get along because it's the quickest way to get back out again. You can relax a little—not like with the first-timers.'

Moss took another sip of tea and made a noise of agreement. It was the old, old story. The first-timers were the ones who had to be watched in C Hall—the youngsters who thought they could make monkeys out of the screws, the older characters who every now and again went berserk under the shock of confinement. By comparison, men like Humbie, men who knew the drill, were almost automatic candidates for jobs as passmen—and it was the passmen, the privileged, trusted prisoners, who practically ran any jail.

The prison officer shrugged. 'Ach, when a man's wife gets killed like that and he's stuck in a cell . . .' He stopped and glanced round as the door opened. 'Here we are, Inspector. You'll just sign this receipt for him, eh? And can we have him back before noon? Otherwise it means having to organize a late meal for him.'

'I'll try,' said Moss dryly. He scribbled his signature on the release form then turned to his new charge.

Frank Humbie had been allowed to change back into civvies for his trip to the outside world. He wore a dark brown suit and his tie was knotted loosely at the unbuttoned collar of his shirt.

'Ready?' asked Moss.

Humbie nodded and held out his right wrist.

Moss reached for the handcuffs in his hip pocket, thought again, and shook his head. 'We won't bother. Just don't try anything.'

A quick flash of gratitude crossed Humbie's face. 'I won't.'

49

They were the last words the man spoke until the patrol car arrived in Fortrose housing scheme and pulled to a halt outside the flats in Gradient Terrace.

.　　　.　　　.　　　.　　　.

Seen in daylight, Glasgow's Fortrose scheme could be almost intimidating in its size and dull uniformity. It sprawled its brick and concrete bulk over what had once been rich grazing for three of the best dairy farms in the West of Scotland. But the cattle and the farm cottages had given way to towering blocks of flats and lower almost endless lines of terraced, identical four-storey houses, all knitted together by a grey web of roads, paths and overhead lighting cables.

It was still spreading. A street of neatly curtained homes would end in a swamp of mud, throbbing cement mixers and half-completed buildings. Fortrose had been building for two years. When it was finished, the equivalent of a new medium-sized town would have been grafted on to the city—a town of people rescued from the filth and squalor of overcrowded, stinking, tumbledown slums.

Fortrose meant such luxuries as a bathroom in every home, hot water from a tap, being able to leave a baby sunning in its pram without worrying about rats. It meant an end to whole families living and sleeping in one damp room.

It also meant petty vandalism, bricked-up staircase windows, smashed street lights and, after the first ecstasies, a chronic boredom. The planners had built houses and built them well. But in all Fortrose there was not one cinema, one dancehall, one bar or café. When it was finished, there would be a community centre and a playing field. Until then, it was a place in which to sleep, to eat—but for many, not much more. Its busiest point was the bus terminus from which a constant fleet of vehicles ferried Fortrose's population back to the city to work and play.

Its greatest pride was the laughter of its children, their strong limbs and sun-tanned faces.

Its greatest tragedy was the sight of the old people who, torn from the only life they'd ever known, headed back

50

every other day to taste and savour the slums they couldn't do without.

Phil Moss knew all that and more. He'd been born in a Gorbals slum—so, for that matter, had another, earlier detective called Pinkerton who'd had some degree of success once he'd emigrated. But he took a long, slow, ever-fascinated look around before he nudged Humbie and they left the car.

A knot of women were gossiping near the entrance to the flats. One of them, a buxom grandmother, called a greeting and Humbie acknowledged it with a listless wave of his hand as he passed into the building.

'Frank, I'd better warn you.' Moss eyed his charge with a touch of sympathy as the elevator whined them upward. 'The flat is still in a mess—just as we found it. Things have to stay that way for now.'

'Okay.' Humbie pursed his lips. 'What about Agnes?'

'Agnes?' Moss raised an inquiring eyebrow.

'The girl—my daughter,' said Humbie shortly. 'She'll know by now?'

'She's been told,' nodded Moss. 'Joe O'Brien gave us her address last night. She'll be flying down this afternoon —she can visit you as soon as she arrives.'

'No.' Humbie blurted the word. 'Tell her to stay where she is.'

'But she's——'

'She's not to get involved.' Humbie's mouth twitched nervously. 'You think it's a good idea to let a kid of seventeen get mixed up in this kind of a deal? Reporters, cameras, people gaping at her? If you want to do her a favour, keep her up where she is—well out of it.'

'All right, I'll try,' agreed Moss. 'I'll 'phone the hotel. But it's her decision—we can't stop her if she refuses.'

When the lift stopped, he nudged Humbie along the corridor to the door of the flat. It was opened for them by a uniformed constable, who gave a brief nod of recognition then stood back to let them enter.

'Through to the living room, Frank,' said Moss, guiding Humbie by the elbow.

The man stopped just inside the room and stared at the disorder, his face pale but expressionless as Detective Constable Beech came towards them from the window.

51

'What d'you want me to do?' asked Humbie quietly.

'Just look around, Frank. Take your time, see what's missing—if anything.' Moss crispened his voice a little. 'Was all the Glen Ault cash in the back of the television set?'

Humbie chewed his lip for a moment then gave the slightest of nods.

'All right.' The Millside second-in-command gestured Beech nearer. 'Stay with him, let him look, touch if necessary. But nothing more.'

'Yes, sir.' Beech cleared his throat suggestively and stepped a little to one side. 'There's just one thing . . .'

Moss followed him back to the window. 'Well?'

'It's the girl next door,' muttered Beech, keeping one eye on Humbie, who hadn't moved. 'Sheena Cador, the blonde kid with the——'

'I know who you mean,' grunted Moss. 'What about her?'

'She was at the door about half an hour back. Wanted to talk to you or Chief Inspector Thane.' Beech shrugged. 'She wouldn't tell me what about—said she'd wait for you.'

'Probably thought you were too young.' Moss grimaced, remembering his previous brief meeting with the girl. 'I'll go round. But remember, watch Humbie—every move he makes.'

A throb of music was coming from the flat next door as he rang the doorbell. He tried again, the music was cut short, and a moment later the door opened.

'Oh—it's you!' Sheena Cador's smile faded a little as she saw him. 'Is Mr Thane no' back yet?'

'He's busy.' Moss squeezed past her into the flat. 'Detective Constable Beech says you've something to tell us.'

'Beech . . . is that his name?' She grinned. 'He's young for a cop, isn't he?'

'He's young, he's married and he's got two kids,' said Moss dourly. 'Right, Sheena, what's it all about?'

'Come through an' I'll tell you.' She led the way, her chunky teenage shape trapped in an outfit of yellow narrow-legged slacks and matching sweater. Not a hair of the beehive hairdo was out of place—Moss wondered briefly if she had to sleep in a chair to keep it that way.

'This'll do.' She stopped and lounged back against the wall as they entered the living room. Breakfast dishes still covered the table, magazines littered the carpet, and a record player sat silent in one corner.

'Where's your mother?' asked Moss.

'Out. Away into town—she does it most days,' shrugged the girl.

'And you? Shouldn't you be at work?'

'I got paid off—I was late a few times,' she said casually. 'Like a fag?'

He shook his head and waited while she lit one. 'Well?'

'It's about last night. Suppose I was to tell you something, would my mum have to know?'

Moss hesitated. 'Depends on what it is. Does it involve her?'

'No—but she'd probably half-kill me.' The girl gave a hoot of laughter at the thought. 'Here, sit down and I'll tell you anyway.' She saw him settled in an armchair then perched herself on a low stool opposite. 'You know I was out last night? Well, I'd a date wi' Danny Farrell—he lives down the road a bit.'

'Is that what's worrying you?' asked Moss.

'Uh-huh—Mum thinks he's a layabout. Anyway, neither of us had much cash, so we just walked around for a spell until it was dark then came back here about ten o'clock an' nipped up to the drying room.'

'Where?' Moss tried hard to follow her stacatto delivery.

'The drying room, up on the top floor—the clothes drying place.' She chuckled. 'If she'd known I went up there with Danny . . .'

Moss knew what she meant. When architects tackling the problem of laundry facilities made the top floor of some of the multi-storey flats a vast drying room with racks, heating pipes and mechanical ventilators they also unwittingly created the finest refuge for courting couples since the back row in cinemas.

The drying rooms were warm, sheltered, usually unused after dark. There had been outraged complaints from tenants' associations about moral dangers—but the drying rooms were now part of the lore of the new housing developments, and the experiment of fitting locks on their doors only meant the locks were broken.

'How old are you, Sheena?'

'Seventeen.' She looked at him with a sudden frank-eyed wisdom beyond her years. 'Don't worry, Inspector—when I settle it'll be for a wedding ring. Understood?'

'Understood,' said Moss.

'Right.' She reverted to a giggle. 'Anyway, Danny an' I went up—only we were too late.'

'Somebody else was there?' At last, Phil Moss began to realize the significance of her story.

'That's it. Another couple—it was dark, of course, but there was enough moonlight comin' in to see them. And listen'—she wagged a dramatic forefinger—'after what happened to Mrs Humbie, I asked around a bit this morning. Whoever they were, that pair weren't local.'

'You can't be sure.'

'No?' Her voice held an emphatic certainty. 'I know what goes on, mister.'

'All right, let's take it as a possibility,' mused Moss. 'Did you go close enough to see them properly?'

She shook her head. 'First come, first stays—that's the rule around here. Danny an' I walked around for a bit longer, then I came home.'

'Can you describe them—even roughly?'

'Not enough to make you happy. The woman had dark hair an' a white raincoat. She was—och, I didn't see her face proper, but I'd know her again all right, if you know what I mean. She'd a pretty good figure. The bloke with her . . .' She shook her head. 'He was just a bloke, an' they were cuddled up pretty close.'

'It's still better than nothing,' Moss told her.

'And you don't need to tell my mum?' asked the girl. 'It's not the rumpus that bothers me—it's the way she'd get herself worked up. She's going to do herself an injury one of these days.'

'Let's not make it happen this time,' agreed Moss. He gave her a wan half-smile and left.

.   .   .   .   .

Colin Thane arrived on one lift coming up from ground level as Moss stepped out of the other after a trip to the drying room.

'Nice timing,' grinned Thane. 'Been exploring?' The

grin faded as his second-in-command sketched Sheena Cador's story.

'Pretty interesting,' agreed Thane. 'They could have arrived here, found Jean Humbie was still out, and then gone up top rather than go through the business of having to leave and enter the block again. Well, get someone to have a talk with Danny Farrell. Dan Laurence's team can give the drying room a going over—we might be lucky.'

'I doubt it,' said Moss gloomily. 'There's nothing I could see—not even a cigarette end. How about you? Any progress?'

'I don't know.' Thane eased his hat back on his forehead. 'I paid a call on the top brass at the Glen Ault offices —Greenlaw and his cashier. And I had a word with Dalziel's girl-friend.'

'Barbara MacPhail?'

Thane raised an expressive eyebrow. 'Meaning?'

'Jean Humbie was at Dalziel's lodgings last night asking about a woman visitor—and the only woman who ever went there was the MacPhail girl.'

'And Barbara has dark hair.' Thane gnawed his lip for a moment. 'Phil, there was something odd about that Glen Ault place. Did you ever go somewhere and feel that people were nervous as hell at the mere fact you were around? Polite, fairly helpful, even friendly—but wanting rid of you?'

'Huh.' Moss gave an involuntary twinkle. 'It's an occupational hazard. Most people regard having a cop around as a social disaster.'

'It was more than that, Phil,' insisted Thane. 'There's something else nagging at my mind, but I'm damned if I know what it is. Something that just doesn't add up.' He shrugged. 'Well, at least the rest was straightforward. I looked in at Headquarters on the way here. The post-mortem report on Jean Humbie is ready. But no surprises—she was coshed from behind then manually suffocated. Time of death about 10.15 p.m.'

'Quarter of an hour after Sheena and boy-friend found the drying room occupied——'

'And about the same length of time before Joe O'Brien says he arrived,' nodded Thane. 'The rest of the report's routine.'

'And the Scientific bods?'

'Nothing yet.' Thane had experienced his biggest disappointment over that. 'No prints, no handy strands of hair lying around—nothing. Dan's sending a couple of men back out to fingerprint everyone in this block. Then he'll start eliminating the prints he got from the elevators. But that's a pretty forlorn hope.'

'Which leaves us with the couple in the drying room,' mused Moss. 'Like me to have Barbara MacPhail brought in?'

'Not yet. I want another talk with Joe O'Brien first. Where is he?'

'Out,' said Moss shortly. 'I left a message that we'd be back.'

'We can collect him once we're finished here.' Thane thumbed towards the flat door. 'Well, let's see how Humbie's making out.'

Frank Humbie had finished his grim inspection. He was sitting on the couch in the living room, smoking a cigarette, Detective Constable Beech in close attendance.

'Well, Frank?' asked Thane as they entered.

Slowly, wearily, Humbie rose to his feet and shook his head. 'Nothing.'

'Beech?'

'I took him right round the place, sir,' reported Beech stolidly. 'Made sure he looked everywhere.'

'Thanks.' Thane turned back to their prisoner. 'Frank, how many people knew about the Glen Ault job?'

'Jean didn't, if that's what you mean,' said Humbie listlessly. 'She didn't know a thing.'

'Not even where the money was?'

'Damn you, no.' The man glared up with a sudden concentrated hate and despair.

'Who else knew about the job?' persisted Thane.

'Just—just Dalziel.' Humbie took a deep breath. 'You haven't got him yet?'

'No. Where d'you think he might have gone, Frank?'

'Me?' The man stared at him. 'What do you think I'm made of, Chief Inspector? Do you think I'd sit here an' keep my mouth shut if I'd any ideas?' He rose from the couch fists clenched by his side. 'Is this finished? It's—I don't want to stay here. I can't take any more of it.'

56

'We'll leave it for now.' Thane nodded. 'Take him back, Beech.'

Detective Constable Beech took Humbie's jacket sleeve in a deceptively light finger and thumb grip and began to lead him towards the door.

'Mr Moss . . .' Humbie hung back for a moment. 'You'll remember . . . about Agnes, I mean?'

'I'll remember,' agreed Moss. 'On you go, Beech—and get a receipt for him at Barlinnie. If we don't stick to the drill we'll get complaints from Headquarters.'

Thane waited until prisoner and escort had gone. 'What was that about?' he demanded.

'His daughter. Humbie doesn't want her down here.'

'That makes sense.' Thane grimaced at what might lie in store for the girl. 'Well, let's go and collect Joe O'Brien. We'll take him back to the office—and once we're finished with him, you and I can eat.'

Phil Moss gave a thankful beam and followed him out.

When their car reached the Eagle Sporting Centre the Millside chief let Phil Moss go in alone. He sat back in the Jaguar's soft leather cushions, wrestling in his mind with a growing, ridiculous possibility. It wasn't strong enough to be a hunch. It hadn't even the full dignity of a serious doubt. It revolved around young Dalziel and Barbara MacPhail, Frank Humbie and his wife Jean. Yet it only began there. . . .

The car door clicked open and he looked up, momentarily startled. The look on his second-in-command's face did nothing to help.

'O'Brien's hopped it,' said Detective Inspector Moss bitterly. 'He came in, got my message, but said he couldn't wait. Packed a bag and disappeared.'

'No word there?'

'None. All the fellow he left in charge knows is that there was somebody waiting outside for him, somebody with a car.' Moss felt in his pocket, found one of the aluminium glycinate tablets, and swallowed it whole. He had a horrible feeling that both he and his ulcer were about to start working overtime.

.   .   .   .   .

They were back in the Millside C.I.D. office within five minutes, and at the end of another five Joe O'Brien's name and description were clacking out on the teleprinter network. With it went a request that if located he was to be kept under observation until Thane could get to him. Two other moves got under way at the same time—running a check on Joe O'Brien's movements during the nights of both the robbery and the murder, and keeping a watch on the Eagle Sporting Centre on the off-chance that its suddenly unco-operative little manager might try to pay a quick return visit.

'If we even had an idea about the car that picked him up,' mourned Phil Moss. 'Colin, I don't buy the idea he murdered Jean Humbie. He'd probably take the money if he got the chance—but I don't see him killing for it.'

'It wasn't a fortune, if that's what you mean.' Thane scowled at the telephone on his desk. Sooner or later it would have to ring, sooner or later one of his team could be counted on dredging up a fact, a hint, a possibility. But until that happened, this was the time he hated—the time of complete guesswork. 'Phil, I'm not saying O'Brien's directly involved. But there's a chance he knows more than he told us and decided there was trouble brewing if he stayed.'

'Trouble? He'll find plenty now.' Moss levered himself up from his chair and gave a grunt. 'Well, time I did my good deed for the day.'

'Huh?' Thane looked blank.

''Phoning Humbie's daughter,' explained Moss patiently. 'I promised, remember?'

'It's okay to go through the motions, Phil. But I want her to decide to come here.' Thane's mouth tightened a little under his companion's glance of surprise. 'All right, the decent thing is Humbie's way—to have her stay at her job in that hotel, well away from all of this. But I want one member of that family near and handy.'

'What can she tell you?' protested Moss.

'I won't know until I've seen her.' Thane barked the words across the room, then gave a half-apologetic sigh. 'Look, Phil, have you seen MacLeod's latest report?'

Moss shook his head. 'How's he making out?'

Thane flicked the telephone message form that had been

lying on his desk when he came in. 'Not very happily. When Jean Humbie walked out of here yesterday we know she went to see O'Brien at the billiard hall. Later she turned up at Dalziel's lodgings—but the rest of the time? All MacLeod has is that she took a taxi from the city centre out to Fortrose. The driver says he picked her up in Sauchiehall Street about nine-thirty and that she wanted to be taken home to Gradient Terrace. But she changed her mind a couple of streets short of there and paid him off in Stanford Avenue.'

'Well, it's always something——'

'It would be—if we knew why she did it. MacLeod can't get a lead.' Thane stubbed his cigarette in the already overflowing ashtray. 'They got to Stanford Avenue about nine forty-five. Minutes later she's 'phoning Uncle Joe—unless he's lying.'

'Telling him to come out, that she's got what she wanted!' Moss swore softly. 'Then she goes home, where there's already a man and woman waiting for her.'

'Where we think they were waiting for her,' corrected Thane absently. 'But where did she go in Stanford Avenue?'

Moss shrugged. 'Well, it would be dark by then—not many people out and about.'

'That could be it!' Thane gave a triumphant snap of his fingers. 'Suppose she saw someone in the street, someone she thought might help her!'

'It's possible.' Moss scratched his thin thatch of hair. 'But does it matter—does any of it matter? The woman was trying to get Frank off the hook. We know he's on it to stay.'

'But she'd found out something, Phil. Whatever it was, we've got to get it.' Thane pondered for a moment. 'The beat man for Stanford Avenue might be able to help.'

He lifted the telephone. A few words with Inspector Campbell in the latter's cubbyhole kingdom down in the uniformed branch duty room produced the answer, once the quiet-voiced roster officer had had time to consult his lists.

'Andy MacPherson's the night beat constable around there,' reported Campbell. 'He's pretty reliable.'

'I know him,' agreed Thane. 'Can you get him in here during the afternoon?'

'Well'—Campbell could never be rushed—'will you need him for long?'

'A few minutes.'

'I'll have a car pick him up,' agreed the uniformed branch inspector. 'But if it's going to interfere with the roster let me know—things are tight enough as it is.'

'It won't,' promised Thane cheerfully. He hung up and gave a wry grin. 'Usual enthusiasm—but he'll do it. Better make your 'phone call, Phil. Then if there's anyone handy maybe we could get some sandwiches brought in.'

Phil Moss went out with a rebellious mumble on his lips. He knew what the sandwiches would be like. They always came from the café across the street—thick, fat-streaked, under-cooked bacon rammed between anaemic brown bread stroked with a faint veneer of butter. 'Slaughterhouse Specials' was the C.I.D.'s close to true description—and he'd suffered their effects only too often.

Left alone, Thane stopped himself from lighting another cigarette and settled to inking a restless, untidy listing of names on the scrap pad before him. He circled some, bracketed others, trying to concentrate on a pattern. Phil had put it neatly. Frank Humbie was firmly on the hook—yet why had Jean Humbie been suddenly so sure of her ground, why had she turned up at Dalziel's lodgings? And her words to O'Brien—she'd found what she wanted, even though it left her angry. If that meant a link between Humbie and Barbara MacPhail—he shook his head. She was Dalziel's girl—and Humbie was an over-fleshed middle-aged ned.

But a dark-haired woman and a man had been waiting at Gradient Terrace, and they had to be found.

The intercom on his desk gave a short buzz and brought him down to earth again. He flicked the unit's talk switch.

'Yes?'

The duty orderly's voice crackled over. 'There's a Mr Greenlaw here, sir—he'd like to see you personally.'

'Bring him through.' He closed the switch and waited, frowning.

When the Glen Ault managing director was ushered in,

Thane greeted him coolly but politely. 'Something wrong, Mr Greenlaw?'

'I'm not sure.' The tall, immaculately dressed executive took the chair he was offered and hesitated for a moment before he came to the point. 'Our night watchman was in at the office a little while back—he always draws his pay at noon on Fridays. According to him, Mrs Humbie turned up at the warehouse about nine last night.'

'Did she now!' Thane showed his interest. 'What did she want?'

'That's why I came,' said Greenlaw, a tinge of reluctance in his voice. 'It's—well, I thought you'd better know, though I'm not sure what it means. She wanted Barbara MacPhail's home address.' Greenlaw shrugged. 'Well, the watchman refused, of course. She argued for a moment or two then went away.'

'Does the girl know about this?'

'Barbara?' Greenlaw shook his head. 'I told the man to keep his mouth shut.'

'Well, tell him that's what I say, too.' Thane sat back in his chair. 'It interests me for more reasons than one, Mr Greenlaw.'

'You can't really think Barbara's mixed up in all this!'

'I don't know who isn't.' Thane gave a trace of a grin. 'But I'm glad you told me. Mr Greenlaw, while you're here maybe you can help me on something else. You mentioned you've had one or two outbreaks of pilfering. Humbie's been with you about a year—how much stuff has been taken during that time?'

Greenlaw shrugged. 'Nothing of any quantity, just a few bottles of liqueur every now and again—that sort of thing is pretty well inevitable. We called in the police once, when half a dozen cases disappeared from a delivery van. It wasn't Humbie's van, and your people nailed a fellow for the job. The other times—well, I decided it wasn't worth making a fuss. And I've made a pretty careful check of stocks since the safe was robbed. Dalziel and Humbie haven't been stealing us blind, if that's what you're wondering.'

'Good.' Thane rose and held out his hand. 'Well, thanks for coming.'

'Pleasure.' Greenlaw prolonged the grip. 'What's happening, Chief Inspector? Making progress?'

'Wish we were,' said Thane soberly. 'But there's still a complete blank as far as Dalziel is concerned.'

'Well, if I can help . . .'

'If you can, we'll be in touch.'

George Greenlaw gave a nod of understanding and went out. As the door closed, Thane stood for a moment, gnawing gently at his lip. Then he walked over to his desk and lifted the telephone again.

.   .   .   .   .

The receiver was back down when Phil Moss reappeared about five minutes later, a paper-wrapped package in one hand.

'Humbie's daughter is still coming,' he reported sourly. 'I don't think she's desperately keen—I could probably have stopped her. And I got the sandwiches. They're the usual.' He stopped, frowning. 'Hey, why the hat? Where are you going?'

'Out,' said Thane briefly. 'I'm going to have lunch with an exciseman.'

'You mean in a restaurant?'

'It's usual enough.'

'But the sandwiches . . .' Moss's mouth fell open.

'You have 'em, Phil,' said Thane gently. 'Spoil yourself.'

He had gone before his second-in-command could marshal the exact words necessary to illustrate his feelings.

The Customs and Excise office for the north-west area of Glasgow was a small, unpretentious unit housed in a neat red-brick building in the dockland area, only two doors away from the granite bulk of the Seamen's Mission hostel. In many ways it was like a police station in miniature—when Thane entered the outer office a ship-to-shore radio was crackling a message, a pair of blue-uniformed Waterguard men were talking in quiet monotones to a worried-looking Merchant Navy officer, and an electric kettle was steaming on the floor just behind the reception counter.

The girl at the counter had been expecting him. She made a brief telephone call, and a moment later John Kelso came through from one of the inner offices. The

mild eyes beamed a greeting through the spectacle lenses.
'I usually eat at a little place round the corner,' he said
almost apologetically. 'It's pretty plain, but it's quiet. . . .'

'If I wasn't here I'd be having brought-in sandwiches at
my desk,' Thane assured him.

He followed the plump exciseman back out into the
bright sunlight. Kelso stopped on the doorstep, sniffed the
air, and shook his head. 'Rain on the way.'

'My garden could use some,' said Thane absently.

'But I start a week's leave tomorrow,' complained Kelso.
'Still, I could be wrong. . . .' His voice trailed into a hopeful silence.

The restaurant round the corner was a large room behind a baker's shop. The walls were of panelled wood,
dark-stained, and the decorations were ancient, heavy-
framed reproductions of Victorian landscapes. As Kelso
had promised, only few of the tables were occupied—and
the food, when it came, was plain but good.

'All right?' queried Kelso anxiously.

Thane nodded and tackled his meat and two veg. with
a hungry intensity. 'Let's eat first.'

By mutual consent they didn't stray beyond small talk
until they were at the coffee stage.

'I was—well, embarrassed about this morning,' said
Kelso, finally, stirring a heavy loading of sugar into his
cup. 'Of course, Greenlaw's a fairly thrusting type.'

'You know him pretty well?'

Kelso sipped his coffee and seemed satisfied. 'Greenlaw?
Yes, he's been in the liquor business for quite a while now.'

Thane considered his companion carefully. He'd had
few dealings with the Customs and Excise organization,
but despite Millside Division's dock area that wasn't too
surprising. Customs and Excise could look after their own
problems. Kelso was a surveyor—that gave him a rank
roughly equivalent to Thane's, and in some ways more
power and responsibility than any policeman.

A Customs and Excise man could demand or force
entry to any house or building in the course of his duties
and search it without having to worry about the need for
a warrant. He could arrest a suspect, have him lodged in
prison for any one of a wide variety of offences. He could
seize and impound any article or goods he wished, he held

a direct Queen's Commission—all in all, the Customs and Excise force had a sobering strength. It was a strength, however, used sparingly with a heavy and automatic disciplining of any enthusiast who went too far without adequate reason.

'Well?' Kelso had been watching him too. 'Wondering what to tell me and what to keep to yourself, Chief Inspector?' He chuckled. 'I feel the same sometimes about your people. I'm fairly new in Millside Division, but I was on the south side of the river until a few months back. Same line of business, of course—excisable spirits.'

'How'd you get into the excise game in the first place?' asked Thane, frankly curious.

'Ten years at sea and a wife that wanted me ashore.' Kelso tapped on a spectacle lens. 'Eyesight trouble settled it. So I gathered a bundle of character references, sat exams, took the training course—book-keeping, chemistry, engineering, the legal side—and that was me under way. I started off with two years as assistant living-in officer in a distillery up in Skye, then other spells at Inverness and around Beauly.'

'And now the Glen Ault place?'

'Well, it's one of the warehouses in my district—but it's in rather a different category.' The exciseman accepted one of Thane's cigarettes before he went on. 'You know, whisky's a strange thing. A chemist might say it's basically just ethyl alcohol. But the distilling and the blending is an art, a piece of magic. There's the malt spirit from barley, the "silent" spirit from grain, and anything up to a score of these raws blended together to get the right subtlety of taste. Then there's the things you can't define like the breath of peat and air and mountain water—no wonder people write poetry about the stuff. The plain fact is that the whisky we make in Scotland can't be duplicated anywhere else—and nobody on earth knows why.'

'Different blends, different palates,' murmured Thane. 'You should meet our Chief Superintendent at Headquarters. He rates himself an expert.'

'Some people are,' nodded Kelso. 'I've seen men who could sip a glass of the raw and tell the district, the distillery, even the year it came from. I've seen other men pretend the same thing and be downright liars.

'But you know what whisky really means to the Customs and Excise Department? It means three hundred million pounds a year in collected duty. When you buy a bottle and take it home, threequarters of what you're paying is sheer tax . . . unless you're lucky enough to live abroad. Whisky's one of the biggest single sources of internal revenue this country's got. So our job's to watch it, watch it every moment of the time it's made, the years when it's just lying in the warehouse maturing or blending, keep an eye on it almost to the moment when it goes down somebody's throat.

'That means living with it—every distillery has an exciseman who has his home inside the distillery area. We hold all the keys, sometimes the only keys, and we've got to account for every drop. You know, there's even a standard table to allow for natural evaporation—and if as much as a pint too much is missing out of a thousand gallons then we've a full-scale investigation on our hands!'

It amounted to a speech. But Thane had heard men launch out like that before, men whose work had developed into a way of life.

'You're thorough, I know that,' he said slowly. 'But every now and again you hit trouble. Whisky's an easy commodity to dispose of once it's stolen.'

'That happens, but not often,' agreed Kelso. 'The distillers see to that. Say a load of whisky is stolen from a distiller—well, we still charge them the duty due. The only exception is if the whisky is destroyed by accident and they can prove it happened, prove it enough to satisfy us.'

Thane gave a thin whistle. 'That's pretty savage, isn't it?'

'Maybe. But it works—and then, we get information from all sorts of odd sources.' The exciseman gave a chuckle. 'You're not the only people who get tip-offs from contacts, Thane. And with us, it's usually well worth their while. Customs and Excise can be fairly generous in their handouts.'

'With three hundred million a year from whisky you can afford to be.' Thane thought glumly for a moment of his own meagre budget allocation for 'Gratuities re Information'. 'Still, what about Glen Ault?'

'What about them?' Kelso's mild brown button-like eyes

65

were wide and inquiring. 'The safe-breaking, even this murder business, doesn't come into my orbit . . . and I'm not complaining about it. Anyway, you're looking for this lad Dalziel, aren't you?'

'I wouldn't tell you how to spot an illicit still,' said Thane pointedly.

Kelso gave a mock wince. 'All right. It's an old firm, good background, financially sound. The previous owners were a pair of maiden ladies through in Edinburgh. They were killed in a car crash two years ago, and the business had to be sold for death duties—that's when Greenlaw's company took over.'

'You knew him before?'

'Yes. He was managing a distillery up near Beauly for a spell. But since he took over down here Glen Ault liqueur's really begun selling—product hasn't changed, just the presentation. Good advertising, promotion work, you know the sort of thing.'

'Same secret recipe, eh?'

'That?' Kelso's barrel-like figure vibrated with silent laughter. 'We know what's in it—so do their competitors. Any well-equipped laboratory can do the job. But it's a good story, why spoil it?'

'What about the rest of the staff?'

'Well, the foreman used to be with him at Beauly. I've met Greta Rodell, the cashier—very competent. Talked to this fellow Dalziel a couple of times too. But, no, I can't really help you. We don't have much to do with the firm.'

'No?' Thane raised an eyebrow in surprise. 'What about this business of "living and sleeping" with the stuff?'

'Not with a set-up like Glen Ault.' The exciseman stubbed his cigarette and accepted another. 'Customs and Excise don't allow compounding—mixing up liqueurs—with duty-free spirits. The duty is paid before Glen Ault gets delivery, and once the duty's paid our job's pretty well over.'

'Even for export shipments?' queried Thane. 'I thought they were duty free?' It was a constant irritation, the fact that the only way a Scot could drink his native spirit at a reasonable price was to make a trip abroad.

'Export shipments are duty free and come straight out of tax-free bond—but with a whisky liqueur the duty is still paid first and only refunded once a consignment has been exported. We check all export receipts and invoices, even see the shipments off ourselves—and carry out warehouse inspections now and again to make sure everything's in order.'

'And is it?'

'At Glen Ault?' Kelso nodded. 'Absolutely. I'd stake my pension on it. Why?'

Thane swirled the last of the coffee in his cup. It had gone cold, and a greasy skin had formed. 'Kelso, would you kill a woman for three thousand pounds?'

'Well . . .' Kelso gave a twinkle. 'There's my mother-in-law for a start.' The smile died under Thane's patient, iron-steady gaze. 'Look, I know what you mean. What I don't know is how to help you. I'm sorry.' He glanced awkwardly at his watch. 'Well, it's time I was getting back —I'm expecting a visitor.'

They argued about the bill, finally split it, and went out. Thane left the exciseman outside the restaurant, hailed a taxi, and had the driver take him back to Millside station. The trip had been just another idea which didn't seem to have paid off—but at least he knew he'd found a sympathetic ally.

.   .   .   .   .

There were two messages on his desk when he returned. Thane slung his jacket over the back of his chair, loosened his tie, and frowned at the slips of paper. The first was a summons from Bhudda Ilford—the Glasgow C.I.D. chief wanted him to report to Headquarters at 3 p.m. The other was a long message from Aberdeenshire C.I.D., a complete rundown on Douglas Dalziel, his known friends and relatives, any other past associations they'd been able to gather. He sighed at the first message and ran a pencil over the second, ticking a name here and there as worth checking.

'Have a good lunch?' Phil Moss was standing in the doorway, a thin manila folder in one hand, the other holding a narrow, oblong cardboard box.

'So-so. Didn't add anything to what we've got, though.'

67

Thane shoved the Aberdeenshire list across the desk. 'Who's spare outside?'

'Huh.' Moss found the query more sad than amusing. 'Only Gunn, and he's got a couple of housebreakings to write up.'

'Put him on these Aberdeenshire suggestions, Phil. The housebreakings can wait.'

'Right.' Moss slapped the folder down in front of him. 'I saw Bhudda's royal command. You'll need this—report summaries on what we've got on the Humbie murder.'

'With carbon copy?'

'Aye.' Moss laid the box down with more tender care. 'This was delivered by hand not long ago. For you—marked private, and it gurgles.'

Thane ripped open the package lid. 'Well now . . .' He drew out the contents, a single flagon of Glen Ault whisky liqueur, the bottle glass glinting cool and amber in the sunlight.

'Bribery and corruption,' said Moss cynically. 'Any note with it?'

'Just this. "With compliments, George Greenlaw."' Thane tossed the slip into the wastebasket and considered the bottle with a wary eye. 'Put it over on the filing cabinet for now, Phil.'

'Right.' Moss looked back over his shoulder as he obeyed. 'The beat man you wanted to see is cooling his heels downstairs. Will I get him?'

'Yes.' Thane glanced at his watch. He'd still fifteen minutes before he had to leave for Headquarters. 'What else has been happening?'

'Three false alarms about Dalziel. London picked up one character, but ended booking him for something else. And there's still no trace of Joe O'Brien.'

'And our wandering boy, MacLeod?'

'Still trying, but he's got nothing fresh.'

'Right.' Thane leaned forward. 'Phil, it's time we set up a little identity parade—to try to clear the air if nothing else. Have a policewoman laid on to collect the Cador girl from home. Put her somewhere where she's able to see the Glen Ault staff leave for home at the end of the day. Let's find out if she reacts at all when Barbara MacPhail goes past. Before then I'll have had another talk with the

MacPhail girl, and between the two we might get some results.'

'I'll fix it—and I'll get the beat cop now.' Phil Moss shambled out. His shoes badly needed mending, noticed Thane. There was no sense in mentioning it—the best way was to make a quiet telephone call to his second-in-command's long-suffering landlady, who lived in perpetual fear of her star boarder being arrested for vagrancy.

Police Constable Andy MacPherson, number M.46, marched into the little office a few moments later with a heavy military tread, a bristling moustache, and a uniform which sported two rows of war-service medal ribbons. His heels snapped to attention before Thane's desk and his right arm sang a salute which was pure Guards Brigade.

'Sit down, Andy,' nodded Thane. The salute was an embarrassment, but Andy MacPherson was a man to respect. He'd been a c.s.m. with the Scots Guards at Salerno, he had a son whom he'd put through medical school without help, and he'd have been a police sergeant long ago if he hadn't once given way to his feelings and belted a child-molester so hard on the jaw that the man had been in hospital for six weeks.

'I've given him an idea of what you're after,' said Phil Moss, moving over to the window and leaning back against the blistered paintwork.

'How long have you been on the Stanford Avenue beat?' asked Thane.

'Eighteen months, sir.' Police Constable MacPherson's moustache bristled. 'Ever since some alleged expert decided I was getting too old for real action.'

'Well . . .' Thane smothered a grin. 'Andy, you know what I'm wanting, details of any people who're a regular feature around there.'

'There's one at least,' declared MacPherson, unfastening his tunic pocket button and whipping out a notebook with one smooth movement. 'Patrick Rafferty, aged 64, newsvendor, address—ah—he flicked a page—'142 Cannon Street. Nickname's Pekey, sir—he's got that kind of face.'

'Eh?'

'Like the dog—Pekinese dog. Flat nose, no chin. He works a stance at the corner of Stanford Avenue and Fort-rose Road—starts with the last editions of the evenings,

69

carries right through with the first editions of the morning papers.'

Moss blinked. 'Where'd you get the address, Andy?'

'Caught him selling cigarettes on the side—no licence,' growled MacPherson.

'Charge him?'

'No.' MacPherson returned the notebook. 'I warned him —I run my beat my own way.'

Thane knew what that meant coming from a cop of the old school. No juvenile delinquents or third-rate 'hard men' hauled up in court for a waste-of-time lecture—a good swift cuff on the ear for the youngsters, an occasional backyard thumping for the would-be thugs, and crime statistics stayed low. 'He was there last night?'

'Saw him myself, sir. And the previous night too. He's a nosey old devil, but friendly.'

'What time last night?' demanded Moss.

'About twenty-two hundred hours, sir.'

'Ten o'clock,' translated Moss, and drew a momentary shrivelling bristle of the moustache.

'We'll get him in,' decided Thane.

'Better wait until he starts work,' advised MacPherson sagely. 'He hangs around the betting shops most after-noons—depending on how the horses run he could be hard to find. But he'll be at his pitch by six-thirty tonight.'

'We'll be there,' promised Thane. 'That's all, Andy. Thanks for coming in.'

'Sir.' The heels clicked, the arm swung, and MacPherson made his exit.

'I wish he wouldn't do that,' shuddered Moss as the door closed.

'Gives you an inferiority complex,' agreed Thane, slowly fastening his tie and pulling on his jacket again. 'Well, time for Bhudda's tea-party, Phil.'

'Take your own booze along,' suggested Moss acidly.

Colin Thane glanced at the glinting liqueur bottle on the filing cabinet. 'For once I don't think he'd appreciate it, Phil—not unless I took it to him with Dalziel hand-cuffed to the other wrist.'

And at the moment, he told himself gloomily, that wasn't much of a danger.

4

THE inevitable cluster of reporters were stationed outside the Police Headquarters building in St Andrew's Square. Some were the regular police calls men, who spent most of their working lives drifting between the Headquarters canteen, the Custodier's office and the various departmental counters gathering a paragraph here, a paragraph there. Others were younger men of the news desk murder teams— once the first-flush hours of a murder hunt were over, all knew from experience that the best place to watch was the Chief Superintendent's office, that whatever might happen outside, whatever their personal contacts with Divisional men, the word that mattered most would come from Headquarters. Their cars parked in rough formation, their radios occasionally coming to life with a harsh pleading from an edition-conscious office, they watched, waited, and played an occasional, half-hearted game of Chase the Queen with a pack of tattered, time-worn cards.

The Millside car's arrival with Colin Thane aboard brought them hustling over. Thane knew most of them by sight, nodded to Jock Mills of the *Bugle*, one of the few who could claim a 'special relationship' with Millside Division, but brushed aside their queries with a quick shake of his head. He escaped through the C.I.D. bar office, stopped for a moment in the corridor beyond to straighten his tie, then pressed the signal button outside Bhudda Ilford's door.

The green 'enter' light spat back at him immediately and he went in.

'Well, at least you're prompt,' rumbled Chief Superintendent Ilford. The head of Glasgow C.I.D. was enthroned behind his big, old-fashioned desk, the long, narrow room was an inevitable litter of discarded files and reference books, and Ilford himself, his massive form encased in a dark blue suit with stiff white collar and maroon

71

silk tie, showed all the animosity of a caged bull. 'What's the latest?'

Thane told him. Ilford listened, his face expressionless, his hands automatically stoking a black-bowled pipe with tobacco from a zip-fastened pouch.

'And that's all?' queried Ilford as the recital ended. 'Huh.' He lit the pipe with a kitchen match, took a few silent puffs, and his face became more benign. 'Well, sit down, man. You're cluttering up the place.'

Thane took the chair opposite. The room was dark, dull, and in need of redecoration. But even the mention of the idea was usually enough to raise Ilford's hackles . . . he liked things as they were.

'I'm not pretending it's an easy one.' The city's C.I.D. chief sucked on his pipe, his gaze lowered towards his paunch in that look of near-meditation which had earned him his irreverent, mis-spelled nickname. 'But dammit, this thing's shaping like a casualty list—one dead and two missing. Dalziel and O'Brien . . . there couldn't be a link between them?'

'There might, but I doubt it, sir.'

'You mean you don't know,' growled Ilford. 'And this girl MacPhail?'

'Our witness—the Cador girl—will be watching her leave this evening.' Long experience held Thane's replies to pure fact.

'Even if she identifies Barbara MacPhail as her "dark-haired woman" from this drying-room it won't mean much.' Ilford's pipe had gone out. He used another match to get it going. 'You saw the wolf-pack outside?'

Thane nodded.

'I'm thinking of using them—before they use us as targets in a nasty little criticism campaign. "The police can catch a common little four-by-two burglar, but not the thug who murders his wife." It's ready-made.' He scowled. 'Maybe it doesn't worry you, Thane. But I'm the punchbag as far as the Chief Constable's concerned, not to mention the police committee, the magistrates and anyone else with time on their hands. I'm going to issue Dalziel's photograph and description—with the tag that he "may be able to help in inquiries". The television people could help too.'

'But the courts . . .' Thane winced at the notion. Defence counsel had had more than one field day in Scottish courts with that type of situation, claiming advance prejudice of juries.

'There's no question of witnesses' identification being affected,' reminded Ilford heavily. 'For a start, we haven't got any.'

'I'd like to leave it, sir. For another twenty-four hours at least,' said Thane quietly.

'Can you give me a reason?'

He shook his head. 'Not yet, except that I've still at least two people to interview.'

'Hmm.' Chief Superintendent Ilford considered the matter. He made a rule of interfering as little as possible with his Divisional men's decisions—provided they seemed the right ones. 'All right. But there's something else. When Humbie got back to Barlinnie this morning he made a song-and-dance about contacting his solicitor, who happens to be a pretty shrewd operator. The solicitor was round on the Chief Constable's doorstep in double-quick time. You've to stay away—no more questioning, no more taking him out to the flat. His client "has had enough shock and strain to last a life-time".'

'Can they bar us—just like that?'

'Yes and no,' said Ilford slowly. 'Humbie doesn't have to answer questions, especially when he's already charged with an offence. He doesn't want to see anyone, cop or conjuror. His solicitor could seek a court order to back it up—but he'd "rather avoid that and the accompanying publicity".'

'I'll bet.' Thane puzzled over the situation.

'Humbie's had it rough,' mused Ilford. 'Probably blames himself for his wife's death—remorse about having the money in the house, that sort of thing. Let's avoid the court order possibility, Colin.' He gave a quick fold of a smile. 'That way, if you ever really need to get to him, the way's still open. Now, what do you plan to do next?'

'I've a couple of calls here, sir. Then I'm going out to the Glen Ault office again. . . .'

'Barbara MacPhail?' Ilford nodded approval. 'Good. Need help in any direction?' He chuckled. 'I'd like to see over that warehouse myself—I must be one of their long-

est-standing customers. It's a fine liqueur—just that fraction silkier than the rest.'

'Greenlaw sent me a bottle this afternoon,' volunteered
Thane.

'Oh!' Ilford sucked his lips at the thought. 'Mind you,
it's not quite what it used to be. Quality's deteriorated a
little; like everything else these days.' He knocked out his
pipe in a shower of sparks. 'Right, keep in touch—I've a
meeting to attend, but I'll be back by five.'

.   .   .   .   .

To reach the Scientific Bureau he had to leave the old
Central building and cross the street to the main Headquarters block opposite. That meant running into the cor-
don of pressmen again. They stirred as he passed, but
settled back as he gave a negative shake of his head. They
didn't worry. They could wait—they were always ready to
wait.

Once through the revolving door of the main building
and past the constable on door duty he relaxed a little.
The corridor was busy, Headquarters staff mingling with
men he knew from several of the divisions. As he boarded
the elevator, a faint odour of frying fish reached his nostrils from the canteen area.

The Scientific Bureau's territory stretched over most of
the top floor—a place of low ceilings and artificial light.
Once the elevator had delivered him, he headed through
to Dan Laurence's office, rapped on the glass door, and
went in.

'Aye, I thought you'd be around.' Superintendent Laurence was in his shirt-sleeves, his white hair unkempt, the
inevitable long-ashed cigarette dangling from his mouth.
He'd been standing by a bench microscope, but he turned,
thumbing towards the inner door which led to the main
laboratory area beyond. 'Five minutes earlier, and you
could have joined in the wake. We've just finished all the
Humbie productions, and the result's zero, zero all the
way. We've still a few unidentified prints from the lifts
at Gradient Terrace, but whoever did this was damn' careful. Mark my words, by the time we've checked the milk-
man, the postman and the rest that'll be another dead
end.'

'What about the drying room?' asked Thane.

'Another waste of time.' Laurence flicked the cigarette with his tongue, and a full inch of ash fell to the floor.

'So?'

'So we try again,' snarled Laurence, angry at his failure. 'There's always interchange, Colin—the job is finding it.'

Dan Laurence and Professor MacMaster, the University forensic expert, were both regular preachers of the gospel of interchange, about the only thing they'd ever been known to agree on—and Thane was already among the converted. He'd seen it work in even the most bizarre situations. Put simply, the theory of interchange was that no act was without its consequences, that anyone who visited a place, however fleetingly, either left some trace of his visit or took away some other trace which linked him with it.

Interchange could be as fine as dust or as obvious as a knife-wound. It applied to people and things alike, it was almost as positive as a natural law—but it had to be first found and then understood.

'Dan, were you out at the original Glen Ault robbery?'

'That?' Laurence shook his head. 'Man, I can't be everywhere—I keep clear of what looks like run o' the mill stuff.'

'But the report you got—did it have to be a two-man job? Was there any trace which could be read a different way?'

'Somebody else involved as well, you mean?' Laurence sighed. 'Ach, wait a minute.' He found the file he wanted, read it through, and looked up. 'It depends what's on your mind. But all we've got are traces of two different sets o' glove patterns—and, of course, Humbie's prints on that bottle cap.' He reached his jacket down from a hook on the wall. 'Well, I'm taking a trip out to Gradient Terrace. Coming along?'

'Later maybe,' said Thane. 'I've other things to do first.'

From the Scientific Bureau he went down to Records. Most of the big, quiet room was occupied by the banked cabinets where over a quarter million men and women were listed in multiple cross-reference based on habits and history, description and convictions plus, in at least one in four cases, by fingerprints and photographs. But Thane

75

passed them by and went to the corner occupied by the reference library section.

He asked the civilian clerk for the latest edition of the Register of Scottish Companies—and when he handed it back it was with the interesting knowledge that the Glen Ault Whisky Liqueur Company Ltd, nominal share capital twenty thousand pounds, had only three director-share-holders : George Greenlaw, Greta Rodell, and a Jamieson Roth, chartered accountant.

'Having an accountant on the Board doesn't mean much,' shrugged the civilian clerk, who was a self-taught expert on a vast variety of subjects. 'He's usually just a front-man for some outside interest—could be a bank, a property company, or a private syndicate. He's simply their nominee and does what he's told. Anything else, Chief Inspector?'

'Not today.'

The clerk gave a perfunctory smile and turned back to his crossword. He needed a five-letter word meaning 'an aquatic worm' and he'd been stranded with it for more than half an hour.

.   .   .   .   .

The Millside duty car was still parked outside the Head-quarters building, its driver half-asleep behind the wheel. The man stirred and stifled a yawn as Thane got aboard.

'Where now, sir?'

'The Glen Ault place in Wood Street,' said Thane shortly. 'If you don't mind, that is.'

The driver grinned, but made a mental note to avoid tramping on his passenger's temperament. When the Mill-side C.I.D. chief began growling it paid to take notice—and it was also a sign that something was brewing. He started the engine, and slid the Jaguar into gear.

The sky was beginning to cloud over, and by the time they arrived at the warehouse a thin scattering of raindrops was beginning to fall. It looked as though John Kelso's forecast was going to be accurate.

Barbara MacPhail was once again at the reception desk when Thane entered the liqueur firm's office. 'Back again, Chief Inspector?' She shook her head and the dark hair danced. 'I'm sorry, Mr Greenlaw's out. I can't say when he'll be back.'

'It doesn't matter, Barbara. I came to see you—can you leave the desk for a spell?' he asked.

She nodded, went through to the main office, and returned with a plump young typist. 'Sue can look after things till I get back, and there's a room along the hall we can use.'

He followed her along to a small, cell-like room which had most of its space occupied by two desks and chairs. 'This is the salesmen's office,' she explained. 'They're both out most of the day.'

'Fine.' Thane leaned back against the nearest of the desks. 'Barbara, did you ever meet Mrs Humbie?'

'Yes—just once, though, when she came here to the office.' She refused his offer of a cigarette.

'Next, then. Can you think of any reason why Mrs Humble would come here last night and start a row when the watchman wouldn't give her your home address?'

She flushed, but her gaze was steady enough. 'She . . . she did that? No . . . no, I can't think why.'

'How well did you know Frank Humbie?'

'Humbie?' The girl showed bewilderment. 'He was just one of the drivers, someone I spoke to now and again.' She frowned. 'I did meet him once away from work—but that was simply when Douglas and I bumped into him in an hotel bar.'

'All right.' His whole manner remained carefully neutral. 'Mind telling me your movements after work for the last two nights?'

'I——'

'I'd ask him first why he wanted to know,' said a crisp, familiar voice behind him. He turned. Greta Rodell was standing in the doorway, a glint of interest in her eyes as she added, 'And, Barbara, some people might think that's the sort of question you don't answer unless you've got a lawyer at your elbow.'

Thane sighed. 'Hello, Miss Rodell.'

'I heard you were here,' she said in frugal explanation. 'I thought I'd find out what was going on.'

'As a director of the company?' he asked.

'Partly, yes.' She regarded him with neither warmth nor

77

rancour. 'So you've been checking up on me too? Well, I could have told you if you'd asked—it's no secret.' She sat on the edge of the desk opposite, her long slim legs swinging in a gentle whisper of nylon. 'Like me to stay, Barbara?'

'I—I don't mind.' The younger girl took a deep breath. 'I share a flat with a girl-friend, Chief Inspector. We stayed in on Wednesday night—that's our regular evening for tidying the place up, doing washing and ironing, anything like that.'

'And last night?'

'I was out, alone.' She looked at him defiantly. 'I suppose you want to know where I went?'

He nodded. 'Please.'

'I was looking for Douglas—going round places we sometimes went to, just in case he'd show up. But he didn't.'

Greta Rodell stopped her leg-swinging and frowned. 'I thought there was supposed to be nothing serious between you and Dalziel.'

'There isn't,' said the girl quietly. 'But he was in trouble —I thought if I saw him I might be able to help.'

'After he robbed the firm, and—well!' The blonde cashier gave a half-amused smile. 'I'd call it unusual, Barbara. But it's your business.'

'And mine, I'm afraid,' said Thane. 'What time did you get home?'

She shrugged. 'After eleven—I can't be sure.'

'Your flat-mate would know?'

She nodded. 'She was there when I got in.'

'And these places you went to?'

'An art gallery, a couple of cafés, a park . . .' Her lips tightened. 'Do you want me to make out a list, Chief Inspector?'

'It would help.' He looked at her for a moment, then gave an encouraging twinkle. 'We'll check—but it's such a damn' flimsy story it pretty well has to be true, doesn't it?'

'Better take your chance, Barbara, and go while he feels that way,' advised Greta Rodell crisply. 'Any objection, Mr Thane?'

'None.'

The dark-haired receptionist took a deep breath,

nodded, and went out. But the older woman was in no hurry to follow.

'Well, what was that all about?' she demanded. 'You practically scared the kid to death.'

'But not you?'

She gave a throaty chuckle. 'I've been around a few years more than she has.'

'It doesn't show.' He made the reply she obviously expected.

'I've a beauty shop bill which says it shouldn't.' She opened her handbag, took out a cigarette, and let him light it for her. 'You still haven't told me what's going on. Shouldn't you be concentrating on looking for Dalziel?'

'We are,' he said dryly. 'But there are routine inquiries.'

'In other words, why don't I mind my own business?' She shrugged. 'Well, anything else you want while you're here?'

'I'd like to talk to your foreman.'

'Ed Yuill?' She shook her head. 'He's out on a delivery run. Humbie in jail means we're a driver short, and the new man we've hired doesn't start till Monday.'

'Yuill's been with you quite a while, hasn't he?'

'Yes. George brought him down from his old job at Beauly—George managed a distillery up there for a spell.'

'I can see Yuill again . . . it's nothing important.' He dismissed the matter casually and reached for his hat. 'It came as a surprise finding you were a director. I suppose it shouldn't—but there can't be many women directors in the whisky trade.'

'A few.' She treated it as a compliment and smiled. 'It was almost an accident. I'm a widow—the Miss Rodell is strictly for business. George is an old friend, we got together, and managed to float the extra money we needed from a finance house.'

'And your third director?'

'One of their accountants—but he only shows up at quarterly meetings.' She stubbed her cigarette. 'You have to go?'

'I'm behind schedule already.'

'Pity.' She inspected him with interest. 'I'd have liked to hear something about you for a change. Well, don't hesitate about coming back—any time. You know your way out?'

He nodded. She came to the door of the room with Thane, smiled again, then left him and headed back towards the stairs. He watched her go, then walked along the corridor towards the exit.

'Mr Thane.' Barbara MacPhail was waiting by the reception desk. 'That list you wanted—it's ready.'

He took the piece of paper she handed him, glanced at it, then stowed it away in an inside pocket. 'Thanks.'

'The times may not be exactly right . . .' she began.

'We'd be more suspicious if they were spot-on,' he reassured her. 'And if things are as you say then why worry?' He grew more serious again. 'Barbara, you're still quite sure you can't think of any reason why Jean Humbie would want to see you?'

'No. I'm positive—I hardly knew her.'

'How about Douglas? Did he know her well?'

'I don't think so.'

'When was the last time you were out with him?'

She frowned for a moment, remembering. 'About two weeks ago. We had another date, but he cancelled it. He said he was busy on some work of his own, but——'

'But you weren't so sure?'

'I just didn't know.' She looked down at the tiled floor, avoiding his gaze. 'There was something on his mind, I knew that. But whether it was work or . . . well, someone else, I couldn't tell. You can't be sure what another person's thinking about.'

'And sometimes it's just as well,' said Thane cryptically. 'Goodbye, Barbara.'

It was still raining when he reached the street. He was hurrying across the pavement to the duty car when a dark red Rover coupé purred in to stop behind it. The man in the Rover waved to attract his attention, and Thane waited while George Greenlaw climbed out and came towards him.

'Looking for me, Chief Inspector?'

'No, not this time.' The rain was quickening a little, and he stood with one hand on the duty car's door handle. 'I came to see Barbara MacPhail.'

'Oh.' Greenlaw gave a nod of understanding. 'Well, I

80

hope you made out better than I did—I've just been at Barlinnie Prison. I thought . . . well, despite all that's happened I wanted to see Humbie. I wanted to say I was sorry about his wife.'

'But you didn't get to him,' nodded Thane.

Greenlaw's eyes narrowed a little. 'You know, then? They told me when I got there that he was refusing to see anyone and that unless I had a'—he searched for the phrase—'a visit-request letter from him I couldn't get in.'

'We're all in the same boat,' said Thane.

'Well, perhaps it's understandable.' Greenlaw shrugged. 'The man must have quite a lot on his conscience.' He brushed some of the rain from his suit. 'I'd better get in and see what's on my desk. We stop work for the day in half an hour.'

Thane said goodbye and climbed into the duty car while Greenlaw disappeared into the Glen Ault building. What Greenlaw had done could be in character, he supposed—but there weren't many who'd go out of their way to sympathize in person with an employee who'd gone crooked on them.

'Where now, sir?' asked the driver for the second time.

'Round the corner from here, but not too far,' said Thane, relaxing back in his seat. 'And toss over that microphone.'

.   .   .   .   .

Twenty minutes later, after a cup of coffee in a corner café a few streets away, Colin Thane boarded the small apparently down-at-heel van which had coasted to a stop beside the duty car. The man at the wheel was dressed in overalls with an open-necked shirt, the signs on each door marked the van as belonging to a delivery service, and its two-way radio was carefully hidden beneath the driving seat.

A turn of a handle opened the partition door which screened the rear of the van from view and he squeezed in past the driver.

'Everything all right?'

The plain-clothes policewoman sitting on a small bench seat beside Sheena Cador gave a nod. 'Everything fine, sir.'

81

'Thanks for coming, Sheena.'

The girl brightened a little. 'Nobody told me I had much of a choice—but it's okay.'

'You've been told what to do?'

'Watch people leavin' the Glen Ault place and see if I spot the woman who was in the drying room.' She peeled the paper from a strip of gum and began chewing. 'Here, I've been hearin' all about being a Betsy'—she saw Thane's blank puzzlement—'a Betsy, you know, a lady cop. Sounds quite a life.'

'Does it?' Thane exchanged a grin with the police-woman. 'You fancy the idea?'

'Well, it's better than foldin' Christmas cards. That was my last job.' Sheena Cador considered the possibility. 'A Betsy—well, why not?'

Thane tried hard to picture the beehive hairdo under a uniform cap. But somehow he couldn't—he just couldn't.

.　　　.　　　.　　　.　　　.

The observation van drew up and parked a few yards away from the Glen Ault office. The driver took out sand-wiches, a flask of coffee, and a science fiction paperback and settled back. His was the easiest part of the procedure.

Inside the small, enclosed body the air was already stale and smoke-filled. Thane restrained himself from another cigarette and concentrated on one of the pin-sized peep-holes bored in the side of the vehicle. As the minute hand on his watch neared the hour, a young soldier in army khaki strolled across his vision then stopped and leaned back against the side of the van. Thane saw Sheena Cador's mouth opened in protest, and he reached over in time to clap a hand firmly across her lips. She pointed angrily to her peephole, blocked by the soldier's back. He nodded, dragged her over to another peephole, then freed her mouth. She glared at him in the gloom but resumed her vigil.

At five o'clock on the dot the first of the Glen Ault office staff began to leave. The soldier detached himself from the van, crossed over and was joined by the young typist Thane had seen earlier.

'Sorry, Sheena,' murmured Thane. 'I couldn't let you yell while he was there.'

'You've made a mess of my lipstick,' she hissed back.

More people were leaving the building. He waited tensely as Barbara MacPhail came out wearing a white raincoat. She stopped by the pavement's edge, hesitated a moment, then set off alone down the road.

'Well, Sheena?'

'Nobody yet,' she said, boredom in her voice.

'What about that girl with the white coat?' asked the policewoman quietly. 'She's dark-haired.'

'No. She's too slim,' said their reluctant witness. 'How much longer does this go on? I'm hungry.'

They waited another ten minutes. Almost the last people out were Greenlaw and his cashier. Greta Rodell spoke to the Glen Ault managing director for a moment, then Greenlaw climbed into his Rover and drove off, while the blonde went her separate way.

'Who's the big fellow?' asked Sheena, stretching her cramped limbs.

'Name's Greenlaw. He runs the firm—why?' asked Thane in turn.

'Just curious—he's got a nice car.'

Thane sighed and rapped on the partitition. The driver opened the hatch door a fraction, looked in, and grinned. 'Finished, sir?'

'Finished,' agreed Thane. 'Take me back to the duty car, then make sure this girl gets transport back to Gradient Terrace.'

'What's my mother goin' to think if the police bring me home?' protested Sheena.

'The policewoman will take care of that,' he reassured her. 'There's nothing to worry about—you've been helping us with inquiries.'

She wasn't impressed. 'Look, if you want to do me a favour just drop me off near a bus stop somewhere an' I'll make my own way back.'

They did.

Frankly, decided Thane, he'd had his fill of interviewing women for the day. Folded and refolded, his breast pocket handkerchief barely managed a thin line of white once he'd wiped his hand clean of Sheena Cador's lipstick. Add the Rodell woman being coy and Barbara MacPhail being scared and he felt a sudden thankfulness for his relatively uncomplicated home life.

But it wasn't over. As he walked into the Millside C.I.D. room the duty d.c. crossed hurriedly towards him. 'Inspector Moss is in your office, sir. He's got Humbie's daughter with him.'

'Right.' From sheer habit Thane stopped to run his eye down the big, leather-bound incident book in which every C.I.D. job had to be logged. It had been a quiet afternoon —a couple of bag snatches on the east end of Main Street and a doctor's car stolen were the only fresh items listed.

'Any drugs in the car?' he asked.

'Not this time, sir.'

That, at least, made a change. He closed the book and went through.

At eighteen, Agnes Humbie was in many ways like her mother. She had the same red hair, a thin face which was strikingly like the old photographs Thane had seen in that morning's papers, and a disposition which held at least a trace of the same fiery temperament. Her hair was tied back in a ponytail, she wore no makeup, and her dress was a severely practical jersey and skirt.

'I'll get some mourning black tomorrow,' she said once Phil Moss had carried out the introductions. 'What arrangements have been made about the funeral, Chief Inspector?'

'It's not as simple as that,' said Thane, skirting round the truth of the post-mortem dissections and all the other gory trappings of the forensic investigation involved.

She listened to his explanation and firmed her lips. 'How long will it take?' Then, in a crisp, business-like fashion, she added, 'In case it matters, my mother always said she'd want to be cremated.'

'Then I'd say at least another week.' Cremation posed its own obvious problems in an unfinished investigation. 'How was the flight down, Agnes?'

'All right.' She was ill at ease. 'Mr Thane, why won't my father see me?'

'Phil?' Thane glanced across at his second-in-command.

'That's how it is,' shrugged Moss. 'I met the plane at the airport and took Agnes out to Barlinnie by car. The governor made the approach himself—but Humbie says no.'

'We can't make him see you,' said Thane slowly.

'It doesn't matter.' The words came bitterly.

'Agnes.' Thane waited until he was sure he had the girl's attention. 'Did your mother contact you at all when he was arrested?'

'No.' Her mouth worked nervously. 'I didn't even know he was back in jail until . . . until after I heard about the murder.' She hesitated. 'Do you know who did it?'

'We're not sure,' said Moss cautiously. 'Not yet.'

'What about my dad? What'll he get?'

'The courts are human. They could feel he's already had part punishment,' Thane shrugged. 'I wouldn't like to say, but they might go easy on him.'

'He deserves all he gets.' Her bitterness boiled over. 'That's why I want to see him—to tell him he can rot in there as far as I'm concerned.' She saw their surprise. 'What's so strange? Since the earliest I can remember, life has been cops barging into the house, him being marched off, and us left with no money coming in. I was four years old when I first caught on to what was happening—the other kids in the street told me all about it. And rubbed it in. I lived with it—but soon as I was old enough I got out. I've had enough. I've had enough for a long time.'

'Your mother stuck by him,' reminded Thane gently. 'She must still have loved him, whatever he'd done.'

'She did.' The eyes snapped fire. 'And she got murdered for it.' The girl rose to her feet. 'Well, I've got to thank you for the lift from the airport—it saved me a taxi.'

'You can't stay at the flat,' said Phil Moss. 'We're still working there.'

'I'll go to Uncle Joe's. He'll put me up.' She turned to leave.

'Joe O'Brien's out of town,' warned Thane. 'We're trying to locate him at this moment.'

The news brought a touch of a smile to her lips. 'You mean he's keeping out of the way? Knowing him, that's no surprise. But it's all right—I've got a key to his place. He's got a couple of rooms in behind the billiard hall.'

Phil Moss frowned. 'It's not——'

'Not suitable for a young girl?' She swept that aside in

contempt. 'We're a different generation, Inspector. We take care of ourselves, by ourselves. You'll let me know about the funeral?'

'We will,' promised Thane.

'Fine.' Her eyes hardened. 'If my father has the nerve to show up at it . . .' She left the rest unsaid, and they were glad. 'Goodbye, then. I'll get my suitcase on the way out.'

The glass in the door quivered as it slammed shut behind her. Detective Inspector Moss winced. 'Not exactly what I expected,' he admitted.

'She had to graduate through a pretty hard school,' mused Thane. He settled down in his chair and swung his feet up on the desk with a sigh of pure bliss. 'Well?'

'I still don't like the idea of her being around that billiard hall,' frowned Moss.

'What makes you think I do?' Thane took out his cigarettes, lit one, then tossed packet and lighter across to his companion. 'I'd have a Betsy in beside her if I thought she'd accept.' He saw Moss's blank look and chuckled. 'That's Fortrose talk for a w.p.c. But the next best thing is to warn the men who're already watching the hall for Joe O'Brien coming back. Tell 'em to make sure she comes to no harm.'

'Fair enough,' nodded Moss. The mention of Fortrose reminded him of another matter. 'There's a report in from young Beech. I sent him to see Danny Farrell—young Sheena's boy-friend. Farrell confirms this story of the couple in the drying room, but he can't even begin to describe them.' A rumble from his stomach area brought a more pressing point to the fore. 'We're due out at that news stance in about an hour. Do we eat first? I mean eat —not another dose of sandwiches.'

'Why not?' Thane regarded his second-in-command benevolently. 'By the way, I've decided to spare your wind and limbs, Phil. I'll take care of the news stance on my own.'

'Leaving me to mop up some other dirty job,' concluded Moss with a growl. 'Well, what is it this time?'

'A full check on the Glen Ault company. I want to know how much of the money used to buy the place was their own and how much of it came from the finance house involved. I want to know how their bank balance stands, whether they've a good credit rating, anything you can dig up on Greenlaw, Greta Rodell or their foreman.' He stopped, his brow furrowed. Phil Moss stayed silent, knowing there was something more, knowing that Thane wanted to tell him, to tell someone, but that he would do it only in his own time.

Thane took almost a minute to himself, the cigarette burning unheeded between his fingers. Then, at last, it came. 'Phil, I don't like this one, I don't like one thing about it. The pattern's wrong, it doesn't make sense.'

'But the facts——'

'The facts. I know.' The big Millside detective swung his feet down from the desk. 'Phil, I'm damned if I believe them.'

'Did you tell Ilford this?'

'No. I've nothing to back it up with.'

'Well . . .' For once his companion was at a loss. 'I'll make the checks. But right now I think we should eat.'

'Let's do that.' It was off his chest, and Thane felt relaxed. 'I want to 'phone home first and say hello to Mary. Fix up about the girl, Phil—I'll be out in a minute.'

He waited until Moss had gone out, then lifted the telephone and had the switchboard get his home number. The telephone at the other end of the line rang a couple of times, then he heard the click as the other receiver was lifted.

'Mary?'

'Who else?' His wife's voice chuckled over the wire. 'When are you coming home?'

'I don't know. Not till late, maybe not tonight.'

'I see.' He sensed as much as heard the resignation in the words. 'The papers say there should be an early arrest.'

'Then the papers know more than I do. How are the kids?'

'Fine—they're just going to have tea.'

'I'm going out with Phil,' he said absently. 'We'll stoke up somewhere.'

'Good,' she said approvingly. Mary Thane had two golden rules as far as her husband was concerned—he had to have dry socks and a full stomach. The rest she was prepared to take on chance. 'Well, you'll get a better meal

87

than we're having. I baked one of those fancy layer cakes for Kate, but it turned out a disaster.'

He grinned at her disappointment. 'New recipe?'

'No—the usual,' she told him. 'It was the damned baking powder, I think. I ran out of the stuff and borrowed a new brand from Mrs Marshall next door. It was the same but different—you know what I mean.'

'Let's say I've a vague idea.' He glanced at the clock on the wall. 'I'll need to go, Mary. Say hello to the kids for me.'

'I'll put your picture on the mantelpiece . . .' He heard her sound a kiss over the wire. 'That way they'll remember what you look like. 'Bye, Colin.'

'Goodbye, dear.' He hung up, stubbed his cigarette, and went out to join Moss.

.   .   .   .   .

The junction of Fortrose Road and Stanford Avenue was a busy time and place on any week-night. It was close to the turning point for the housing development's main bus route, it was where boy usually arranged to meet girl —and at 6.30 p.m. the last tide of homecoming workers was mixing with the first wave of Fortrose residents heading back into town for an evening's enjoyment.

Police Constable Andy MacPherson puffed out his massive chest until the tunic buttons strained, and scowled around him, moving on at least half a dozen loitering youngsters in the process. His massive legs spanned one of the bundles of string-parcelled newspapers and magazines which had been dumped by a delivery van, but there was still no sign of the man they were intended for.

'He should be here by now, sir,' he rumbled. 'Not like Pekey to be late—not like him at all.'

'Maybe he's in a pub somewhere,' suggested Thane, comfortably conscious of the meal under his belt. He'd arrived by car to find MacPherson already waiting at the news stance, which was little more than a canvas shelter perched on a small plot of waste ground left by some planning oversight when the terraced houses around had been laid out.

'Pekey Rafferty?' MacPherson stroked his moustache. 'No, sir. He bets before work, but only drinks after—there are plenty of shebeens open in the wee sma' hours of the morning if you know where to look.'

'Here?' Thane knew the Fortrose development had its black sheep. They'd broken up a reefer party in one house, and there'd been half a dozen kids on a rum and Purple Hearts binge a few months back. But unlicensed drinking dens were usually confined to the older parts of the Division.

'Well . . . not on my beat.' MacPherson scowled around again then crooked a massive forefinger. A youngster in jeans and a saddle-stitched black shirt shuffled reluctantly towards them.

'Seen Pekey?' demanded MacPherson. 'And stand up straight, lad—come on. How long've you been here?'

The black shirt twitched into a slightly more upright position. 'Me? Twenty minutes, maybe more. Since before his papers came, anyway.' The youngster brightened. 'Think he's had an accident? Fallen under a bus, eh?'

'That's our worry, not yours.' MacPherson dismissed the boy and turned back to Thane. 'I don't know, sir. There could have been an accident, I suppose——'

They let another ten minutes pass, and by then Thane had had enough. 'Still got that address, MacPherson?'

'Aye.' The beat constable burrowed in his notebook. 'Here it is, sir. 142 Cannon Street. Eh . . . want me to come along?'

'No. You stay here in case he shows up.'

Constable MacPherson nodded understanding. He watched Thane move at a jog-trot over to the waiting duty car. As the car moved off, making a fast U-turn back in towards the city, he sucked in a breath, clasped his hands behind his back, and settled to his vigil.

.   .   .   .   .

Cannon Street is in old Millside—the typical of a layer of Glasgow left out of both guide books and slum sagas. The tenements are old and their stonework needs repointing. The landlords take their pound of flesh and complain about giving half an ounce in return. But the communal entries and stairs are scrubbed clean, the landings are pipeclayed every Saturday night, and the worn lace curtains are washed religiously every second Monday.

Cannon Street was a street of old houses which still clung to pride—and was, Thane admitted, rather a surprising address for a character like Pekey Rafferty. But it was also a place where every other window seemed to have a housewife busy watching the world go by.

'Round the next corner and stop clear of this lot.'

His driver grinned and obeyed.

Thane walked back. It was, he decided, still a chancy evening from the weather standpoint. The rain had died, but there were enough clouds around to make the whole atmosphere dull and overcast. He thought again of Kelso, and grinned at the Excise surveyor's bad luck.

Nearing the last tenement before the corner with Cannon Street, he walked through the passageway close to the back of the building, stopped, and gave a nod of satisfaction as he saw the strip of communal drying green beyond. The older parts of Glasgow were all built to the pattern, a hollow square of homes with a drying green in their centre—a pattern which saved the need for any direct frontal approach to a house.

Finding the back entrance to 142 Cannon Street was no problem, and he stepped quietly into the cool gloom of the tenement and began checking door-plates, moving up the stairway with the minimum of noise.

The door with the worn, well-polished brass plate labelled 'P. Rafferty' was two floors up. Thane rang the bell, waited, tried again, then gave a turn to the door handle and found it locked. There was a drill for that kind of situation in a place like Cannon Street. He lifted the doormat at his feet, saw only bare concrete, and replaced the mat with a shrug. He tried the letterbox, and his fingers first brushed then held the length of string dangling behind it. A moment's effort, and he had the doorkey in his hand. He unlocked the door and went in.

The hallway was tiny and dark, with only two rooms leading off it. He tried the first, and looked into a small kitchen cum living room, neat but deserted. He closed its door and tried the other, a bedroom.

As he stepped inside, he sensed a flicker of movement—then a heavy blow took him on the back of the neck and he pitched forward into a cloud of blinding pain.

5

He was lying on the floor with something cold and wet draped across his face, and a voice which seemed vaguely recognizable was speaking to him from a long distance away.

'Wake up, damn you . . . sir.' The wet covering was removed, he heard a splash of water, and then the cloth descended again.

Colin Thane gave a spluttering groan, clawed the rag away, and tried to sit up, his head still throbbing and his vision swimming.

'Take it easy, now.' Detective Sergeant MacLeod's anxious, familiar face peered down at him. 'What happened, sir?'

Thane clenched his teeth, finished the job of sitting up, then explored his neck and scalp with gentle fingers. A king-sized bruise was beginning to gather, but otherwise he seemed intact.

'Where's that cloth, Mac?' He took the cold, damp pad and applied it thankfully. 'What's the time?'

'Quarter past seven, sir.'

'Hell.' That meant he'd been out for almost ten minutes. 'Give me a hand up.' He let MacLeod half-carry him across to the bed, and sat thankfully on its edge. 'What the devil are you doing here anyway?'

Detective Sergeant MacLeod gave a faint sniff which could have been translated in several ways. 'I came to see if this man Rafferty was at home, sir.'

'Why?'

'Because Mrs Humbie came here early yesterday evening,' said MacLeod patiently. 'Of course, I didn't know you were working on the same line, Chief Inspector.'

'I wasn't, not directly.' Thane tried to rise, groaned at

the effort, and decided to wait a little longer. 'How'd you trace her here, Mac?'

'Part routine, part luck.' But MacLeod was more than a little pleased with himself. 'I tried the bus route nearest to Joe O'Brien's billiard hall and found a conductor who remembered a woman like her getting on his bus last night. She stuck in his mind because she'd only a pound note and he'd no change—he let her travel free. Mrs Humbie—this woman anyway—got off at the Cannon Street stop, and from there I just asked around. She went into a dairy across the way to ask where Rafferty lived.'

'What time?'

'About five last night, sir.'

'Good.' Thane moved very slowly this time, got to his feet, and stayed there. 'You did just one thing wrong, Mac.'

'Sir?'

'Why the hell couldn't you have been here fifteen minutes earlier? Then it would have been your head that got clouted.'

Detective Sergeant MacLeod didn't seem to find it funny. And all he could add to his story was that he'd arrived to find the front door closed and had used the same 'key in the letter-box' routine to gain entry. He'd seen no one leave the building as he came in.

They made a laborious check through the two-roomed flat, but whoever had attacked Thane had been careful, too careful, to leave any trace of his visit.

'Leave it,' decided Thane reluctantly. 'Let's try some of the neighbours.'

There was no reply from the flat next door. But as they turned away a small, grey-haired woman came plodding doggedly up the stairway towards them with a leather shopping bag in one hand.

'That's my door you're knocking at,' she announced. 'And if you're selling anything, I'm not for buying.'

'Police,' explained Thane briefly. 'Any idea where Mr Rafferty is?'

She blinked. 'Well, you folk should know if anyone does.'

'Eh?' MacLeod showed his impatience and got a firm glare in return.

92

'If you don't know what goes on in your own business . . .' She shook her head. 'There was a policeman
round at me this morning. Mr Rafferty's in the Central
Police cells—for the usual, being drunk. What I'd like to
know is why he always gives my name as a friend when
he's in that state. I've no money to pay his fine.'

'When was he picked up?' demanded Thane.

'Och, sometime in the middle of the night,' she told him.
'According to the policeman he was found wanderin' along
Argyle Street, singing his head off.' She gave a sad shake
of her head. 'Yet he's a nice quiet soul when he hasn't got
money for drink.'

'I'm sure of it.' Thane thanked her hastily as the throb
in his head built up again. He briefed MacLeod to check
round the rest of the tenants in the building on the slim
off-chance that one of them might have noticed a stranger,
then headed back to the duty car.

.   .   .   .   .

The turnkey at the Central Police Office walked with a
limp that dated back to when he'd been on point duty
and had got in the way of a skidding truck. He jangled the
bunch of keys in his hand and hobbled along the white-
tiled corridor which led to the cells, talking as he went.

'We'd have boosted him out to Barlinnie with the rest of
the morning court mob,' he explained cheerfully. 'But
Pekey Rafferty always manages to raise his fine eventually,
and it saves a lot of bother this way.'

'What did he get?' asked Thane.

'The usual—two pounds or twenty days,' grinned the
turnkey. 'Here we are.' He selected one of the keys from
his collection, unlocked the cell door nearest them, and
stuck his head inside. 'Visitor for you, Pekey.'

'Eh?' Rafferty shuffled forward. He was thin, unshaven,
bald and hollow-cheeked, clad in a worn tweed suit with
large leather patches at the elbows.

'Chief Inspector Thane from Millside Division,' said the
turnkey. 'Better put your teeth back in, Pekey—it helps.'

'Aye—aye, I'll do that.' The man turned away, burrowed among the blankets on his bunk, and returned with
the dentures in place and displayed in a hopeful smile.

'Has somebody paid my fine, eh?' He looked at them for a moment, and the smile faded. 'No, you wouldn't be here for that—not a C.I.D. big-shot. Is it about Frank Humbie, then?'

Thane glanced at the turnkey and raised an eyebrow.

'He's sober enough now,' confirmed the officer. 'But he was as high as a coot this morning.'

'Has he seen any newspapers since he came in?'

'No. Room service is poor around here.'

Thane switched back to the newsvendor. 'Mrs Humbie first, Pekey. You saw her last night?'

'Twice. She'll have told you about it, eh?'

'She's dead, Pekey. She was murdered last night.'

'Murdered!' Rafferty stared at him unbelievingly for a moment then solemnly crossed himself. 'She was a decent woman, that one.'

'Tell me about meeting her,' prodded Thane. 'When was the first time?'

'She came up to m'house about five last night.' The man moistened his lips, still shaken. 'After that, the second time I saw her was coming on for ten o'clock. She passed me in a taxi, out at Stanford Avenue—then the taxi stopped, and she walked back to talk to me again. Said she just wanted to make sure she had everything right. . . .'

'Everything right about what?'

'About me seein' Frank the night he was lifted for the robbery job,' said Rafferty. 'Did she not tell you?'

'She didn't get the chance.'

'Oh.' The little man sighed. 'I could use a drink—medicinal, like to help me over the shock.'

The turnkey gave a curt but friendly laugh. 'Nothing doing, Pekey. You were on rotgut last night—a glass of anything and you'd be paralytic again inside five minutes.'

'When did you see Frank?' demanded Thane. 'Let's have the story—I haven't time to waste.'

'I'll tell it just the way I told her. I was at my pitch in Stanford Avenue a bit after midnight when Frank walks up, says hello and buys a paper. He talked about the dog-racing for a minute, then went on home.'

'You mean he'd been at the dogs?'

Rafferty shook his head. 'No. But he was keen to know the results. Said he had to tell his wife he'd been there.'

'And where had he been?'

'Well . . .' The newsvendor sounded almost embarrassed. 'He didn't say, an' I didn't ask. But I heard a car draw up just before he appeared. It went past a matter o' seconds later.'

'What kind of car?'

Rafferty shrugged. 'Ach, I didn't bother. Just a wee black car, that's all I know. Except that there was a woman drivin' it. The thing only clicked wi' me when Frank turned up. If he'd been out wi' some woman in a car he wouldn't want his wife to know, would he? Not at that time o' night.'

'But you told Mrs Humbie?'

'Well, aye . . .' Rafferty gave a reluctant nod. 'She slipped me a couple o' quid and said it was important, that telling what I'd seen might get him out o' jail.'

'That was when she came to see you the first time?'

'Uh-huh. I didn't start on the booze, mind, until after I'd finished wi' the papers. That's a wee rule o' mine—the work comes first.'

'You said Frank Humbie bought his paper not long after midnight.' Thane felt the tension gathering within him at the implication that involved 'How sure are you of the time?'

'I'm no' just sure, mister—I'm positive,' said Rafferty wearily. 'Look, I don't even have to think about it. I get two loads o' morning papers. The first is dumped off at 11 p.m., the second lot at half-twelve, always dead on the dot. Frank Humbie was on his way home long before the second load arrived.'

'The woman in the car, Pekey—can you describe her?'

'Mrs Humbie asked that too,' said Rafferty ruefully. 'Hammered away at it. All I could tell her was this dolly-bird in the car had dark hair, maybe kinda long—though I'm no' awful sure about it.'

He couldn't expand on the description, and there were only two more questions to ask.

'What gave Jean Humbie the idea to come and see you?'

'Ach, she remembered Frank comin' in wi' the paper an' sayin' he'd got it from me.'

'Did you tell anyone about her coming to you?'

Rafferty looked pained. 'No—at least, I don't think so.

But I'm a wee bit hazy about some o' last night, if you know what I mean, like.' He brightened. 'Here, any chance o' gettin' my fine paid now? Fair's fair, eh?'

Thane's left hand strayed to the lump on his head. 'Stay where you are, Pekey,' he advised. 'It's a whole lot safer than outside.'

'And the meals are regular,' added the turnkey. He had the cell door shut and locked before the newsvendor could answer.

.   .   .   .   .

Colin Thane sat silent while the duty car took him out to Gradient Terrace. He ignored the traffic, his mind struggling to put the new facts into order. If he was much nearer the truth, it was purely because the confusion was growing—for if Rafferty was right, if that newspaper was in Humbie's flat, it meant Jean Humbie hadn't lied, that her husband had been home before the getaway car had driven away from the Glen Ault offices.

But what would that do in turn to the rest of the evidence, the so-called hard facts he'd already found himself instinctively distrusting? He was still forcing his thoughts towards an answer, still coming up with only wildly improbable theories, when the duty car drew up outside the high block of flats. He sat on for a moment while the driver waited, curious but prudently silent. At last, he made a token decision.

'Radio in and have D.I. Moss meet me out here,' he ordered. 'Pass it as urgent.'

He'd left the car before the uniformed man had time to nod.

Up on the twelfth floor, a constable opened the door of the murder flat. Thane brushed past him and into the living room, where a joyful rumble reached his ears.

'Ruddy telepathy,' greeted Dan Laurence, rising from behind the television set. 'I was just going to try and get you out here.'

'Oh?' Thane glanced around and headed towards the bundle of newspapers piled on a shelf.

'Damn it, don't you want to know why?' barked Laurence irately.

'In a minute, Dan . . .' He flicked his way through the newspapers and sighed. There was no Thursday morning edition in sight. 'Any other papers around?'

'To hell with the newspapers,' hooted the Scientific Bureau chief. 'Listen, will you! I said there was always interchange, didn't I?'

'Uh-huh.' Thane still looked around.

'Well, I've found it,' said Laurence. 'Come here.'

That was different. He crossed obediently to the television set. 'Well?'

'These screws,' said Laurence, pointing to half a dozen small bronze screwnails, each now nestling in a separate plastic envelope. 'They were used to hold the back-plate to the set, and the back-plate was removed, right?'

'To get to the money.' Thane's attention hardened. 'What about them, Dan?'

'Something ruddy peculiar,' growled Laurence. 'This is a rented set—and the rental firms don't like customers pokin' around in the guts of their TVs. So a good few of them always put a wee dab o' red paint on each screw-head, almost like a seal. If the paint's disturbed, they know somebody's been trying to fix things themselves.'

'What's that got to do with it?'

'Just this.' Laurence was enjoying himself now. 'These screws have only one set of markings—and even under an ordinary jeweller's glass there's no chance of mistake in that fact. Whoever did it used a small-bladed screwdriver, badly worn on one shoulder of the tip. I've got my interchange, Colin. Find me that screwdriver and it's as good as a fingerprint. But that's only part of it. Can you tell me how the devil the money got inside the set in the first place, when the back was only taken off once?' He looked at Thane for a moment, then his exuberance gradually faded. 'You don't seem very surprised!'

'I'm not, Dan,' said Thane, his voice harsh and low.

'You're not?' Laurence goggled at him.

'It was a fake,' said Thane bitterly. 'A fake just as much as the way Humbie helped to frame himself for robbery— a robbery that has to be a cover-up for something a damned sight bigger. We fell for that part, Dan. And the only thing to go sour about it was that Jean Humbie got

97

in the way.' He broke off as the duty car driver bustled into the room. 'Want me?'

'Yes, sir.' The driver had been hurrying. 'I radioed for D.I. Moss, but he's out in a car himself. He's gone to O'Brien's billiard hall—he says he may have a lead on where O'Brien's hiding.'

'Right.' Thane began heading for the door. 'Let's get over there.'

'Colin . . . !' Dan Laurence let out a despairing wail. 'What the hell's going on?' He was too late. He swore pungently, got down on his knees again, and gathered up the screwnails in their envelope.

. . . . .

Most people would have called it a tedious task, but Phil Moss tackled his check on the Glen Ault company with an unperturbed dedication. Armed with a list of names and telephone numbers, some of them gleaned from the Fraud Squad at Headquarters, he spent over an hour on the telephone. When he'd finished, the receiver was hand-hot, his ear felt numb, and he'd gathered a scribbled collection of facts and figures still scattered in unrelated confusion.

He pulled a fresh sheet of paper toward him, then swore softly as the telephone shrilled again. He let it ring for another moment before answering.

'Moss.'

'Gunn here, Inspector.'

'Well?' Moss sucked his lips. D.C. Gunn was currently on watch outside the Eagle Sporting Centre and was overdue for relief. But there was no relief man available.

'It's Agnes Humbie,' said Gunn, his voice underlaid by the background noise of traffic. 'She left the billiard hall about ten minutes back.'

'Where'd she go?' Moss cradled the receiver against his shoulder and concentrated on drawing three neat lines across the sheet of paper.

'That's why I'm calling,' explained Gunn. 'She walked along to a hire-car office in Main Street. I checked once she'd left—she has a car and driver hired to take her out to Aberfoyle in an hour's time.'

Moss gave a soft whistle and abandoned his chart. Aberfoyle was twenty-five miles north of Glasgow, strictly a tourist village on the fringe of the tree-lined hills of the Queen Elizabeth Forest. It had scenery, a few hotels, but not much more. 'Where is she now?'

'Back in the billiard hall,' said Gunn. 'I looked in to make sure—she's talking to the hall attendant. I'm in a 'phone box across the street.'

'Right. Stay there and I'll come over.' Moss broke the connection, flashed the station switchboard, told them where he was going, then hung up and headed for the door.

There was no duty car available outside the front office. But one of the traffic patrol cars was in the Millside parking lot, its crew inspecting a wrecked motor-cycle whose rider would face a string of charges once he left hospital. Moss unashamedly pulled rank to cadge a lift and five minutes later he was dropped off beside D.C. Gunn, who was standing in a doorway fifty yards away from the billiard hall.

'She's still inside?'

Gunn nodded. 'Nobody's come out lately. What about the hire car?'

'Go round and tell them it's cancelled. I'll talk to the girl—if she goes anywhere tonight we're providing the transport.'

The Eagle Sporting Centre was always busy on a Friday night. When Moss pushed open the door and went through, lights gleamed at every table in the smoke-filled hall. The constant clicking of cue against ball was the main sound to be heard. He looked around and then saw the girl. She was standing beside the hall attendant's desk, talking to Joe O'Brien's sullen-faced young assistant. A small cluster of Eagle regulars lounged around, waiting for tables to become vacant.

'Agnes . . .' Moss walked over, beckoning to her.

She turned, frowned, said something quickly to the hall attendant, then came towards him. 'Well, Inspector? Still worried about me?'

He shook his head. 'Not as long as you tell me why you want to go to Aberfoyle.'

'Who says I'm going anywhere?' she asked abruptly.

99

Detective Inspector Moss gave a sigh. 'We know about the hire car. And we're still looking for Joe O'Brien.'

'Maybe I just feel like a run out into the country,' she fenced clumsily. 'What's it got to do with you?'

'A lot,' he snapped, losing all that was left of his patience. 'Don't you want to help us find who killed your mother?'

Agnes Humbie's chin set stubbornly. 'If Uncle Joe could help he would.' She started to walk away, and he reached out an arm to stop her.

'Less of it, mister.' A bulky, beery-breathed labourer suddenly shoved hard against him. 'Leave the kid alone—unless you want your face shoved in.'

'Get lost,' agreed another of the Eagle's regulars, detaching himself from the watching cluster. 'That's Joe's niece.'

'Now look——' began Moss.

'Look, nothing!' The nearest man swung a wild massive fist. Delivered sober, it was a punch which would have knocked Moss back across the nearest table. But the wiry Millside man dodged, then used his right leg and a quick wrist-lock. His bulky opponent crashed forward, his head banging hard against the underside of the billiard table.

The second regular, swaying unsteadily, stopped to grab a cue from the nearby rack. The hall had gone suddenly quiet, games abandoned, and Moss ducked back as his new antagonist came in, swinging the cue butt-end foremost.

'Cut it out—I'm a police officer!'

'Eh?' The man stopped short, blinking. 'Here, Agnes—is he?'

She nodded. 'But don't let that stop you as far as I'm concerned.'

'Well, eh . . .' the man hastily lowered the cue and swallowed hard. 'Sorry, friend. We were just——'

'Looking after her, I know,' snapped Moss roughly. 'Don't be so ruddy quick off your mark next time.' He glared at the other would-be protector, struggling up from the floor. 'Better take care of your friend.'

'Ay, right.' Muttering, the man shambled over to obey. Around them, the tables came back to life. Amusement over, there were games to be won.

'Let's get down to business, Agnes,' said Moss wearily. 'Where's your uncle? What's he been up to?'

'Ask Matt Pierce, the hall-man,' she snapped. 'He knows.

'I'll do that. But you're staying.' He took her arm again and led her across to the attendant's desk, the onlookers parting to let them through.

'Back again?' O'Brien's assistant, resplendent in his evening rig of sharply cut 'mod' suit with a narrow black string tie, snickered as they reached him. 'I thought the big fella was really goin' to clobber you across the chops.'

'You'd have enjoyed that, wouldn't you?' Moss crooked a thin, commanding forefinger. 'Out from behind that barricade, sonny. We're going to have a little talk—in private.'

'Eh? I can't leave the tables——'

'Out.' Moss grabbed the hall-man by the lapels and yanked him clear. 'Where's O'Brien's office?'

'In at the back—an' watch the material, pal.' Pierce scowled and anxiously smoothed his jacket. 'This lot set me back a bundle o' cash.'

'Then you wouldn't want to get it ripped, would you?' grinned Moss happily. 'Let's go.'

The hall-man sighed and led them to O'Brien's office, a little cubicle of a room near the entrance. Moss guided the girl in ahead of him, then nodded. 'Close the door.'

'Okay.' It slammed shut.

'Now then,' rapped Moss. 'Where's Joe O'Brien?'

Matt Pierce gave a sickly frown. 'Well, it's a bit difficult——'

'Tell him,' sighed Agnes. 'Uncle Joe will understand.'

The hall-man shrugged. 'He's at a place nearby Aberfoyle, the Ardmoor Hotel. But he told me to keep my mouth shut about it—except to let Agnes know once she got here.'

'Is he alone?'

'No. He's there wi' a reporter called Eastgate, Mario Eastgate. One o' the Sunday papers is payin' Joe a packet for his story.'

The girl gave an angry hiss. 'You didn't tell me that part.'

'Joe was goin' to do his own explainin' when he saw

101

you,' explained Pierce uneasily. 'He just offered me twenty quid to keep my mouth shut.'

Moss grunted. 'Who else have you told?'

'Nobody, so help me. I was only doin' Joe a favour—though he did say there'd be more money around if I kept the hall runnin' till he got back.'

'Then has anyone else been trying to find out where he is?' demanded Moss, his dislike of the young hall-man growing by the moment.

'Well . . .' Pierce gnawed his lip. 'Another reporter's been on the 'phone a few times. A bloke called Carter.'

'What paper?'

Pierce frowned. 'I don't know—never bothered to ask.'

'And he didn't bother to tell?' Moss lifted the telephone lying on an old chair by the door and began dialling the *Evening Bugle* office number. He was lucky. When the *Bugle* switchboard answered, the operator said that Jock Mills was out—but she had a number where he could be reached. Moss thanked her, broke the connection, redialled, and gave a grunt of relief when he heard the red-haired crime reporter's voice answer the call.

'It's Phil Moss of Millside, Jock. I need a little help. Who's Mario Eastgate?'

'Him?' Mills gave a wry chuckle over the line. 'He's new here—one of the London mob usually, but he's up on a circulation-boost attachment, with money to burn.'

'He does crime stuff?'

'He ghosts it,' corrected Mills. 'You know how it is. The average ned can hardly scrawl his name on a cash receipt, so Eastgate writes the story for him.' His interest grew. 'I heard he had some angle on the Humbie case. What's he been up to, Phil?'

'Nobbled a witness,' said Moss briefly. 'Another name, Jock. Do you know a reporter called Carter?'

'No—but hold on.'

Moss waited, hearing an indistinct mumble of voices at the other end of the line. The office door opened, and Colin Thane looked in. He saw Moss on the 'phone, nodded, entered the room, and closed the door.

'Phil?' Jock Mills came back on the line. 'Sorry, can't help. I'm at a pal's house—six of us are having a poker session. We're all in the business, but nobody knows a Carter.'

'Thanks, Jock.' Moss remembered the formula to keep the red-haired newspaperman happy. 'You'll get first bite at the story when we can talk about it.' He hung up.

'What story?' queried Thane, glancing at Agnes and the hall attendant. He chuckled. 'Phil, I hear you've been fighting again.'

'Huh.' Moss found no pleasure in the reminder. 'O'Brien's hiding out with a pressman near Aberfoyle. Our little friend with the hand-chiselled suit knew about it all along.'

'Did he?' Thane eyed Matt Pierce in a way which made the young hall-man take a step back. 'And who's this Carter character you were talking about?'

'Somebody pretending to be a reporter and anxious to know where O'Brien is,' paraphrased Moss. 'Did you tell him anything, Pierce? Don't fool around with the answer —if you do, it could mean real trouble for you.'

'I didn't tell him.' A bead of perspiration ran down the hall-man's forehead, then another. 'So help me, I didn't.'

'Let's hope you mean it.' Thane moved to the telephone, unscrewed the mouthpiece, and slipped the diaphragm plate into his pocket. 'That's just in case you've thought of warning Joe. And we've a man outside, so don't try anything clever that way.'

'What about my uncle?' demanded Agnes, a new concern in her voice. 'If there's somebody else looking for him——'

'We're going to see him now,' said Thane. He grinned. 'You stay here for the time being, Agnes. You seem to have plenty of protectors handy.'

Phil Moss didn't argue.

.   .   .   .   .

The road from Glasgow to Aberfoyle is reasonably fast, though it has at least its share of narrow winding turns and short straights where overtaking calls for a firm accelerator and a trust in luck. As the police Jaguar swept north, eating the twenty-five-mile distance, Thane first radioed

Headquarters and put them in the picture, then settled back against his seat and told Moss what had happened at Pekey Rafferty's house and afterwards.

'Pekey was lucky—and so were you,' agreed Moss, clinging to the upholstery as their driver did a neat four-wheel drift round an inviting bend. 'Hey, do we need to go so fast?'

'The sooner we've collected Joe O'Brien the happier I'll be,' said Thane grimly. Up front, the driver heard him and, without any change of expression, happily settled down to overtake a cream Mercedes purring unsuspectingly ahead.

'How's your head now?' asked Moss.

'It could be worse.' Thane shrugged. 'Whoever thumped me only did it because I was in his way of getting clear. But if Pekey had walked in . . .' He left it unfinished. 'Somebody's covering up, Phil. Covering up every way he knows, whatever the cost.'

'And Frank Humbie?' Moss winced as they swept past the Mercedes. 'If that money-bag and the withdrawal slips were planted at the flat after his wife was killed . . .' He struggled to grasp the wider implication. 'What the heck's going on, Colin?'

'Start off that Jean Humbie knew Frank was home too early to be involved in the Glen Ault robbery, whatever the evidence,' growled Thane angrily. 'Then, after she saw Pekey, she must have told somebody she had confirmation —and that somebody decided to silence her and sew the case up still tighter against her husband.'

'But if Humbie knows this, and he's bound to——'

'It takes a pretty powerful reason for a man to hear his wife's been murdered and still stay silent,' said Thane, his face a frowning mask. 'But we helped, damn it. Who let him play along with the idea that the Glen Ault cash had been hidden in the television set? We did—we told him what we'd found!'

'His own wife.' Moss murmured the words. 'There's only one reason I can think of that's strong enough to keep him quiet. Murder—murder equals murder. Douglas Dalziel?'

'Dalziel,' agreed Thane. 'He has to be dead, Phil. And that has to be the reason why Humbie daren't talk—because if he does he's risking his own neck.'

'But why kill Dalziel?' Moss sighed. The situation was

getting too much for him. 'Why kill a small-fry office clerk——'

'The answer has to be somewhere around the Glen Ault place, Phil. What did you find out about them?'

'Nothing that seems to matter.' Moss helped himself to a pill from his reserve supply and sucked it gently. 'They're A.1 financially. Greenlaw and the Rodell woman put up more than half of the purchase price when they took over, and the finance company regarded it as top-class investment—still do. Greenlaw's been most of his life in the whisky trade and knows his job.'

'What about Yuill?'

'The foreman?' Moss shrugged. 'Couldn't get much on him. He was a charge-hand at this distillery in Beauly, no complaints from anyone. Greta Rodell's more interesting. She's forty-three, according to the agreement deeds they signed. She used to visit Greenlaw up at Beauly, and gossip was they were more than friends. But Greenlaw has a wife in Edinburgh who doesn't want him around but won't let him go.'

'She said she was a widow. . . .'

'The Rodell woman? That's genuine. Her husband was killed in the Normandy invasion.'

Over the county border into Stirlingshire, climbing the gentle scenic heights of the Campsie Fells, their pace was slowed by a steady flow of family cars trundling along on evening outings. But the Jaguar wriggled through and settled back into its six-cylinder stride over the rich, flat farmland beyond. Its passengers sat silent, jolted now and again as the big car kissed the occasional corrugated length of tarmac which told of soft peat below the road's foundations. Trees and mountains loomed ahead, Thane caught his first glimpse of the massive shoulders of Ben Lomond, and then the driver slowed and pulled in at the roadside to consult his map.

'I make it next turning on the right, sir—then about a mile on to Ardmoor Hotel.'

'Good.' As the car moved off again Thane lit a cigarette and nudged his companion. 'Phil, wake up.'

'Huh?' Moss blinked and yawned. 'I wasn't sleeping . . . just giving my eyes a rest. Nearly there?'

Thane nodded. Ardmoor Hotel, a big, old-style mansion

105

house of grey stone with whitewashed outbuildings, was already ahead. The size and scale of its surrounding gardens showed the type of owner who'd once called it home, but a high neon sign and the compact, modern filling station beside it spoke the language of the mansion's new use.

The car crunched up a short gravelled runway and stopped beside the entrance door. They got out, stretched their legs, and then entered the hotel while the driver steered the Jaguar towards the parking area.

'Can I help you?' The receptionist was a friendly blonde with her hair piled Britannia style. Her desk-top was a slab of synthetic marble, and the parquet flooring around was covered by a scatter of sheepskin rugs.

Thane showed his warrant card and watched her face change to cool surprise. 'You've two guests, a journalist called Eastgate and a man O'Brien?'

Her eyes twinkled. 'I'd an idea they might be involved. Yes—they've had dinner. They'll be in the bar. The public bar, Chief Inspector. Mr O'Brien says he doesn't believe in drinking sitting down.'

They thanked her and followed the signs on the walls. The public bar was at the back of the hotel, busy and narrow, with a high glass ceiling.

'There he is . . .' Phil Moss stopped in the doorway and nodded towards the far end of the bar counter. Wreathed in smiles, a pint mug of beer in his grip, Joe O'Brien was in animated conversation with the tall, sleek-haired man by his side. 'Do we break up the party?'

'Straight off,' growled Thane. He strode down the length of the bar, a burly, angry figure, Moss following close behind. Joe O'Brien stopped talking for a moment to take another long gulp of beer—and as he saw them, the gulp changed to a choking swallow.

'Well, Joe?' Thane rested one hand on the bar counter, blocking the little man's retreat. 'Like to introduce us to your friend?'

'Eh . . . sure, sure.' O'Brien eyed him nervously. 'This is Mr Eastgate——'

'Mario Eastgate,' grinned the reporter confidently. 'Police?' The accent was English, the suit impeccable, his manner irritating.

106

'Police,' agreed Thane heavily. 'Chief Inspector Thane, Glasgow C.I.D.—and I don't like pressmen who muck around with my witnesses.'

'Muck around?' Eastgate's grin remained. 'Joe's signed a contract, Chief Inspector. This is a business transaction.'

'I get five hundred quid,' declared O'Brien eagerly.

'For what?' asked Moss.

'His story, of course—human interest stuff,' said Eastgate quickly. 'There's a tremendous sympathy for the agony of this family. Husband held in prison, wife murdered by his own accomplice, daughter left alone. . . .'

'I've read the kind of thing before.' Moss didn't bother to disguise his contempt. 'What I can't understand is how anyone enjoys it.'

'Plenty of people do——' began the reporter, flushing.

'Does your paper make a habit of hiding witnesses when they're needed in a murder investigation?' demanded Thane, his voice ice-edged. 'Eastgate, I could slap a handful of charges on you for this.'

'You're outside your area, Chief Inspector——'

'True. But if that's the way you want it I can arrange to have a couple of county men here in double-quick time. I'll give you an alternative, though Lord knows why. Get out of here, out of this hotel, out of this case—and stay out.'

'But the contract . . .' Eastgate stopped short at the look on Thane's face. His eyes blazed an impotent fury for a moment, then he sullenly put down his glass and walked away.

'But—hey, what about our deal?' asked O'Brien in a sudden panic.

The reporter looked back in mid-stride. 'Sort it out with them,' he advised bitterly.

O'Brien watched him go, and groaned. 'Mr Thane, that's five hundred quid walkin' away. Did you have to do it?'

'Did you have to disappear?' countered Thane without sympathy. 'Come on, Joe. Let's find a place to talk.'

Miserably, the little billiard-hall manager drained the rest of his beer and let them escort him out of the bar. The residents' lounge was small but empty. Thane settled himself in a chair by the window, O'Brien gloomily following his example while Phil Moss kept in the background, standing near the door.

'Notebook, Colin?'

Thane shook his head. 'No—we'll get a formal statement from him later.' He swung back to O'Brien. 'All right, Joe, you left the city in a hurry. Was it purely the newspaper offer—or was there something more?'

Joe O'Brien shrank back in his chair. 'I told you everything that happened. . . .'

'About Jean's death, maybe.' Thane watched him closely, sensing the little man's nervousness, probing for the cause. 'What about the money that was supposed to be in the TV set?'

'I didn't go near it!' Once again, the sheer indignation in O'Brien's voice dismissed the far-out possibility.

'Then what about Frank?' Thane saw the man's mouth twitch a little at the corners. 'You know something about Frank, don't you? That he wasn't in the Glen Ault robbery, wasn't there at all?'

'Eh? I thought . . .' O'Brien goggled at him. 'What's the idea, Mr Thane?'

'You tell me, Joe.' He tried a fresh tack. 'And tell me about the racket Frank's involved in.'

'I can't—I just don't know.' O'Brien crumpled. 'Look, Mr Thane, I only know about the money he's been makin' —and that's just because he wanted to make sure there'd always be someone on the outside who could look after Jean an' the girl.'

'How much money?'

'About seven thousand quid that I know of—there could be more.' O'Brien shrugged. 'That's one o' the reasons I suggested Aberfoyle when this reporter character said he wanted me out o' town. The money's in a bank account in Aberfoyle. Ach, I wasn't goin' to tell Eastgate about it. But I wanted to make sure the arrangements still stood.'

'Start from the beginning, Joe,' said Thane softly. 'And Phil, maybe we'd better have your notebook after all.'

His second-in-command nodded, already reaching into his pocket. He had the book open and a pencil poised as O'Brien began talking.

Frank Humbie had opened an account with the Bank of

108

Central Scotland's Aberfoyle branch about a year back—soon after he began working for the Glen Ault company. It was an interest-free current account to avoid tax problems. Humbie had used his own name, had given his occupation as salesman, had explained that he'd no permanent address—and Joe O'Brien was authorized to draw cash at any time.

'The idea was that if Frank got put away for a long spell then I'd start payin' out to keep Jean okay,' O'Brien explained.

'Quite a responsibility,' said Thane dryly. 'So he trusts you—or were you to draw commission?'

O'Brien flushed. 'We had a bit o' an arrangement,' he faltered. 'But I'd have done it for free, an' that's the truth. Jean—well, Agnes now, is the only blood kin I've got.'

No, Frank Humbie had never told him how the money was earned. His first guess had been that Humbie's delivery trips made ideal cover for a roving series of house robberies. But he'd decided the cash came too regularly for that kind of operation.

Why choose Aberfoyle for the bank account?

'Frank said he had to come this way regular, an' it was nice an' clear of town.' O'Brien ran a hand across his mouth. 'He reckoned the whole game would dry up after another year—an' then he was goin' to buy a house around here, think up a story for Jean, an' settle down.' The little man forced a smile. 'Frank knows most of the places roun' Aberfoyle, that's for sure. Told me about this hotel, for a start——'

'You mean he had a room here?' asked Moss, resting his hand for a moment.

'No. But he came in for a drink every now an' then.'

Colin Thane carefully lit a cigarette, giving himself time to think. 'Joe, what other places did he mention? How about a house, a farm, anywhere like that?'

O'Brien frowned. 'Can't rightly remember any in particular—but he told me about a spot aroun' here that gave him the shivers. He had a bucketful in him an' was a bit wandered—but he certainly made it sound fierce.'

'Where is this place, Joe?' demanded Thane.

'You can see it out the window—'least the beginnin' of it. The low ground between here an' the hills. It's called Flanders Moss, an' accordin' to Frank it's one helluva big swamp.' O'Brien perked up a little at their interest. 'Theres a bloke in the bar knows plenty about it—he's a trapper out on it. I'd a talk wi' him while Eastgate was away phonin' someone.'

Thane went to the window. The sun was low on the horizon and the hills were etched by lengthening shadows. All he could see in between was a flat, featureless expanse, devoid of any sign of life. He pursed his lips and nodded. 'We'll have a word with your trapper, Joe.'

.　　　.　　　.　　　.　　　.

The trapper was a lean, sun-tanned youngster with large, capable hands and wearing an old army battledress over a wool jersey. He came into the residents' lounge with a tolerantly puzzled air, accepted the drink Thane had waiting on him, and sipped it cautiously.

'Alistair MacSorn,' introduced Moss, who'd done the collecting. 'He's employed by the Forestry Commission.'

'And you work in that bog-land over there?' asked Thane.

'Most of the time,' nodded the trapper. 'The Commission's reclaiming part of it, and my job's to keep down the vermin and such-like.'

'Then we're in the same business,' said Thane softly. 'Tell me about it.'

'Och, it's simple enough.' MacSorn gave a friendly grin. 'Do you know what a moss is like, Chief Inspector?'

'I've got a Moss of my own,' Thane returned a wisp of a smile. 'He's standing beside you.'

'Eh? Aye, just so.' Still puzzled, the trapper scratched his chin. 'Flanders Moss is peat bog, thousands of acres of the stuff. It used to be even bigger, but some of it's been reclaimed for farming, and now the Forestry folk are working on more. They're using swamp tractors and skid ploughs, draining sections, planting trees, that sort of thing. Animals can play the devil with young trees, the far-

110

mers don't like the idea of having too much wild-life on their doorstep, so I keep the population down to minimum.'

'Are there paths across Flanders Moss?'

'A few.' MacSorn tasted his glass again. 'There's an old road or two, what used to be a railway line, and a handful of tracks.'

'Any houses, buildings?'

MacSorn shook his head. 'Not around this part, and with good reason. Go off the paths and you're in trouble, real trouble. Sometimes the deer come down from the hills to the Moss, Mr Thane. They have their own ways—but I've seen a deer sucked under before now, and shot the poor brute as a mercy.'

'Yet people visit it, don't they?'

'They do. There's the Forestry folk, a trapper or two like myself, botanists, naturalists—even the odd courting couple, though it's a damned dangerous way of making sure you're alone with a girl.'

Thane glanced at Phil Moss and gave a slight, grim nod. 'Alistair, what about the night before last? Were you out there?'

'Out as usual, checking and resetting the traps,' agreed the younger. 'There was a fox in one, but nothing more.'

'Did you see any stranger, any stranger with a car?'

MacSorn thought for a moment. 'Aye, there was a car out along the Kelpie path. I noticed it just before I found the fox. That kept me busy for a bit, and the car had gone by the time I'd finished.'

'What time was that at?'

'Late on—dusk. Say about ten o'clock.'

'This car, Alistair,' probed Thane. 'Ever seen it there before?'

The trapper shook his head. 'I was a long way off and it was getting late. But when a car goes as far out as the Kelpie path it usually means the driver knows the Moss.'

'Could you take us there?'

'Well, there's my traps,' frowned MacSorn. 'But if it's important——'

'It's important,' agreed Thane heavily. He saw the trapper drain his glass, ready to go, and told him: 'But we'll need to wait a little. I'll have to get some of the local police along.'

'You think there's something important out there, is that it? 'MacSorn rubbed his hands together. 'What is it you're after? A safe or something?'

Thane shook his head. 'Not a safe, Alistair. A body.'

6

SHADED a deep, sickly green, Flanders Moss shows on the
ordnance maps as a broad band stretching across much of
the waist of Scotland. Running eastwards from near Aberfoyle, mile after mile of flat, empty wasteland, it is a freak
left over from the Ice Age, a place once submerged by the
sea. It has been nibbled at by farmers and attacked by re-
claimers, yet only now, gradually, is its main bulk being
tamed. Shunned by roads, shielded by marsh and scrub,
the vast peat-bog has long had its own mythology of death
and disaster, wandering spirits and vanished travellers.

Colin Thane, who had lived all his life in Glasgow only
thirty miles away, had never seen it before . . . and this was
no surprise. People either knew Flanders Moss as part of
their existence or were blissfully unaware of it, so over-
whelming was the majesty of the hills and mountains
beyond.

They waited at the Ardmoor Hotel until a Stirling
County car arrived with a sergeant and two constables
aboard. One of the constables remained behind with Joe
O'Brien, the sergeant had a brief conversation with Alistair
MacSorn and then, the trapper aboard, Thane's car led
the way with the Stirling car following.

In minutes they were driving down a narrow, bumping
ash-surfaced pathway between thin flanks of hedging
which gave glimpses of brown, watery peat-bog on either
side, bog which was a riot of flowering myrtle and a heavy
buzz of insect life.

'Turn here,' said the trapper quietly. 'And, Mr Thane,
your driver won't be minding if I tell him to stick very
close to the way. The Forestry folk use swamp buggies
around here—and even they can bog down.'

Thane's driver needed no second telling. He crawled the

113

Jaguar along, his eyes glued to the narrow route, his thoughts on the joys of a city-centre traffic jam. Mud spattered over the windscreen as they jolted from one broken pot-hole to another.

'And turn here again,' said the trapper, pointing to the left. The track worsened and grew narrower.

'Eh . . . how do we turn to come back?' asked Phil Moss warily.

'We don't,' said MacSorn. 'This goes on and joins another path which will take us out.' He asked the driver to slow still further, watched the bog-land carefully, then nodded. 'Just a wee bit more now—where that high myrtle shows a break.'

They pulled in, the county car followed their example, and Thane waited until the sergeant and constable reached them.

'Tyre tracks,' he said shortly. 'That's what we need first —and this path has soft enough shoulders.'

The county sergeant, a brawny, red-faced man, found the tyre marks a little way beyond where they'd halted. The impressions were clear. A small car had stopped on the left side of the path, the treads neatly defined except for the break where the wheels had spun for a moment as it got under way again.

'Keep clear of them,' warned Thane. 'We'll need moulage casts later.' He took a cautious step on to the peat beyond, felt the ground give gently beneath him like a soft, deep carpet, and moved a little further out. He stopped, looked around, then experimented, rocking his weight up and down. For a dozen feet and more around, the whole surface of the peat began a swaying rise and fall in nightmare fashion.

'Nasty,' agreed Moss, squelching over to his side. 'Hey, look there. . . .' He pointed to a low clump of heather, with a giant dragonfly resting on the topmost spray. Detective Inspector Moss took a first step towards the insect—and Alistair MacSorn suddenly materialized beside him, holding him firmly by the arm.

'Not that way, Mr Moss.' The young trapper had a thick ash stick in his other hand. He stabbed at the seemingly solid carpet inches ahead, the stick slid down deep and easily—but when he pulled it free again there was an

114

audible suction as the bog showed its reluctance to give the stick back. The wood was wet and peat-smeared.

'Thanks.' Moss whitened.

MacSorn shrugged, his face expressionless. 'You want us to search around here, Chief Inspector?'

'Yes.' Thane pursed his lips. 'But I don't want to lose anyone in the process.'

'This is my world, Chief Inspector.' MacSorn's voice made it clear he preferred it that way. 'I'd be happier if the rest of you stayed with the cars.'

They did.

MacSorn had made his own preparations. From the county car he brought a bundle of long, jointed rods, part of the Ardmoor Hotel's chimney sweeping brush. He screwed half a dozen rods together then began to walk around, his eyes scanning the vegetation. He stopped close to one clump of scrub and began to feed the brush rods down into the watery pool beside it, using the rods like a sensitive probe. He shook his head, tried again, then moved on to another spot.

They watched him while the dusk deepened and the sweet, sharp perfume of the myrtle plants wafted over to beat down the mechanical smell of the cars. Thane lit a cigarette and used its smoke to fend off the more persistent of the midges and other insects which began to cloud around them.

At last, when MacSorn was about fifteen yards out from the path, he fed the rods down for the umpteenth time, stopped, waved, and gave a shout. 'There's something under here—and the weed around has been crushed down!'

The county sergeant had a rope and grapnel iron coiled ready. Thane nodded grimly. 'Try it.' Then he led the way himself, one slow, cautious step at a time.

Night had fallen by the time they finished the task. A black, slime-coated shape was dragged out of fifteen feet of peat-bog while the cars' spot-lamps blazed to illuminate the scene. They placed the dead man by the side of the path, peat-water dripping and oozing from his clothes— and Colin Thane gently used a rag to wipe away the thick film of slime from the face.

They'd found Douglas Dalziel.

'It's not often we can recover a body out here,' mused

young MacSorn. 'But then, it's not often we have much of an idea where they went in. Say somebody goes out walking and strays . . . well, on the top it looks all the same. But the crust is maybe feet deep at one place and only a fraction of an inch a step or two along.'

'Aye, it's a treacherous place,' agreed the county sergeant. 'Like Alistair says, it's what you can't see that matters—it's all the same, yet different.'

Thane looked up, his eyes suddenly cold as crushed ice. It was the third time that day he'd heard something similar—first there had been Bhudda Ilford, then Mary. Each time it should have meant more to him. But now he knew what had to be done, what the result should be. He rose to his feet, rubbed the smears from his hands with the rag, and threw it down.

'Colin?' Moss had read the signs from his face.

He nodded. 'I think I've got it, Phil. Let's find a 'phone —I need help, a lot of it.'

'Eh . . . the nearest 'phone's back at the hotel,' said MacSorn. He cleared his throat apologetically. 'This man we've found, Chief Inspector—would he be dead when he went in?'

Thane nodded. At least he hoped so, though that would be for the post mortem to decide. But for the moment, the important thing was to get to the telephone—and then head back to the city.

.   .   .   .   .

It was near midnight before the Millside Division car reached the Glasgow boundary on its homeward journey. As the car crossed into home territory again, the driver automatically made a radio check with Headquarters Control—and Control in turn had a message waiting for them.

'Car one-seven. Chief Inspector Thane. From Chief Superintendent Ilford—your parties are now waiting at number forty-eight, four-eight, Graeme Street. Acknowledge, one-seven?'

Thane took the microphone, confirmed, and treated himself to the luxury of another cigarette. 'That's it, Phil. They're ready for us.'

116

'What's this Graeme Street place?' Moss yawned, not bothering to look up.

'I don't know,' admitted Thane. They were heading in past Fortrose now. The streets were almost deserted, and few lights burned in the homes around. He saw a drunk leaning against a street lamp. The man waved happily but unsteadily as they passed. 'I left that part of the arrangements to John Kelso—Customs and Excise have their own ways. He rammed the fact down my throat hard enough.'

'Huh.' Moss curled back in the corner of his seat. He was tired, he was hungry, his gastric juices were stirring, and, for the moment, his general enthusiasm was low.

Graeme Street, when they reached it, was a row of big, old-fashioned houses in the West End. Each house had its privacy of high hedges and well-kept garden, but No. 48 alone was a blaze of light. A string of cars was parked outside it, two with police drivers waiting half-asleep behind the wheel. The Millside car pulled in at the rear of the others and its two passengers headed for the house.

'Here's your answer, Phil!' Thane stopped by the gate pillars, read the bronze plate on one by the glow of the street lamps, and gave a thin whistle of understanding. 'Strathclyde University—Research Annexe, Department of Food Technology. Kelso's been busy all right.' Strathclyde was a technical research centre with few equals.

The short, gravelled pathway led to a stained-glass front door. Thane reached for the old-fashioned bell-pull, but the door was already opening.

'Ah!' Chief Superintendent Ilford swept them with an impatient glare then waved them in. 'You took your time about getting here. I've been hanging around twiddling my thumbs for the last twenty minutes.'

'I'd things to arrange with the County Force before we could leave.' Thane tried to inject an unwilling note of apology into the words. Bhudda Ilford was always the same when he was dragged away from home at night—but leave him out of things and there were liable to be fireworks.

'If what you asked me to do is a sample, heaven help them,' grunted Ilford. He slammed the door as they entered.

'Any problems involved, sir?' asked Moss.

117

'If there weren't, it would be a miracle. And this Excise fellow Kelso is clucking around like a wet hen—something about being due to start a week's leave tomorrow.' Ilford sniffed at the idea. 'Well, Colin, what have you arranged about O'Brien? Let's not have him disappearing again, eh?'

Thane nodded, glancing around the long hallway in which they stood. 'There's a Stirlingshire man staying with him. I've arranged for a car to collect Agnes Humbie and run her out to join him—then we'll tuck them away in one of the Loch Lomondside hotels until we need them.'

Ilford approved. 'Fine. Well, I haven't got all the detail you want, but I'm expecting it soon. And let's hope this part gives us results.' His face darkened. 'If it doesn't, I'm going to have both the Customs people and the University senate wanting to know what we've been playing at.' He turned abruptly to Moss. 'How's the ulcer standing up to all this?'

'It could be worse, sir.'

'Hmm. Remind me to tell you about a cousin of mine. They opened him up last week, chop-chop, everything's fine.' Ilford was already leading the way as he spoke, oblivious of his junior officer's pinch-lipped fury. 'Last door on the right. Here we are.'

There were four men and a girl already in the room they entered. Dan Laurence was nearest the door, perched on a high-legged laboratory stool. The cigarette between the Scientific Bureau chief's lips wagged furiously as he talked to Kelso, but the exciseman's attention seemed mainly focussed on what the others were doing. Two men in white laboratory coats were busy at a bench while the girl, a radiant brunette, fed a fresh roll of graph paper into the front of what looked like a cross between a refrigerator and an aircraft control panel.

'All present,' announced Ilford loudly. 'Ah—Professor Rose, these are the two men to blame for tonight's exercise. Chief Inspector Thane, Detective Inspector Moss.'

Professor Rose, the taller of the two men who'd been working at the bench, crossed over and shook hands. He had bright, keen eyes, a head of grey, close-cropped hair, and an obvious excess of nervous energy.

'I've no complaints,' he told them. 'This is something

out of the usual, and I'm all for change. Over there's Charlie, one of my lab assistants. . . .' Charlie gave a thin, sombre nod. 'And the young lady feeding that contraption we're going to use is Barbara, my secretary. She's too busy to say hello.' A raised eyebrow from the brunette threw doubt on the matter. 'Anyway, we're still getting set up. Amuse yourselves for a couple of minutes, but don't touch anything in case it goes bang.'

Dan Laurence wandered over as the University man returned to his task. 'Found yourself another body, eh, Colin?'

Thane nodded. 'Found's the word. But I didn't expect you to be here.'

'Me?' Laurence was almost offended. 'You couldn't keep me away. Old MacMaster wanted to come too, but he's on a retainer from Stirling County for p.m. work, and they've whistled him in for duty.'

'I'd heard.' Professor MacMaster might have been rather left out of things at the first post mortem, but Thane knew the thin, acid-tongued pathologist's reaction would be to put an extra effort into his new task. He looked around him. 'What's all this stuff, Dan?'

'I'm wondering that myself,' chimed in Moss. 'I know we asked for facilities, but——'

Bhudda Ilford heard them and chuckled. 'It's a new one on us all. For information, this is the University's gas chromatography unit. But don't ask me what the hell that means. Mr Kelso'—he raised his voice and the exciseman turned, blinking at them through his thick spectacles —'mind explaining what's going to happen?'

Kelso eased his short, bulky frame nearer. 'I'll leave that to Professor Rose,' he said mildly. 'But this is the best way of solving your problem, Thane—and the quickest. I've done what you asked. I brought a sample of the bulk whisky used in Glen Ault liqueur—they always buy from the same firm, Brannoch Distillery on Islay, and I managed to draw some of it from stock in one of the Glasgow bonds.'

'And the bottle of Glen Ault?' queried Thane.

'I got that myself,' rumbled Ilford. 'Collected the one in your office.'

'Oh.' Thane saw the grin lurking in Ilford's face, but

119

refused to rise to the bait. 'Kelso, you're sure their whisky always comes from this Brannoch outfit?'

The exciseman sighed. 'It's my business to be sure. I told you whisky duty was refunded on export shipments of liqueur. We've got to know whose whisky they're using and when it was bought. There are records kept for all distilleries.'

'That sounds a fair-sized job,' commented Laurence.

'It is—there are one hundred and ten distilleries in Scotland. Legal operations, that is—I'm not counting moonshiners.'

'Backyard stills.' Laurence chuckled. 'Remember the one in the church?' he asked Ilford.

The C.I.D. chief grunted. 'Damned if I can ever make anyone believe the story's true,' he complained. 'A church in the middle of Glasgow, the church officer running a still down in the basement, and using the central heating pipes as his worm for distillation!'

'I've heard of that one,' agreed Kelso. 'Was the rest of it true?'

'About the tap behind the minister's pulpit?' Ilford gave a slow, crinkling grin but was stopped from answering as Professor Rose bustled over.

'Ready, gentlemen?' the food technology expert rubbed his hands. 'Let's start our little experiment.'

Kelso softly cleared his throat. 'Professor, they'd like to know what's going to happen. I said I'd leave it to you——'

'Of course.' Professor Rose welcomed the chance. 'The apparatus we'll use is a gas chromatograph—that thing over there. It can give an infinitely fine detail analysis of of any compound or substance we can convert to liquid form. The results come via the stylus pen and the graph drum. We get two readings in one—something like a barograph effect. The height of the graph tells us the particular chemical ingredients we're dealing with, and the width of the peaks tell us the quantities present.'

'And it can work, even when the whisky's part of a mixture like this?' queried Thane doubtfully.

'It can work,' Rose assured him. 'I'll give you an indication. Present us with a chunk of bread and we can say whether the flour was made from Canadian or Russian grain—or grain from any other country, come to that. The difference is in the characteristics of the fatty acids present. The machine gives the readings, and it's only left to the human element to interpret them using known standards. I'll give you another example, another little experiment Mr Kelso was interested in. Charlie went out of the room and drank a glass of whisky. When he came back, I took a sample of his breath—and then identified the brand of whisky from the fumes.' He chuckled. 'That took time, much more than you've got right now. All I'm going to do is take a basic run at chromatographic patterns. Follow me?'

'Eh . . .' Phil Moss hesitated and glanced at Thane. 'Professor, you mean you're going to find out what's in the whisky?'

'Correct.' Rose beamed at him like an aunt about to award a currant bun to a favourite nephew. 'The essential fact is that few things in this world are chemically pure. What makes one whisky different from another isn't the basic alcohol but all the tiny aromatics and chemical traces from the water, the grain, the distiller's plant, any number of things. They're so many, so complex, so downright inexplicable that the idea some people have of making whisky in a test-tube's downright ridiculous.'

'Amen to that,' agreed Bhudda Ilford heavily.

They crossed over to the chromatograph. Charlie the laboratory assistant hoisted a thick, three-foot-long glass tube into position, pointing downwards inside the machine. He checked its stability, then attached a rubber coupling to the top end.

'First sample,' said Professor Rose briefly. 'Identified by Mr Kelso as whisky from Brannoch Distillery. It's been put into the tube along with a standard filtration packing.' He turned his attention to the chromatograph apparatus, pressing a switch here, triggering a relay there. The machine came to life with a quiet, steady hum, control lights blinked, the graph drum began a slow rotation, its stylus line still steady. The University man began talking, explaining while he worked.

Pushed on by the argon gas being injected from above, the whisky sample percolated down through the tube's composition packing in a very special way. Filtered out by the packing element, the smallest molecules came first, then the next smallest and the next again . . . as the pressured whisky neared the bottom of the tube it was a vapour now separated into order of constituents, fine moleculed substances first, largest last. At the foot of the tube the vapour jetted out across a platinum wire exactly one third the diameter of a human hair—a wire carrying an electrical current too weak to bring a glow to the smallest of torch bulbs but more than enough for its purpose. Its normally steady 125 milliamp flow varied as the passing vapour caused the platinum conductor to go through minute expansion and contraction.

They saw the stylus pen begin jumping as it measured each and every tiny variation in current—and then at last the graph settled back to its normal steady line.

'Stage one,' said Professor Rose. 'Barbara . . .'

The brunette removed the used section of graph chart. At the same time his other assistant began removing the first glass tube and fitting a second.

'We'll run the liqueur sample next,' said Rose absently, already studying the first set of results. 'Hmm. Mr Kelso, I've a feeling we did a graph on this Brannoch stuff once before. Am I right?'

The exciseman nodded. 'It was one of the batch you ran for me six months back—remember the baseline data I needed when I tried to organize the plain spirit pattern index?'

'Yes . . . I thought so.' Rose saw all was ready and moved back to the chromatograph. 'I'd better warn all of you that this next graph is bound to be different, whatever the whisky used. The essences added in compounding a liqueur will come into play. They're also liable to mask some of the whisky characteristics. Still . . .' He seemed about to say more, but shook his head, gave a brief smile, and set to work.

Once again the argon gas flowed, pushing the sample vapours down over the platinum wire. Needles quivered, the machine hummed gently, and the stylus jerked its wavering path.

When it was over, Rose tore the graph paper clear himself, took the two sets of results to the laboratory bench,

122

laid them side by side—and then looked up with a sudden, testy frown as the laboratory door creaked open.

'Mr Ilford . . .' The uniformed constable in the doorway paused apologetically. 'Sorry to interrupt, sir. Telephone call—Headquarters say it's urgent.'

Bhudda Ilford cursed under his breath, shrugged towards the others, then followed the man out. Professor Rose set to work again. He didn't take long, and when he looked up there was a broad grin on his face.

'Chief Inspector, come and take a look at this.'

Thane went quickly to his side, the others crowding round.

'These two graphs show characteristics.' Rose tapped the nearest. 'This is the pattern for the Brannoch distillery sample. Notice the high peak?'

Thane nodded. The graph line jumped almost to the top of the paper little more than an inch from its start.

'We call that a sigma peak. It's not completely unusual, but it's sufficiently odd to have stuck in my memory from the last time we examined a Brannoch sample. But even if I'd never seen it before, no matter what else might change, I can tell you that sigma peak should be in the Glen Ault liqueur.' Rose stopped and shoved the second graph forward. 'Well?'

'It's not there,' said Thane softly, triumphantly.

'Damn all sign of it,' agreed Dan Laurence.

'None,' confirmed Rose. 'Thane, I can't tell you the brand of whisky that was used as a base in this liqueur sample, not without further tests which could take days, maybe even weeks. But I can say this . . . it wasn't the Brannoch blend.'

Phil Moss eyed the graphs with the ancient distrust of man faced with machine. 'You're sure? On just these readings?'

'Positive. That peak represents a tiny, probably almost inexplicable, difference in the distilling process, the type of difference that makes Brannoch a good whisky when an equally tiny difference might make it the other way. Nothing to do with the ingredients. This could be something as simple as a dent in the distillation vat.'

'Brannoch Distillery's one of the oldest on Islay,' reminded Kelso. 'The reason for that difference could be anything—maybe even that a workman dropped a hammer against a vat a hundred years ago and caused a dent.'

'A dent?' Thane stared at the graphs, fascinated.

'A very important dent,' said Kelso solemnly, taking off his glasses and giving them a slow polish on the end of his tie. 'I've been at a distillery where a new vat was to be installed—and where the specification demanded that every dent and bump on the old one had to be copied to within a thousandth of an inch.'

'Well, I won't argue.' Dan Laurence glanced pointedly at his watch and steered them back to practicalities. 'So they're not using the whisky they should. What's the link-up, Colin?'

'Kelso knows,' said Thane quietly. 'The answer's stolen stock, a large-scale operation and a pretty clever one.'

'But . . .' Kelso's face reflected his reluctance to accept. 'But they couldn't. We take precautions, we check their export shipments, I know they're still buying their usual supplies from the Brannoch distillery. . . .'

Thane shook his head. 'You said they use duty-paid whisky—and that your interest finishes when the duty is collected, that you only become involved again if there's a refund due. All right, what's to stop them operating a legitimate export trade, keeping it within a reasonable percentage of what they're supposed to be producing with their legitimate whisky stock—but at the same time boosting their home market sales a hundred per cent or more with stolen liquor?'

'Nothing, I suppose.' Kelso gave a slow, weary sigh. 'They'd have to fiddle the book-keeping side of the business, falsify invoices, run two separate sets of accounts. But it could be done.'

'Robbery, fraud and tax evasion,' mused Phil Moss. 'Well, it's a good start. Still, we've got two murders on our hands. Would it be worth even one?'

Thane leaned back against the bench. 'You tell him, Kelso. If I stole a lorry-load of whisky how much money would be involved?'

'Let me see.' Kelso did some fast mental calculation. 'A usual load would be thirty casks, each containing one hundred gallons. In total that's enough to fill eighteen thousand bottles. At that rate, one lorry-load would have a commercial duty-paid value of about thirty-five thousand pounds.'

'And two lorry-loads seventy thousand pounds and so on,' said Thane grimly. 'Satisfied about motive now, Phil?'

Moss gave a wry grin, nodded, then picked up the graph charts. 'Looks like we're going to need these, Professor Rose. But what about this rogue whisky? When's the soonest you can put a label on it?'

Rose didn't believe in idle promises. 'I can't say. The job would be easier if I had an unadulterated sample— this Glen Ault liqueur's as complex as they come. They use a lavender and mint basic essence, with a percentage of orange and citronella, which makes it damnably difficult. Then there's the whisky itself. The blend could be simple or complex.'

There at least, they knew what he meant. Identifying a single whisky from a distillery was one thing. But the average bottle which reached the retail market was a whisky which had passed through the hands of at least one blender and could contain liquor from up to a score of distilleries. Some had as many as fifty single whiskies skilfully balanced one against the other to develop the sought-after flavour . . . and there were something like three thousand registered brands of whisky on the market.

'Remember there's more than four hundred million gallons of whisky lying in tax-free bond in this country, maturing,' murmured Kelso. 'Enough to float a navy—and another seventy million gallons being produced each year. Thane, you'd better realize what you're asking.'

'I know it.' He already had an idea which would simplify things, simplify them in more than one direction. But the door opened and Bhudda Ilford came in before he could even begin to explain.

'Colin was right,' Dan Laurence told the Chief Superintendent happily. 'This Glen Ault mob's using a different whisky.'

'Then this should help.' Ilford tapped his breast pocket. 'I've got your list now, Thane . . . all major whisky thefts reported over the past five years.'

'And one of them was near Beauly?' asked Thane anxiously. A lot depended on the answer.

'Just the way you guessed,' confirmed Ilford. 'An entire

125

load vanished three years ago. The driver left his vehicle outside a transport café while he had a meal and the load was hi-jacked. Lorry found later, empty and abandoned. The driver seemed in the clear.'

'Ed Yuill?'

'The same Yuill, Glen Ault's foreman,' agreed Ilford savagely. 'And a year later Greenlaw leaves the Beauly distillery, sets up business on his own, and takes Yuill along as foreman.'

'Which shows how Greenlaw raised the cash to buy the Glen Ault business—even if he was smart enough not to use it all.' Thane's relief was complete, the last hurdle to his theories removed. 'And the overall picture, sir?'

Ilford had that too. When he contacted Records with a priority request he usually got results. 'Whisky thefts have been on the upswing for long enough—you know that. It's negotiable, like liquid gold. Plenty of people will buy at cut price and no questions asked. But I had Records tackle it the way you suggested—a statistical and geographic breakdown. You were right again. There's been an abnormal increase over the past couple of years—bulk whisky stolen in transit, warehouses raided, but never twice in the same part of the country. Each operation was big enough to matter yet never quite spectacular enough to have a major impact outside the particular area.'

'And the total, sir—enough to keep a firm like Glen Ault going on increased production?'

'More than enough.' Ilford glanced around the room. 'Professor Rose, you and your people have given us a lot of help. We're going to need more—but you'll say nothing of this for now, please.'

Rose nodded. 'I'll answer for my staff. Anything we can help with at the moment?'

Ilford shook his head. 'We're finished here for tonight. We'll go back to Thane's office—and I'd like you to come too, Mr Kelso.'

'I think I'd better.' The exciseman's voice was low and hesitant. 'There's a reason—though it didn't seem to matter until a minute or two ago. I was expecting a visitor this afternoon, Thane may remember I mentioned I'd an appointment. We were talking about contacts and tip-offs.'

'I remember,' agreed Thane.

'This was—well, one of these contacts. A man who telephoned about a week ago, wanting to know if we had to reveal where information came from and whether there would be any reward if he gave us a lead to an evasion of excise duty. He wouldn't say more or tell me who he was—just that he'd have the proof I needed for this afternoon.'

'He didn't show up?' asked Laurence, raising a shaggy eyebrow.

'No, and there was no word from him. I thought it might have been a hoax or that he'd been too frightened to show up. Both can happen.'

Colin Thane broke the long silence that fell over the room. 'You're trying to say it could have been Douglas Dalziel who made that appointment.'

'It might have been. It was a young man's voice.' Kelso gave a helpless shrug. 'We'll never know, will we?'

'We'll know,' promised Thane. He meant it. He knew what had to be done—and more important, how to do it.

.　　.　　.　　.　　.

The harsh tar of Millside Division's 1 a.m. tea brew had a bite strong enough to scald away any tendency to sleep. Four mugs of the warm brown liquid, brought along by the night-shift orderly, were lined up on Thane's desk as he held what amounted to a council of war.

Bhudda Ilford occupied Thane's usual seat—but that was because the big, overstuffed leather chair was the only really comfortable one in the room and the city C.I.D. chief, though prepared to sit back and listen, was determined to do it in fitting style. Thane, Moss and Kelso were grouped around but Dan Laurence, deciding the Scientific Bureau had no immediate role to fill, had gone home to snatch some sleep.

'There's plenty to do, but a lot of it has to wait until it's properly morning,' decided Thane, stirring his tea with the aid of a pencil. 'We've Dalziel's body—but we need a relative for formal identification. That means bringing one of them down from Aberdeenshire.'

'But no publicity about it,' warned Ilford. 'The one advantage you've got at the moment is that Greenlaw and his people still think we're blind to their set-up.'

127

'I'll keep it that way,' promised Thane. 'Phil, you'll make the arrangements—and give the county boys an extra warning.'

Moss nodded. 'Will do. What about running a check on the hotels around Aberfoyle? If Humbie spent so much time there, the odds are Greenlaw and the others might have done the same.'

'Greenlaw should be easy enough to remember,' muttered Thane half to himself. 'A tall man with one side of his face paralysed and probably with a slightly ageing blonde along for company. Yes, it's worth trying.' He glanced at the clock on the wall, then at Kelso. 'What about your week's leave?'

The exciseman shrugged. 'As long as somebody helps me explain to my wife—well, these things happen.'

'Good. What about Glen Ault? Do they work Saturday mornings?' Thane gave a mild grunt of satisfaction at Kelso's nod. 'Then that takes care of one or two problems. One is that we've been so busy chasing around for a dark-haired woman that we've overlooked the obvious.'

'How?' Ilford's curiosity was immediately roused.

'Women,' explained Thane. 'Give the average woman ten minutes and the materials and she can make herself look like anything from a sheepdog to a ruddy fashion-plate. And the quickest, easiest way for a blonde to change her appearance is to stop being a blonde.'

'A wig?' Ilford didn't particularly enthuse at the idea.

'A wig, a dark headscarf, a close-fitting hat . . .' Thane shrugged at the rest of the mysteries available. 'If we stop attaching too much significance to this dark-haired description then we're simply looking for a woman—and that woman could be Greta Rodell. If we find she owns a car . . .'

'Leave that one with me,' decided Ilford. 'I'll put some of the Motor Vehicle people on it—and on a check round the hire-and-drive offices. They can ask about Greenlaw and Yuill while they're at it. If they come up with any-thing, we've got those tyre marks from Flanders Moss . . . though we can ignore Greenlaw's usual transport. A dark red Rover is too conspicuous. Now, what next? Frank Humbie?'

Thane shook his head. 'I'd like to tackle him myself, but

there are other things first, sir. I'm going to have the Cador girl back in the observation van when the Glen Ault staff arrive for work this morning—and this time she'll be told not to concentrate on hair-styles.' He swung towards Moss. 'Phil, here's another job I want you to pass on. Get someone round to the bank handling Glen Ault's account. I want to know if their staff received any advance warning that Glen Ault would want three thousand in cash on Wednesday—and if so, how long notice was given.'

'There's a way I could help,' volunteered Kelso, who'd been sitting silent, sipping his tea with a wary caution. 'Before they could produce extra stocks of liqueur they'd need to buy in extra materials—bottles, essences, even labels. I know most of the suppliers in the trade. I could check the orders they've received—and it wouldn't take long to work out just how big an operation has been going on.'

'That could cut a lot of corners.' Thane decided it was time to coax the mild-eyed man the first few steps towards what he really wanted. 'But I'm going to ask you to do something else. Professor Rose said it would make things easier if he could get a direct sample of the whisky from the Glen Ault warehouses——'

'That needs a search warrant,' reminded Moss soberly. 'If we do that, we're tipping them off.'

'And the evidence we've got still has plenty of holes in it.' Bhudda Ilford gave a heavy frown of disapproval. 'No, I'm against it—in fact, that's an order.'

'We'd need a warrant,' said Thane with a surprising grin. 'But Customs and Excise wouldn't. Right, Kelso?'

'I—well—yes, we can enter suspected premises on our own authority.'

'Enter or break in?' prompted Thane.

'Break in, if necessary.' Kelso grew even more unhappy. 'But the service rules are that between 11 p.m. and 5 a.m. we have to be accompanied by a police officer——'

'You will be,' promised Thane warmly. 'Got your sampling kit with you?'

'Yes—but it isn't so simple,' protested Kelso. 'If you're right and I drew a sample which was identified as stolen then I might get a pat on the back. But if something went wrong I'd have my tail kicked in no uncertain fashion.'

'We'd have to be caught first,' mused Thane cheerfully.

'And three of us could make sure that didn't happen.' Moss came to his support. 'If neds can do it every other day and get away——'

'Then we can,' finished Thane. 'Well, John? What about it?'

John Kelso looked from one man to the other. He eyed Bhudda Ilford in a silent appeal and received a bland, blank stare. He sighed, and it was settled.

'I'll leave you to it,' said Bhudda Ilford briskly, rising to his feet. 'I'm going back to Headquarters. Colin, I want a word with you first—outside.'

Thane followed him out into the main office. The bulky C.I.D. chief stalked almost to the inquiry counter then stopped and cleared his throat abruptly. 'Two things on my mind. Frank Humbie's fingerprints on that bottle cap is one—it has to be a plant. But if they're smart enough to cook up that kind of deal then we're going to be up against some pretty watertight alibis.'

'That's why I don't want to scare anyone,' said Thane quietly. 'Not until we've got more than just the taste of proof. I want to have everything watertight.'

'Watertight?' Ilford's eyes twinkled. 'There's precious little water involved in this.' He thumbed over his shoulder towards Thane's room. 'What about Kelso? I heard what you told him. But I've a suspicious mind. You've another ploy in view at Glen Ault, haven't you?'

Thane scratched his chin, feeling the day-old stubble. 'Well, now that you mention it, sir, I thought——'

'Don't tell me. I don't want to know.' Ilford gave a hasty shudder of horror. 'Just do me a favour. Don't get caught.'

.   .   .   .   .

When it comes to organizing a break-in, being a cop offers certain advantages. Thane used every opportunity available, including a selection of items from Millside Division's collection of souvenirs from past robberies. The duty car which took Moss, Kelso and himself on their expedition stopped a street away from the Glen Ault warehouse, and a moment later the local beat constable rendezvoused with them as arranged. He was a young man, it

130

had been a long, boring night until then, and he was enthusiastic for a personal reason.

'What you say leaves me looking a mug over that last robbery,' he said bitterly. 'I don't mind getting a bit of my own back, sir.'

'Then here's your chance,' explained Thane. 'We're going in through the office to the warehouse, but by the time we're finished it'll look . . . well . . .' He hesitated and glanced towards Kelso, but the exciseman was safely out of earshot with Phil Moss. 'All you've got to do is go to the warehouse and keep the watchman talking as long as you can. If anything goes wrong, make a song and dance about chasing us. But for Pete's sake don't run too fast.'

'I'll remember,' said the constable solemnly. 'It shouldn't be too difficult. The old fellow's got a hut near the warehouse gates, and I usually check he's okay once in the night. He's mad keen about football. All I've got to do is tell him Rangers aren't doing so good and he'll argue till dawn.'

He set off round the corner, a young, confident figure in navy-blue, the flat uniform cap with its diced band at a jaunty, non-regulation angle, his boots ringing on the pavement slabs. Thane chuckled. Less than twenty years back he'd been much the same—only then there'd been the old-fashioned high-domed helmet with its leather chin-strap, while the uniform had included a button-to-the-throat tunic and the thought of a cop wearing a collar and tie would have been classed as heresy.

'Our turn.' He signalled, and the others followed him along the darkened street, Moss only a step behind, Kelso trailing a little to the rear. The night was dry, with a gentle wind and just enough cloud to blanket the moon.

Well ahead of them, the beat cop strode past the Glen Ault office block and stopped at the gate in the warehouse area's high protective fence. They moved into a handy doorway, heard the faint peal of a bell, then saw an overhead light snap on above the gate. A man shuffled into the light's beam, they heard the constable call a cheerful greeting, and a moment later the gate creaked open. The beat man went in, the gate closed again, and the two figures headed back towards the watchman's hut.

'Front door for us?' queried Moss.

'Why not?' Thane saw his wiry second-in-command's teeth flash a grin.

First there was the short walk to the Glen Ault office. Then came a brief interlude with the batch of skeleton keys Phil Moss produced from one baggy pocket. A last quick, cautious glance around and they bundled Kelso through the opened door and followed him inside.

'Close it again, Phil,' murmured Thane. 'Let's not put temptation in anyone's path.' He took a small torch from his pocket and shone its beam around, taking his bearings from the empty reception desk with its covered typewriter. 'We go through the back, along the corridor. Then there's another door, the one that leads to the yard.'

Kelso stirred nervously beside them. 'Wouldn't it be an idea to—well, to have a look through the office while we're here?'

'I doubt it.' Thane flicked off the torch for a moment, conserving the battery. 'Any records we'd find would either be legitimate or so well faked we'd need a team of accountants to break them. No, we came to get whisky samples— let's stick with it.'

The lock on the rear door was no trouble to Moss's keys. Thane eased open the door a fraction, peered out, listened, then opened it wider, wincing at the squeak of hinges. The yard was a black, empty pool with the heavy silhouette of the warehouse block directly ahead.

'Where's the watchman's place from here?' hissed Moss.

Thane pointed towards the little building, a light glowing faintly through its curtained window. 'Ready again, Kelso?'

'I just hope football hasn't lost its attraction,' muttered the exciseman as the door locked behind them, leaving them in the open.

Their feet crunched loudly on the rough ash surface of the yard. A cat yowled at them from somewhere and Moss swallowed hard enough to be heard. True, Kelso was with them and in theory that made it legal . . . but if anything went wrong there would still be plenty of questions.

The lock guarding the side door of the warehouse was the oldest, the simplest, and yet the hardest to open. It finally yielded with a grating rasp Thane permitted himself a long breath of relief as they moved into the building

132

and the heavy, all-pervading odours of whisky and flavourings met their nostrils. He took out the torch again and shone it around. They were in the packing store and bottling section.

'Where do we start?' demanded Moss hoarsely.

'Further along, at the mixing vats,' decided Thane. 'I saw them handling barrels of the stuff there.'

'If I see them that'll almost be enough,' murmured Kelso, his confidence returning now they were back under cover. 'These casks are all numbered and marked.'

The mixing section, with its big, glistening twin vats and its lattice-work of pipes and smaller tanks, glinted like a fantasy nightmare in the beam of their torches. Two of the hundred-gallon casks were lying to one side, empty, their bungs removed. A third was nearby, still loosely plugged with a bung-cork. Kelso put his weight against the wood, rocked the cask with display of unexpected strength, heard the liquid swirl inside, and grunted.

'Half full, no more. Like to put your torch on the lid for a moment?'

Thane did, and waited while the exciseman studied the inked code numbers.

'Brannoch Distillery.' Kelso tutted his disappointment. 'This is legitimate enough.'

'Maybe the cask is,' said Thane pointedly. 'But what's to stop them using it twice over?'

'A refill?' Kelso blinked. 'Yes, it could happen.' He took a flat leather case from his jacket pocket, opened it, and chose a small syringe-like instrument and a length of fine rubber tube. 'This won't take a moment.' He eased out the bung, used the syringe and tube to draw a sample, and fed the spirit into an empty glass phial from the case. 'The main whisky store is further along——'

Thane cut him short. 'Can you check these vats for me? I want to know how much liqueur is ready for bottling.'

'Yes, that's easy enough. But——'

'It could be important.'

The exciseman shrugged, put away his sample, and replaced the bung in its hole. He took the torch, and crossed over to the vats, checking the control dials on each. 'They're fairly low—probably only enough for the half-day

133

working. That's usual enough. Most firms would start a new batch on Mondays.'

'That's what I thought,' said Thane almost complacently.

In the darkness, Phil Moss glanced sharply at his companion and wished he could have been sure of the expression on his face. He knew that tone—and what it meant.

Kelso guided them to the main store, a small corner of the warehouse protected from the rest by a heavy wire-mesh screen which ran from floor to ceiling with a door held by a stout double padlock. Inside, a raised platform occupied most of the space with a couple of hand trucks lying in front of it. About a dozen large whisky casks were on the platform, and much of the rest of its width was occupied by high-piled cans of essence.

Once Moss had dealt with the padlock, Kelso went in and began checking.

'I don't know . . .' He looked around at them after a moment, openly puzzled. 'Most of these casks are empty. They're Brannoch Distillery jobs but—but why bring the empties back in here?'

'How many are full?' asked Thane.

He checked again. 'Just two. Want them sampled?'

'Leave it for now,' said Thane suddenly. He climbed up on the platform, his torch sweeping the wooden floor. 'What's underneath this?'

'Empty space, I suppose,' shrugged Kelso, still puzzled.

'And beyond that wall?'

'You'd be outside, in the warehouse yard.'

Thane frowned down at the platform again. It was a fairly new structure—and it might have been simply a good idea for easier loading and unloading of the big whisky casks. There was no trap-door, no loose floorboard, only a small ventilator grille set close to the wall, a grille hardly bigger than a man's hand. He pointed the torch-beam down it, but could see only rough brick below.

He stood for a moment, perplexed, then made up his mind. 'Phil, look up again—I want to have a try at this from outside.'

They followed him back out of the building and into the yard. The clouds had broken a little, and pale moonlight helped them make their way round the back of the ware-house, along to where three Glen Ault delivery vans were parked in a tight row against the wall.

'It should be about here. . . .' Thane eased between the vans and the brickwork, edged along, and gave a thin whistle of triumph as his hands brushed from brick to metal. 'Here it is!'

The hatch door was low-set, ancient, dirty and neg-lected. It was fastened by two rust-eaten padlocks. But Phil Moss had his first surprise when he found the lock mechanisms were grease-packed and slid open without a sound once he'd got to work on them. His second surprise came when he eased back the hatch and shone his torch inside.

'Colin . . .' He gave a happy sigh. 'This is it.'

From ground level, they dropped down about three feet and found themselves crouching in a low, narrow, cellar-like space, its floor bare, roughly excavated earth—and eight massive black whisky casks lay on their sides along its length.

'Look over there,' said Thane softly, his torch trained on a small hand-pump lying on the floor and the two lengths of rubber tube coiled beside it. 'There's why they keep empty casks in the storage bay, Kelso.' His torch slashed upwards to the underside of the ventilator. The underside of the grill was secured by a sliding catch. 'Open that, and all you've got to do is tap into a cask down here and pump it up into one of the casks on the platform.'

'It's a sweet set-up,' breathed Moss. 'But with the watch-man wandering around——'

'He wouldn't be much of a worry,' said Thane, resting back against the wall. 'Greenlaw could give him an hour or two off at night—more likely at the weekend—and they'd either bring in a new supply by van or get to work filling the empties up there.'

Kelso was hardly listening. Head bent low he moved from cask to cask, muttering to himself. Then he stopped, took out pencil and notebook, and went back to the begin-ning of the line.

'Well?' demanded Thane at last.

'It's fantastic,' declared the little exciseman. 'This one's a

Special Cruachan. The others are four Grallaich Mohrs from Inverness and three Islay Sanctions.'

The Special Cruachan and two of the Islay Sanctions were dry. But only one of the others had been tapped. Kelso drew a sample from the broached cask, then turned his attention to the remaining four. He used a short, strong gimlet to remove each bung in turn, drew off samples into more of his phials, and finally sealed the casks again.

'I'm finished.' He rubbed his hands together and gave a sniff of disgust: 'These things are filthy, wherever they've been.'

'Phil . . .' Thane used a fingernail to scrape the nearest barrel. It was covered in a fine coating of dark, dried slime and mud. Silently, he lifted one foot—and his torch beam shone on the mud still clinging to his shoe, mud from Flanders Moss with the same dark streaks running through it.

They'd found more, much more than he had expected. But he waited while Moss carefully scraped a sample of mud from one of the barrels into an envelope, then nodded towards the hatch. 'Time to go.'

'Lock up?' asked Moss as they scrambled out into the open.

'Lock up,' agreed Thane. 'Then you take Kelso back out the way we came in. I'll stay on for a little—when I leave, I'll come over the fence.'

'But there's barbed wire on top of that lot,' protested Kelso. A new thought struck him. 'Another thing, once I'm gone what's the legal position about you being here? I don't know if I can leave without you.'

Thane clucked his tongue sympathetically. 'Well, there's an alternative. You can stay and see what I'm going to do, and then you'll be an accessary—but I wouldn't advise it.'

Kelso gulped. 'You mean it?'

'He means it,' said Moss gloomily. 'Need any help, Colin?'

'One's enough.'

Moss shrugged. There were times when he knew it was useless to argue. 'Then that's it. Mr Kelso, I think you and I should get going.'

Colin Thane stood where he was until the two men had

136

disappeared into the darkness—then he pulled on a pair of cotton gloves and began.

The delivery vans came first. They were empty but unlocked. He let the air out of their tyres, threw the valves away, found and scattered the contents of the toolkits, but kept hold of a heavy hammer from one. The hammer would be by way of a refinement . . . all he really needed was the piece of white blackboard chalk he had in one pocket and the small but powerful telescopic jemmy which was in the other.

The jemmy was a work of art—though the artist concerned had drawn seven years for attempted bank robbery. Thane inserted it into the hasp of the top padlock on the latch, levered, tried again, and the hasp snapped. He dealt with the second padlock in similar fashion and once again eased the hatch door open. Then he stopped and listened —whatever they were talking about in the watchman's hut there was still no sound of movement from that direction. He grinned, brought out the chalk, and set to work. The words scrawled over the barrels and the brickwork were crude, the spelling illiterate, the lettering sprawling.

Next the whisky . . . he removed the bung from the broached cask, heaved and strained to turn the heavy barrel and chuckled as the liquor began gurgling out. While it flowed, Thane stripped off his jacket, bundled it into a pad, and used it to muffle the hammer blows as he smashed in the lids of the unstopped casks. Each time a lid gave, a miniature tidal wave of whisky torrented out, almost sweeping him off his feet. He staggered back clothing soaked in the spirit, the fumes biting at his nose and eyes. He splashed towards the hatch, tossed the hammer aside, got out, shut the hatch behind him, and hung the broken padlocks as inconspicuously as possible.

Breathing heavily, the whisky-sodden clothing clinging cold and uncomfortably to his body, he took a last glance in the direction of the watchman's hut and quietly walked away.

Three minutes later he had scrambled over the barb-topped boundary fence with no more damage than a triangular tear in one trouser leg. Moss and Kelso were waiting for him round the next corner. So was the C.I.D. duty car. He tumbled into it with them, the car started, and they were on their way.

Phil Moss sniffed the reeking whisky fumes. 'What the heck happened back there?'

'I was arranging things,' said Thane happily. 'Giving my impersonation of a gang of juvenile delinquents—and somehow I don't think Greenlaw's going to complain about it. But if he wants whisky for Monday, well, he's going to have to collect some more from wherever it's hidden—and we'll be along to help.'

'Hmm.' Moss grimaced. 'Did you have to take a bath in the stuff?'

'Why not?' asked Thane solemnly. 'It makes a change.'

They began to chuckle. John Kelso looked at them in bewilderment. It must be the strain, he decided.

7

FOR the second night running it was almost dawn when Colin Thane arrived home. With only a couple of hours available and even that time uncertain, he wouldn't have made the trip but for the whisky-spoiled suit. There was no sense, he knew, in trying to sleep—that kind of half-nap would have left him feeling worse than before. He went through and said hello to the dog, which had begun scraping at the kitchen door as soon as he'd entered the house. But Mary was asleep in the downstairs bedroom, and up above the children were sound enough to have ignored anything short of an explosion.

Moving quietly, listening to his wife's gentle steady breathing, he got what he needed from his wardrobe. He stopped for a moment by her bedside, seeing her by the dim light coming in from the hallway. As usual, she was deep under the sheets with the tip of her nose barely visible and her legs drawn tight up towards her body. He grinned with a touch of envy and went out, closing the door gently behind him.

Once he'd had a bath, had shaved, and was changed into clean linen, a grey sports jacket and tough, matching corduroys he began to feel better. In the kitchen, he made himself a pot of strong coffee, half-burned some toast, scrambled a couple of eggs, then settled down to eat with the dog mooching busily against his knee.

He had plenty to think about. The outline picture was clear enough, even if the details remained vague. Young Dalziel had found out what was going on, had been careless, and the result had been his carefully planned elimination—elimination which offered a complete explanation for his disappearance. How much money had it taken to buy Humbie's part in it? The figure must have been high to get him to accept a possible three to five year jail term.

But if the figure had been high, the whole sum at stake must have been higher still, much higher. . . .

By comparison, Jean Humbie's murder had been a rush job—but still skilfully planned. And ice-cold nerve had been needed to take the gamble that her husband wouldn't talk because of the consequences to himself. By Scottish law, if a group planned murder it didn't matter whose hands carried out the act—they were all equally guilty of the crime.

George Greenlaw and Greta Rodell, the foreman Yuill —it was one thing to know their common motive, another altogether to prove charges of murder against them as things stood. He still lacked the hard, positive evidence needed to link together the whole mass of loose and scattered fact.

That was always the hardest part, the most nerve-racking and frustrating—and the whole challenge of being a cop.

At five forty-five he telephoned for the duty car to collect him. Colin Thane finished the last half-cup of lukewarm coffee, then scribbled a note to Mary to explain the used dishes and the reason for the clothes he'd dumped in the laundry basket. He left the note propped against the coffee-pot, went out, and waited by the pavement's edge in the grey morning light.

.   .   .   .   .

Summer or winter, morning begins at 6 a.m. in Barlinnie Prison. It was six-fifteen when Thane arrived, and Barlinnie had already settled down to the routine of another day. At the gatehouse, the duty officer yawned a tired good morning, phoned his opposite number in C Hall, then regarded Thane with unconcealed curiosity.

'Something special on, Chief Inspector? We had a word you'd be coming. Still, I thought you'd leave it till a decent hour.'

Thane shrugged. 'No choice. . . . How's Humbie behaving?'

'Edgy, edgy. . . .' The prison officer got up, collected his keys, and rammed his hat on his head. 'Well, let's go through.'

Frank Humbie and another prison officer were already

in the interview room when they arrived. His fair, receding hair was unkempt, the small eyes in the plump face were red from lack of sleep, and he stood with his back to the window, scowling aggressively.

'What's the idea?' he demanded hoarsely. 'Listen, Thane, didn't you get the word from my lawyer? I'm through talkin', through wi' seein' anyone—especially you.'

His escort eyed him with a bland watchfulness. 'Wasn't very keen to leave his cell,' he reported laconically. 'Didn't like it a bit, did you, Frank?'

Humbie glared at him. 'I've got my sorrows, mister. More than any of you screws could understand.'

Thane glanced at the two prison officers and jerked his head significantly. They went out, and as the door closed behind them he stood with his hands in his pockets, considering the man in the untidy buff-brown prison rig.

'Well?' Humbie's mouth twitched. 'What d'you want? Come to tell me you still haven't got Dalziel, is that it? My wife dead an'——'

'We've found him.' Thane's voice whip-cracked across the room, cutting him short. 'It's finished now—the play-acting's over. No more cigarettes and sympathy, Humbie.'

'What?' It came as a whisper while the plump face drained of colour.

Thane crossed the room until he stood only inches from the man, inspecting him with a frozen contempt.

'It's over, Humbie—all over. We dragged young Dalziel's body out of Flanders Moss last night. We know about the whisky racket, your bank account at Aberfoyle, all the rest. And we know you were animal enough to go home and lie to us in the very room your wife was killed—lie to us to try to save your own skin.'

Humbie gulped air. 'I don't know——'

'You don't care.' Suddenly he wanted to hit this man, to hurt him physically—because there was no remorse, no shame in Humbie's face, only craven fear and an irresolute panic. 'Your daughter doesn't know what you did—but she loathes you without it. And from where I'm standing, I don't blame her. You're not even an animal—it would defend its mate.'

'I don't know anything—I can't tell you anything.' The

141

words barely rustled out from between dry lips. 'I admitted the robbery, didn't I?'

Thane gave a grim nod. 'And that Dalziel was with you.'

'No—it was a story, just a story,' said Humbie desperately. 'I thought I'd try that line on you when he'd vanished . . . make you think he had the money. I did the Glen Ault job solo. I didn't know about Dalziel. . . .'

'You weren't near the Glen Ault robbery,' snapped Thane, fighting his voice back to a cold, professional monotone. 'Your wife knew it—and was killed when she tried to prove it. Who was the woman with you, Humbie? Who went with you to Aberfoyle to dump Dalziel's body?'

'I did that safe . . . you found my prints. . . .' The words trembled out.

'The break-in was a fake just as much as this pretence that the money was in the television set.' Thane sighed. 'How much were they going to pay, Humbie?'

'I've nothing to say.' It came with a resigned desperation.

'Who killed Dalziel, Humbie?'

'I've nothing to say.'

'Who was the woman in the car, Humbie? Because she was there when Jean was killed.'

The man moaned and shook his head. 'No—leave me alone.'

'How does it feel? You were here, but you killed your wife just as surely as if your own hands had done it.'

Frank Humbie swayed on his feet for a moment, his eyes closed. When he looked up, there was a naked agony lined in his face. He clasped his hands together to stop them shaking. 'Damn you,' he whispered. 'Nothing to say.'

Very slowly, he walked over to the table, pulled out a chair, and sat down. He moistened his lips. 'If you've a charge, make it. If you haven't, leave me alone.'

'All right, that's it for now.' Thane looked at him for another long moment then turned, opened the door, and walked out without a backward glance.

   .   .   .   .   .

Phil Moss was speaking on the telephone when Thane entered the C.I.D. room at Millside Division—and the weary detective was showing signs of a worn-thin temper.

'I don't give a ha'penny hoot,' he snarled into the mouthpiece. 'So it's Saturday and tomorrow's Sunday—what are we supposed to do? Sit around on our backsides and let the rest of the world go paddle at the seaside?'

Thane stood beside him, grinning at the apologetic voice crackling from the other end of the line. But his second-in-command scowled as he listened.

'Listen, Beech, you're supposed to be a policeman. You'll go back in there. You'll be nice and polite the way they taught you at Training College. But you'll tell the girl that either she gets out of bed and gets dressed or you'll drag her out the way she is.' The voice of D.C. Beech crackled again, and Moss barked a humourless laugh. 'That's your problem, laddie. Get on with it.'

The receiver banged down and Moss sat back with a groan. 'Colin, there are times when I wonder why we let him out without a ruddy nanny!'

'What's young Beech's problem?' grinned Thane.

'Sheena Cador. I sent him out to collect her for the observation van routine. She's in bed, she says it's too early to get up—and anyway, when she does, she's going to the seaside with some boy-friend.'

'I thought MacLeod was doing the observation job,' mused Thane. 'Why the change?'

'Ach, I told him to get some sleep first—but he'll take over for the actual watch.' Moss paused and scratched the stubble on his chin. 'How about you? From the look on your face I'd say Frank Humbie wasn't too helpful.'

'Helpful? All I could get out of him was "nothing to say"—on and on like a ruddy gramophone.' Thane swung himself on to the edge of the desk. 'But he's scared now, really scared. He's starting to crack, and when he does—well, he'll talk.'

'Amen.' Moss yawned. 'Got a cigarette handy? Mine gave out an hour back.'

Thane obliged, took one for himself, and they shared a light.

'What's the score now, Phil?' he asked. 'Any change?'

'Not much.' His second-in-command took a long draw at the tobacco. 'Dalziel's father is on his way down from Aberdeen by car—they'll take him straight to Aberfoyle. That's going to be a nasty job for the old fellow.'

'Any sign of the p.m. report?'

143

'Not yet. And Stirlingshire say they can't start asking questions around hotels and the like until the place is properly awake. Things are a little better down here though. Motor Vehicles say Greta Rodell has a driving licence, though she's not registered as owning a car. Yuill has a motor-cycle.'

Thane nodded. The Glen Ault trio might be making a fast fortune, but they were taking care not to make any display of the fact. 'How about hire and drive?'

'They've checked the day-and-night services. But a lot of the smaller firms are only open during office hours—they'll keep at it.' Moss stretched and yawned again. 'The only other thing to be done is that call on Greenlaw's bank manager. I thought I'd take care of it myself.' But he had one tit-bit remaining, characteristically saved until last. 'The Scientific mob were on the line a little while back. The muck we scraped from the whisky casks is an absolute match with the stuff from my shoes.'

'Flanders Moss. . . .' Thane had plenty of reason to welcome the confirmation. 'If that's where the stuff is hidden, then we'll have to be ready for Greenlaw making a trip out there.'

'Aye.' Moss gave a sour twinkle. 'Well, while you were wallowing at home I had a wee word with the Stirlingshire force. If we need them they'll be ready, and that trapper character will be with them.'

'Fine.' Thane stubbed his half-smoked cigarette. 'Greenlaw will need a lorry, Phil—and he can't use any Glen Ault transport. Too risky.'

'There's not much we can do,' protested Moss. 'He can have a truck tucked away anywhere for all we know——'

'Or he could hire,' mused Thane. 'We'll see. Anway, I'll take over for a spell now. You get some rest.'

'But the bank——'

'MacLeod can take care of it.'

'Well, fair enough. . . .' Moss gave in with a degree of reluctance. 'Where'll you be if there's a panic?'

'Either here or at the end of a car radio,' Thane assured him. 'Don't worry, I won't get lost.'

'You're too dam' big for that,' grunted Moss, heading for the door.

．　　　．　　　．　　　．

144

Professor MacMaster's report on the Dalziel post mortem arrived at Millside Division by motor-cycle despatch rider at 8 a.m. Thane thanked the rider and buzzed the duty orderly to organize something approaching breakfast for the man before he headed back to Aberfoyle. Then, alone in his room, he opened the envelope and settled down to read the typewritten quarto sheets.

'The body was that of a well-nourished male apparently in his mid-twenties. . . .' MacMaster's reports always began in the same caution-laden pedantic fashion, and many an unwary student had discovered the hard way how rigorous were his standards. The preamble went on to make a slightly peevish mention of the way in which 'extensive cleansing of mud from the body was required prior to examination'. But if some mortuary attendant had presented the old forensic expert with a neatly washed corpse there would have been hell to pay. MacMaster preferred his subjects to be as found.

Thane grimaced as the report got down to anatomical detail, and flipped through to the final page and its summary.

'Death was due to asphyxia, the result of homicidal suffocation. Small surface bruising and minute under-skin haemorrhage showed that pressure had been applied at the mouth and nostrils with fixation of the lower jaw, apparently in conjunction with fixation of the chest walls. The injury to the skull, noted under para. G., was caused prior to death and in my considered opinion was the result of a blow administered for the purpose of rendering the subject unconscious.

'This report given on soul and conscience. . . .'

Another Burking. Thane growled quietly to himself, turned back to the beginning, and read the report through. There were two other points which mattered. A quantity of beer in Dalziel's stomach had been consumed about an hour before death—that fitted with what they knew. But when it came to actual time of death MacMaster dug his heels in. The conditions in the peat-bog had to be considered. The most he'd commit himself to say was that death 'occurred a minimum of forty-eight hours before examination'.

He tossed the report into the 'pending' tray on his desk,

glanced at his watch, lifted the telephone, and got a line through to the communications room.

'Any word back from the observation van?'

'It's in position, sir,' confirmed the communications sergeant, an exiled Londoner. 'Any message for 'em?'

Thane considered for a moment. 'Yes. Tell them I'm coming out. I'll meet them locally once they've finished.' He pressed the receiver rest down briefly, then flashed the switchboard. 'Helen. . . .'

'Sir?' The day-shift operator had a trick of always seeming slightly breathless.

'Get me Customs and Excise—the local office. I don't have the number handy.' He waited, tapping the desk lightly with his fingers. As he'd guessed, John Kelso was already on duty when he got through.

'If it's about the whisky samples, Professor Rose is running a chromatograph analysis on them this morning——' began the exciseman.

'It isn't,' Thane reassured him. 'But how long till they're classified anyway?'

'Around noon, I expect. I'll bring the results over once they're ready.' Kelso sounded unhappy. 'I've told my wife I'm having to cancel my leave—I'm not exactly popular as a result. Thane, I'd like to know when this'll be over.'

'You're not alone,' said Thane dryly. 'If it's any help, I can't see any panic developing until late afternoon—maybe it won't be until evening. But when it starts, we could need you in a hurry.'

'Why?' There was a sudden edgy caution in Kelso's voice. 'If there's going to be anything more like last night——'

'There won't.' Thane grinned into the mouthpiece. 'But we'll need an exciseman handy if we find ourselves with a load of hi-jacked whisky on our hands.'

'Mmph. It might be wise from everyone's viewpoint,' said Kelso cuttingly. 'And afterwards?'

'After that you can bow out gracefully,' promised Thane cheerfully. 'You'll be ready?'

'All day and at this number.'

Thane said goodbye and hung up. His preparations were nearly complete.

The Glen Ault warehouse opened at 8.30 a.m., the office staff began work half an hour later—and by nine-fifteen the observation van cruised round to rendezvous with the Millside duty car at a spot two streets away. Thane opened the rear door and climbed aboard. Sheena Cador greeted him glumly, with Detective Sergeant MacLeod and the same policewoman as before sitting beside her.

'Sir . . .' MacLeod caught his eye and gave a quick, happy wink.

'Well, Sheena?' asked Thane. 'Any luck this time?'

'She was there,' agreed the girl with a minimum of interest. 'I did it the way these two asked—never minded the shade of hair, just the rest. I showed them the one I meant.'

'Mac?' Thane raised a questioning eyebrow.

'Greta Rodell, sir—she'd no hesitation about it.'

'It's her all right.' Sheena nodded vigorously. 'What next? Will I get to be a witness in court or that sort o' thing?'

'If you've no doubt she was the woman in the drying room,' said Thane with heavy deliberate emphasis. 'This is too important for guesswork, Sheena. If you've any doubt I want to know about it. Remember what you told me before—you only saw her for a moment or two, in a darkened room.'

She took a deep, indignant breath. 'I get yanked out o' bed near enough to the middle o' the night, an' now——'

'We've got to be sure, that's all,' soothed the policewoman.

'An' I am!' Sheena sniffed. 'You should know, even if he doesn't—you don't just label a woman by her face. There's her figure, her legs . . . here, bet I could tell you her hip size, Mr Thane, even though she's corseted up like armour platin'.'

Thane capitulated. 'I'll take your word for it. But the man who was with her——'

She shook her head. 'That's different. He could be this sergeant o' yours for all I know.'

'Then you've done all we want.' He saw no sense in pushing the matter. 'But remember——'

'I know,' she agreed wearily. 'I've to keep my mouth

147

shut. Can I get a lift home this time? I'm tired, an' I haven't even had my breakfast.'

Thane arranged for the policewoman to take her home by taxi, then told MacLeod about the bank inquiry. That done, he went back to the duty car and told the driver to take him round to the liqueur warehouse. His weariness had vanished, and a fresh, brisk confidence was beginning to sing in his mind. The sunlight glinted on the car's chromework and reflections danced on the windscreen. It was going to be another warm day—and a busy one.

·   ·   ·   ·   ·

Barbara MacPhail was on duty at the Glen Ault reception desk. He greeted her cheerfully and asked to see George Greenlaw.

'Just a moment, Mr Thane. . . .' She turned to the switchboard, rang through to an extension, spoke briefly, then came back. 'He's over in the warehouse with Mr Yuill. But he won't be long.'

'Something wrong over there?' inquired Thane casually.

'Nothing that I know about.' She sat back in her chair, serious-eyed. 'That list I gave you, Chief Inspector—the places I'd been. You're satisfied?'

He nodded. 'About you, yes. But I need your help, Barbara—in another direction.' He had to lie now, and hated the fact. 'There's a chance you could help us prove young Dalziel is innocent. Will you do it?'

'Whatever you want, yes.' There was no hesitation in her voice. 'Does it . . . do you mean you've found out where he is?'

Thane shook his head. 'I can't answer that one. But if I tell Greenlaw I want you over at Millside Division for questioning, there's no need to worry. Right?'

She gave a quick, happy smile and he hated himself again. But before she'd time to ask more, footsteps sounded in the corridor and Greenlaw bustled into sight, his face twisted in an oddly handsome grimace of welcome.

' 'Morning, Chief Inspector—sorry to keep you. I had to visit the warehouse for a spell.'

'Problems?'

'Life is full of problems,' said the Glen Ault boss easily.

148

'Most of them happen on Saturday mornings.' He shrugged. 'Some kids got into the parking lot last night. They climbed the fence—don't ask me how—let down some tyres, and generally messed around.'

'No other damage?'

Greenlaw glanced at him with momentary sharpness. 'No—why?'

'Professional curiosity,' grinned Thane innocently. He gave a faint jerk of his head towards Barbara MacPhail, who was once more back at her typewriter. 'Mind if we talk somewhere else, Greenlaw? Privately?'

'Come up to the office.' Greenlaw led him towards the stairway. 'Oh—did you get the bottle I sent?'

'Thanks, yes.' Thane followed him, staying silent until they were in Greenlaw's room and the door was closed. 'It's about the MacPhail girl—and this is strictly off the record. I'm going to need another question-and-answer session with her.'

'Here?'

'No—back at my office. A dark-haired girl was seen at Gradient Terrace just before Mrs Humbie was killed. Barbara MacPhail's alibi for the time doesn't stand up.'

'I see.' Greenlaw frowned. 'Will she—well, will she be coming back from this "session"?'

'She'll be back,' Thane assured him. 'But she knows something about where Dalziel's hiding if anyone does. So we'll throw a scare into her and then watch every move she makes over the weekend.'

'Nasty,' mused Greenlaw, turning towards his desk. He helped himself to a caramel from his box. 'How can I help?'

'Just treat her as before unless she does anything unusual or asks for time off,' said Thane comfortably. 'If you notice anything, don't stop her—but let me know.'

'That's how it'll be. . . .' Greenlaw broke off as there was a short double-rap on the door. It opened, and Greta Rodell glanced in.

'George . . .' She recoiled a little. 'Sorry, I didn't know you'd company.'

'That's all right,' Thane told her. 'I'm ready to leave.' She came in, wearing a vivid blue and cream dress in a pleated nylon. Sheena Cador's words came back to him . . .

yes, Greta Rodell was definitely armour-plated. Perhaps in more ways than one.

'You always seem to be leaving when I appear,' she said with a brittle twinkle. 'Has something fresh happened, Mr Thane?'

'Well . . .' Greenlaw made a show of reluctance.

'Maybe you should know,' agreed Thane heavily. 'I'll leave it to Greenlaw to tell you.' He stopped by the door and glanced back. 'These youngsters you mentioned—the ones who got in last night. I'll have a word with the local beat man about them.'

'It's not worth bothering about. But thanks anyway.' Greenlaw raised a hand in a brief farewell.

.   .   .   .   .

He collected Barbara MacPhail downstairs and helped her into the duty car. Then, as it pulled away from the kerb, he saw her nervousness and felt another tug of sympathy for the girl. 'I had an early breakfast,' he told her. 'Settle for coffee?'

She nodded, and he told the driver.

The restaurant was the same little place behind the bakery shop where he'd lunched with Kelso. At that hour it was almost deserted and he ordered coffee, gave her a cigarette, and then sat back, watching her for a moment.

'Barbara, how do you get on with Greenlaw and Miss Rodell?'

The girl frowned a little. 'Mr Greenlaw can be a bit fierce, but he's all right. Greta Rodell'—she settled more comfortably into her chair—'well, she's more moody.'

'Especially in the last few days?'

She gave a blink of surprise. 'Yes. How did you know?'

He took a deep breath, his judgement of the girl at stake —and success or failure in the balance. 'Barbara, we think the robbery was deliberately faked.'

'Faked?' The hand holding the cigarette trembled. 'But if it was—then why did Douglas run away? And Mrs Humbie. . . .' Her eyes searched his face, and he was thankful for the respite as the waitress clashed the coffee cups down on the table.

150

'There could be several reasons,' he said vaguely once the woman had gone. 'Barbara, you're going to have to trust me on this. I want you to go back to the office. You work the Glen Ault switchboard from your desk. For the rest of the day I want you to make a note of any calls made by Greenlaw, Greta Rodell or Ed Yuill. I want you to listen in any time you can. Don't take risks—but if any of the calls seem unusual I want to know. And when you stop work at lunchtime I want you to come straight round to my office.'

'You think they're involved?'

Thane nodded. 'Yes. And before you ask, getting official sanction to tap a telephone line takes a lot of time. That's why I'm asking you to do it.' He leaned forward. 'Barbara, ever notice anything strange happening back there? Any private meetings when no one was welcome, no matter who they are?'

She blushed. 'Well, sometimes—when Greta Rodell would go into Mr Greenlaw's office. They called it a conference, and locked the door. The powder-vine thought——'

'That there might be a different explanation?' In spite of himself, he chuckled. 'Maybe. Tell me, did Douglas ever talk to you about the firm's books?'

'He never got near them—Greta Rodell does all that side on her own,' declared the brunette. 'Even when she was off ill and Douglas volunteered to keep them up to date, Mr Greenlaw said no.'

'When was this?' Thane carefully laid down his coffee cup.

'About a fortnight or three weeks ago—she was only off for a few days. It was one of those virus 'flu bugs.'

'And Douglas would be left on his own?'

'More or less,' she agreed. 'Why? Does it matter?'

'I think so.' He steered her on to another course. 'Does Greta Rodell have a car?'

She sighed, but answered. 'She doesn't own one, but she has a friend who loans her a car any time she needs it. I've seen her in it.'

'Know the friend's name?'

'No, I'm sorry.' She lifted her cup in both hands and sipped the coffee. 'It's a small black car, if that's any help.'

'It is,' agreed Thane happily. 'Last question, Barbara. Who's her hairdresser?'

'Her hairdresser. . . .' She looked at him, almost giggled, then gradually sobered. 'I don't know—but I could ask.'

'Don't,' advised Thane. 'Just do what I've asked, Barbara —nothing more.'

'And it'll really help Douglas?' The brown eyes appealed again.

'It'll really help.' He looked away, fumbling for change to pay the bill.

.   .   .   .   .

By 10 a.m. he was back in the Division office. The C.I.D. room was livelier on Saturdays, with most of the day-shift team available. Saturday mornings meant no jury trials in the courts, none of his men waiting uselessly in corridors until their time came to give evidence. Thane moved through the room, listened to a couple of jokes, went through the ritual of telling one in return, then at last got through to his own room and closed the door.

There was a message slip on his desk asking him to phone Aberfoyle police, and under it a longer memo from Sergeant MacLeod. He lifted the telephone, asked for the Aberfoyle number, then glanced through MacLeod's report. There had been no difficulty at the bank branch handling the Glen Ault account, but the information was negative. The bank had been given no advance notice of the three thousand pounds cash withdrawal, but they regularly received heavy cash requests from the liqueur firm without prior warning.

'Aberfoyle on the line, sir. . . .' The switchboard girl told him a second time before he came down to earth. He asked for the duty inspector, crumpled MacLeod's memo into a ball, and tossed it into the wastebasket as a gruff Highland accent reached his ears.

'Inspector Kennedy here.'

'Thane, Millside C.I.D.' He leaned one elbow on the desk. 'Any luck with the hotel checks so far?'

'Aye, a little,' said the county man cautiously. 'There's a couple of places say they remember this fellow wi' the

152

strange face. But he was just a customer in for a meal and a drink, nothing more.'

'What about the woman?'

'There was a fair-haired woman along wi' him.' The county officer cleared his throat. 'But this man Humbie's bank account is more interesting, more interesting by far. He had the seven thousand pounds in it right enough, until Thursday afternoon——'

'You mean it's been withdrawn?' snapped Thane.

'Och, no. It's still there—but so is a parcel he handed in that afternoon, telling them it was to be kept in their strong-room.'

'Can you get it?'

'Wi' a wee bit of fuss.' The county officer chuckled. 'That'll be a pleasure—their manager's not inclined to be co-operative, and I'm in the mood for an argument.'

'Let's find out then—though I'll take a bet there's three thousand in banknotes inside.' Thane paused as another thought struck him. 'Has Dalziel's father arrived?'

'He's due within the hour——'

'Take it easy with him, will you?' he asked quietly. 'The family's had a rough time.'

'I'm aware of the decencies,' said the Aberfoyle inspector with a brief touch of annoyance. 'I've a son of my own.'

Thane apologized, said goodbye, and hung up. The sun streaming in the window was beating down on him, and already he felt sticky with perspiration. He loosened his collar and tie, reached for the 'phone again, then stopped in surprise as Phil Moss barged into the room.

'Can't you stay away from here, Phil?'

'I hadn't much option,' complained Moss sourly. 'There ought to be a law against women with vacuum cleaners.'

'Landlady trouble again?'

'She's on a cleaning jag,' confessed his companion. 'I asked for some breakfast and got handed a tin of fruit juice. Juice, with my stomach—the woman's mad!' He dragged a chair over, faced its back towards Thane, and draped himself around it saddle-fashion. 'Ach, it's almost as bad as being married.'

'Worse things can happen——'

'Maybe.' Moss wasn't convinced. He slid a strip of teleprinter paper across the desk. 'Communications sent this up. Motor Vehicles have drawn a blank as far as hires to the Rodell woman are concerned.'

'I expected it.' Thane left the message where it lay. 'We can't get all the breaks.'

'Platitudes I detest—in the morning anyway.' Moss grunted. 'What's been happening?'

Thane told him. Moss gave a thin whistle when he heard of Barbara MacPhail's new role.

'Taking a risk, aren't you?'

'There's a risk,' acknowledged Thane. 'But we need her help.'

'And when she finds out Dalziel's on a mortuary slab?'

Thane winced at the words. 'I don't know, Phil. That's something I can't avoid. When it happens, well, I'm the one who'll tell her.'

He turned to practicalities with a sense of relief. There were problems in arranging a watch on the Glen Ault warehouse. The observation van couldn't hang around the one place all morning, and the Wood Street area didn't lend itself to the usual pattern of acquiring a static observation point.

'Keep the van handy in the neighbourhood.' Moss offered a compromise. 'You say you can't risk one of the regular cars being spotted—right, then a couple of the lads can use their own vehicles. They'll be happy enough at the chance to charge mileage.' He demonstrated on the wall map. 'We're lucky as far as street layout's concerned. They can keep a reasonable distance away, and yet anyone leaving will still have to pass one or other. After that, it's a simple enough shadowing detail.'

Thane gnawed briefly and absent-mindedly on the knuckles of his right hand. 'Fix it,' he agreed. 'Let's take a look at their home addresses.'

Moss got the list from the report file. Greenlaw had a flat in a luxury block in the city's West End, outside Millside Division's area. Greta Rodell lived in a small three-apartment semi-villa on the northern edge of the Division, and Ed Yuill's address was a boarding house not far from the Fortrose district.

'Set up a watch ready for them coming down,' decided Thane. 'Greenlaw's flat is Marine Division territory—ask them to take care of it. They owe us some favours.'

154

Moss made the arrangements. When he'd finished, he stayed at his desk in the main office for a spell, working his way through some of the routine stuff which had accumulated. There were circulars to be marked for filing, drafts for statements from some of the junior d.c.s.—he sighed over the spelling and grammar in a couple, ran them through with a red pencil, and tossed them aside. Headquarters had sent out their usual end-of-week report of stolen property . . . it could wait.

'Sir . . .' The duty orderly had come up so quietly Moss almost jumped. 'Visitor to see you.'

He looked towards the inquiry counter, saw John Kelso waiting, and went over. The exciseman was solemn-faced and rubbed his hands nervously as Moss approached.

'Come on through,' invited Moss. 'Colin Thane's in his room.'

'In a moment.' Kelso hesitated, his voice dropping to a near whisper. 'Moss, I'd like to ask you something first.'

'Well?'

'It's Thane . . .' The exciseman paused lamely. 'He may think he knows what he's doing. But after last night . . . there could have been serious trouble. I couldn't sleep for thinking about what might have happened. Can't you——'

'Control him?' Moss gave a dry sympathetic chuckle. 'Man, if it was possible Bhudda Ilford would have done it long ago. But those chances he takes have a habit of coming off. And he got us both out of the way first, remember? Any time he does something which could backfire, he takes good care nobody else is liable to be hurt.' He shook his head. 'Stop worrying until you have to, that's my advice.'

Thane was on the telephone when they went in, but he hung up a moment later.

'Dalziel's father identified the body,' he told them. 'And, Phil, Humbie's bank opened that parcel—three thousand pounds in it. Probably the first instalment for staying in jail, paid in advance.' He glanced at his watch. 'Hey, you're early, Kelso. It's getting to be a habit around here.'

The exciseman glanced uncomfortably towards Moss. 'The chromatograph results aren't ready yet,' he said apologetically. 'But I've finished checking with the trade outlets who supply Glen Ault—I thought you'd like the results. When you balance essence and glass bottle supplies against

155

the whisky stocks they're supposed to hold then it looks as though they're producing at least one extra bottle of liqueur for every three we've known about—and that's being conservative.'

'Like to calculate it in terms of cash profit?' asked Thane.

'I've already done it.' Kelso took off his spectacles, unfolded a fresh-laundered handkerchief, and began polishing. 'Calculating the whisky at its duty-paid value and subtracting the probable cost of essence and manufacturing——'

'How much?' protested Moss.

'Two hundred and twenty thousand pounds a year—which includes roughly one hundred and eighty thousand in evaded duty.'

Thane gave a whistle of appreciation. 'Quite an operation!'

'You've already collected duty on the whisky, haven't you?' prodded Moss.

'But it still amounts to an evasion on their part.' Kelso saw nothing humorous about it. 'The statutory penalty applies—forfeiture of stock and a fine of double the duty evaded.'

'I wouldn't try to collect it on your own——' Thane broke off as the telephone shrilled. He lifted it and gave his name.

'It's Barbara,' said the low, hasty voice at the other end of the line. 'I think something's happening, Mr Thane—but I'm not sure what.'

'Go on. . . .' He gestured to Moss to pick up the extension earpiece. 'What's wrong?'

'There's been a meeting in Mr Greenlaw's office—I was told he wasn't to be disturbed,' she said quickly. 'Greta Rodell was there, and Ed Yuill was brought over from the warehouse. They were in the room for almost half an hour.'

'Any idea why?'

'No. But I did what you asked. I listened in on their calls. Mr Greenlaw telephoned a number just afterwards and spoke to—well, I think it was a garage. He was talking to another man, about a lorry which had to be ready for tonight.'

'What number did he call?' Thane waited hopefully for the answer.

'I don't know. He asked me for an outside line and dialled from his extension. And I didn't hear all they said —someone came into reception halfway through.'

'You've told us enough,' he assured her. 'Now remember —don't take chances. And come straight here when you finish work.'

'I'll come,' she agreed. 'We stop at twelve. Mr Thane, can you tell me anything more about Douglas?'

'No, not yet. Perhaps when I see you. Goodbye, Barbara —and thanks.' He hung up, pursed his lips, then looked towards Moss. 'Well, say it.'

Moss shook his head.

.   .   .   .   .

Kelso left a little later, with the promise that he'd be ready when they wanted him. They waited, smoked, talked desultorily about things that didn't matter, chased off a couple of reporters who somehow talked their way past the inquiry desk, and watched the clock on the wall.

Two minutes after noon the telephone rang. The observation van had radioed that the Glen Ault warehouse was locking up for the day. The van was tailing Yuill's motorcycle, which had just left, and the warehouse man was heading in the direction of home. The other Millside cars were standing by.

'Watch it for me, Phil.' Thane lit another cigarette. 'Better go down to communications—it'll save some telephoning.'

Moss guessed another reason behind the order. 'And the girl?'

'I'll be here when she comes.'

Moss shrugged. He didn't envy Thane the task ahead. 'If you need any help . . .' he began awkwardly.

'I'll let you know,' said Thane quietly.

Barbara MacPhail arrived at twelve-thirty, flushed and slightly breathless. 'I came as quickly as I could,' she apologized.

'There's plenty of time.' Thane made her sit down, took the lightweight coat she carried over her arm, and carefully

157

hung it on a peg. Her hair shone in the sunlight, her eyes were bright with excitement, and she was eager to talk.

'Did my 'phone call help?' she asked.

'Quite a lot.' He went round to his chair and sat down, watching her.

'Well, there's more. Mr Greenlaw and Ed Yuill had an argument—something to do with trouble in the warehouse last night. I only heard a little of it when I took some letters up for signing, and they stopped until I'd gone.'

All those gallons of lost liquor in the cellar-style hiding place—Thane could appreciate the rumpus that had caused.

'You've done well,' he told her. And now, he thought, it's my turn to repay you, repay you in the most damnable way anyone could imagine.

'Barbara——'

'Oh, there's one last thing,' she chuckled. 'You remember you wanted the name of Greta's hairdresser? She goes to Ballini's, the Italian salon in High Street. Muriel knew.'

'Good.' Thane didn't bother to ask who Muriel was. 'Barbara, you wanted to know about Douglas,' he began quietly. 'I think you've more than earned the right to be told——'

'I hope so.' The eager smile flashed once more.

'The right to be told the truth, Barbara.'

The suddenly sympathetic note in his voice faded the smile from her face. 'You mean there's something wrong? You know where he is, but——'

He nodded. 'We know where he is, Barbara. We found him last night.'

The girl stiffened and bit hard on her lower lip. Then, forcing it out, she asked, 'You mean he's—dead?'

'Murdered, like Jean Humbie.' Thane came round, her eyes following him. He put a hand on her shoulder. 'Barbara, I said you could help him. I meant it—but this was the only way. You couldn't have done what you did this morning if I'd told you the truth. And the best way people can help young Dalziel now is to help put his killers where they belong, in the dock, before a jury.'

Her hands shook as she opened her handbag and fumbled with a tiny enamelled cigarette case. She opened it, took a cigarette, then sat looking at her fingers, dazed.

158

'Here.' Thane snapped his lighter to life. She looked at the tiny flame and slowly shook her head.

'No. I—I don't really want this.' She swallowed. 'You're sure it's Douglas?'

'His father identified him this morning.'

'And you think Mr Greenlaw and the others . . .'

He nodded.

Quietly, she rose from the chair. 'I think I'd better go home, Mr Thane. I—I liked him very much.'

He gave a simple nod of understanding and pressed the buzzer on his desk. 'There's a car waiting. And one of the switchboard girls—she's not a policewoman—will go back with you.'

She looked at him, the pain still in her eyes. 'You organize everything, don't you, Mr Thane? Is—do the police even have rules on how to break bad news?'

He let her go. Then he went over to the window and did nothing for a long time but watch the children at play in the street below.

· · · · ·

The machine had taken over—the 'Big M' the lecturers always emphasized when they were ramming home the facts of life to each class of probationary constables. It was a machine which had as its components men and their equipment. It was as thorough and unemotional as a computor. It was as keen as the vision through the seven-by-fifty lenses of the binoculars trained on three widely different houses, as fast as the signals from the walkie-talkie sets which kept each two-man observation post in contact with Headquarters control, where a relay circuit linked them with the communications room at Millside. It was a machine oiled by sandwiches and coffee, unblurred by tedium—and it was the most diabolic duty any cop could draw.

George Greenlaw, Greta Rodell, Ed Yuill—all three had travelled straight home from the warehouse. The shadowing cars had pulled back, leaving the next stage to the watchers already in position and the other cars which waited at a distance.

At Millside Division, the communications room badly

needed a 'House Full' notice. Colin Thane sat beside the duty operator. Phil Moss leaned against the standby generator housing, sucking a bottle of milk through a straw. Over by the door, Detective Sergeant MacLeod trimmed his fingernails with his teeth and frowned discouragingly at any d.c. who dared to linger in the area.

The radio loudspeaker coughed, and they tensed. But it was yet another service message on the all-car wavelength . . . a couple of fifteen-year-olds missing from home in Govan Division.

'Need their backsides tanned, some kids,' said the duty operator cheerfully. 'Gone off to see the big wide world—well, they'll learn.'

He got no response. He yawned and settled back. If the C.I.D. mob felt temperamental, that was their business. He had his own job to do, and that was enough, thank you.

At three-ten, Greta Rodell left her flat. There was a brief flurry of reports, ending when she returned home with a bundle of groceries.

A Customs and Excise messenger arrived with a sealed letter for Thane. He opened it absently, glanced at the contents, then shoved it across to Moss. John Kelso had received the chromatograph reports on the whisky samples —one was Brannoch, the rest all illegal stock. It hardly seemed to matter now.

They waited, while the radio and the teleprinter each produced the occasional spasmodic message. The clock crawled—until nine minutes past four.

'Romeo-Two to Millside control. Subject C-Charlie has left house and is starting motor-cycle. Over.'

Thane rubbed his hands dry of perspiration, saw the duty operator eyeing him, and nodded.

'Millside Control here. Roger, Romeo-Two. Fox-Two, your subject leaving. Over.'

The shadow car acknowledged from its position. Ed Yuill was moving—and the machine worked on. From the observation post to control, from control to the shadow car, from the shadow car back, the messages passed. Yuill rode off, heading west. There was a crucial minute of silence.

'Fox-Two to Millside Control. Following subject. Over.'

The duty operator acknowledged. The connection had been made, the machine had won.

They switched another car into the shadowing routine, avoiding any risk that Yuill might become suspicious if one vehicle remained behind him for too long.

At four thirty-two, the motor-cycle coasted into a small garage out on Northwest Boulevard. At four-forty, a dark grey three-ton Bedford truck with a canvas hood came growling out. Yuill was at the wheel. At one minute before five o'clock he parked the truck near his boarding house, left it, and went back inside.

Romeo-Two took over again. Thane stubbed his latest cigarette, stood up, and nodded to Moss and MacLeod.

'Our turn. We'll check out that garage.'

'What about Yuill?' queried Moss.

'He'll keep. They won't want to arrive out at Aberfoyle much before dusk.' Thane was already on his way to the door.

.   .   .   .   .

Early evening on a Saturday is always a quiet time around Glasgow. The C.I.D. car, travelling through light traffic, made good time on the journey out to Northwest Boulevard. The 'garage', when they reached it, was a run-down brick building set back on a neglected patch of ground and reached from the road by a strip of weed-broken tarmac.

'All Our Cars Are Guaranteed.' Moss read the display board above the building and gave a cynical grunt. 'I'll bet. Well, there's always a mug around somewhere.'

'From the look of the place they're in short supply around here,' volunteered Sergeant MacLeod from the front seat. He glanced round towards Thane. 'What's the drill, sir?'

'We'll play it by ear,' decided Thane. 'It's no crime to hire out transport—even from a dump like this. Still, you'd better go round the back way as insurance.'

The car purred off the road and stopped just short of the building. Thane ordered their driver to wait, gave MacLeod a moment's start towards the rear, then headed towards the open main door of the garage with Moss at his side. Their footsteps echoed on the concrete floor as they entered the gloomy, unlit building. It was little more than

161

four walls and a roof, with a handful of cars and a few old-model vans spaced along it.

' 'Evening, gents. . . .' The man who popped up from behind the bulk of a blue Ford commercial took a couple of brisk steps towards them then froze, his welcome dying as he recognized his visitors.

'Well now—Bonce! Our old pal Bonce Page!' Thane's teeth showed in a happy grin. 'This is a surprise, eh, Phil?'

'For me too, mister.' The lanky, long-haired ned they'd last seen protesting so vigorously at Millside Division moistened his lips uncertainly. 'What d'you want this time?'

'I don't think he likes us,' decided Moss cheerfully. He took in the dark suit, the blue-striped shirt and the loosely knotted tie. 'Smart, isn't he? This is your working rig, Bonce? I thought you'd be in London by now.'

'You made me miss the flight, an'—well, I didn't go.' Page stayed where he was. 'Look, I'm shuttin' the place for the night. I've got a date in town.'

'So have we,' said Thane agreeably. He glanced around. 'This your own place, Bonce? We didn't know you were a giant of commerce.'

'Funny, very funny.' Page edged closer to the Ford, as if gaining a feeling of protection from its rusting bodywork. 'If it's about Frank Humbie you're here, I've tol' you all I know.'

'We're more interested in a lorry that drove out of here.' Thane's voice suddenly hardened. 'The one with Ed Yuill at the wheel.'

Bonce Page's reaction was immediate and explosive. He swallowed, practically propelled himself off the van, and dived towards the rear of the building.

'Mac!' Thane bellowed the warning and sprinted in pursuit. A small door at the back of the garage flew open, and Detective Sergeant MacLeod burst in. Page's feet skidded as he changed direction, grabbed at a car's radiator to stop himself from falling. He tried to dodge back—but Moss was already there. Page's hand blurred for an instant towards his handkerchief pocket, a white lozenge appeared between his fingers, and he slashed wildly towards the thin, sour face approaching him.

'Phil. . . .' Thane cried a warning, but Moss had already sidestepped clear.

162

The cornered man launched himself off on a desperate new tangent. But Thane had had enough and was in no mood for niceties. He swept into the lanky ned's path, met a slashing cross-stroke from that white lozenge and hammered it aside with one arm, slammed his right fist into the man's stomach just above the belt-line. Page folded forward—and as he tried to pull himself upright again Thane grabbed him by his ample, greasy hair and shoved him back against the nearest car. The man jabbed at him with a knee, and Thane returned the compliment by banging his head hard against the car's door-pillar.

Bonce Page swayed and would have gone down but for Thane's grip. 'All right . . .' He half-gasped, half-groaned the words and stopped struggling.

'That's friendlier.' Thane shoved the man into Sergeant MacLeod's arms and glanced around. 'Where is it, Phil?'

Moss held out one hand and showed the oblong cube of coarse sugar he'd picked from the floor. It was unusually large and looked deceptively harmless. But a sugar-cube slashed down a man's face could cut a rough, deep and scarring path—and since the Offensive Weapons Act had brought in heavy penalties for being found carrying more fashionable weapons several lesser thugs had begun favouring sugar-cubes or full beer bottles. The beer bottle had to be full, of course—that way it was a container. Empty, it remained a weapon.

'Always carry your own sugar around?' asked Thane heavily.

The man cringed away. 'I was goin' to have a cup o' tea before I went.'

'And I thought maybe you were going to give it to a policeman's horse.' Thane grimaced. 'You're in trouble, Bonce. Right up to your neck. We've got Dalziel's body and we know about the Glen Ault racket.'

Page's mouth fell open. 'Dalziel . . . he's dead?' His voice quivered in heightening panic. 'Now listen, Mr Thane——'

'You listen.' Thane's bark cut him short. 'You told us Humbie and Dalziel were in a bar on Wednesday evening.'

'An' they were, so help me!'

'But what about the rest? What about the truck, Page?'

'That's different—it's a straight business deal,' protested the frightened ned. 'I didn't know about Dalziel—an' I'm

163

not tied up in any killin'. You know me, Mr Thane. I'm all for the easy gold, sure—but not that way. It's out o' my class.' He was trembling, his last vestige of confidence gone. 'I do a bit o' work for them an' get paid for mindin' my own business . . . but that's the lot.'

'The truck?'

'I give it garage room an' keep it ready for them.' Page was eager to talk, seeking his own way out. 'Frank Humbie put the job my way, an' they made it worth while. Then Frank got nobbled by your blokes—an' when Joe O'Brien told me I was goin' to be dragged into it I thought the best thing for me was to fade to London for a bit.' He swallowed. 'I 'phoned Mr Greenlaw first. He said I was to keep my mouth shut about the truck, but that it was okay to tell the rest——'

'What about the whisky thefts?'

'Eh.' Page shook his head unhappily. 'I know they're up to somethin'. But that's all, Mr Thane—I mean it. They jus' tell me they want the truck an' take it away. I've got to be here when they get back.'

'And sometimes it's covered in mud?' demanded Phil Moss.

Page nodded. 'They've a car here too,' he volunteered. 'The black Morris over by the door.'

'Who drives it?'

He shrugged. 'Most o' the time it's a woman—a blonde. Her name's Greta.'

'Did she have it out on Wednesday and Thursday? At night?'

Page nodded. 'Till late on, Mr Thane—after one o'clock both nights.'

Thane had heard enough. While MacLeod handcuffed the man's right wrist to the steering column of the nearest car, the Millside chief used the garage telephone to arrange for a patrol van to come out. Then he called Dan Laurence at Headquarters—the Scientific Bureau could be turned loose on something positive for a change, and the black Morris might hold the key to several things.

Phil Moss was at his elbow as he replaced the receiver. 'I've looked around,' said his second-in-command. 'The place is a dump—but there's nothing interesting, unless

164

some of these cars are on the "stolen" list.'

'If there was anything here he'd have told us, Phil.' Thane gave a faint, tight grin. 'He's too scared to start lying.'

'There's a chance Greta Rodell might show up for her car,' mused Moss. 'Still, I asked Page and he doesn't think so—she usually 'phones first, and he meant it about closing up when we arrived. Yuill told him he needn't expect the lorry back before midnight.'

'Then that's it.' Thane beckoned Sergeant MacLeod over. 'Mac, stay on here and look after things until the others arrive.'

'You won't need me at Aberfoyle?' MacLeod was disappointed.

'You're going to have enough on your plate. I want a full statement from Page ready as soon as you can. And when that truck moves out I don't imagine Greta Rodell will be along. Give us just enough time to make sure, then collect her. I want her house really gone over. You know what to look for?'

MacLeod nodded and looked more cheerful.

.   .   .   .   .

They were back again in the communications room at Millside and time was crawling. At eight o'clock John Kelso joined them, tired of twiddling his fingers over at the Customs and Excise office. Moss dozed in a chair near the duty operator and Colin Thane prowled restlessly around, his impatience barely controlled.

It was eight twenty-one when the radio gave the first call that mattered. George Greenlaw had left home. Other messages traced his car until it arrived at Yuill's boarding house. There was a nerve-racking silence of some five minutes, and then Romeo-Two came on the air.

'Greenlaw and Yuill have left house and are driving off aboard lorry. Over.'

The Millside operator gave a brief acknowledgement. There were other messages to be passed now, messages the machine was ready to receive.

'Let Aberfoyle know we're on our way,' reminded Thane, drawing a brief nod from the operator. 'Ready, Kelso?'

The three men were almost at the front door of the station when a sudden shout called Thane back.

'Telephone, sir—it's Headquarters,' said the desk sergeant apologetically.

Thane took the call. When he hung up and rejoined them, his mouth was hard and strangely angry.

'What's wrong?' demanded Phil Moss. 'Who was calling —Dan Laurence?'

'No, Bhudda Ilford,' said Thane grimly.

'At a time like this?' Moss showed his disgust.

'He'd reason.' The energy seemed momentarily drained from Colin Thane's voice. 'Frank Humbie's just been found dead in his cell. He tore up a bedsheet and hanged himself from the window bars.'

Moss whistled his surprise. 'Any suicide note?'

'No.' Thane was thinking back to the morning, to the way Humbie had shown both despair and a stubbornness born of fear. He'd lacked the courage to talk—but also, it seemed, the will to hold out. That had left him only the easy way . . . if there was anything easy about self-strangulation.

But Colin Thane wanted one of the other three, wanted a murderer brought to book in a way he'd seldom felt before.

'Thane?' John Kelso was holding the station door open. Their car was outside.

'Ready.' He nodded, and led the way.

8

THE Bedford truck reached the first fringe of Flanders Moss at nine forty-five, at almost the same moment as the sun began to touch down on the west horizon, turning the land into a savage clash of contrast. To the north, the mountains were an oils on canvas vision of dark shadow and golden-brown shoulders. But the waiting peat-bog lay under a dull, sullen heat-mist, tall vegetation undisturbed by a breath of wind while insects swarmed in a pre-dusk frenzy of activity.

Ed Yuill was still at the wheel. The truck changed gear, its engine-note altered, and it bounced into the rough track which led from the narrow main road. Greenlaw sat beside Yuill, in his shirt sleeves, one arm draped along the open passenger window . . . and a hundred yards away, flat on his belly in the long, reed-like grass, a Stirlingshire constable laid down his binoculars, cursed a horsefly which had just bitten him near the ankle, and began to wriggle back to where his motor-cycle lay concealed.

Two miles back along the road, Colin Thane's car was travelling at a leisurely thirty miles an hour when the radio told them their quarry had arrived. It had been the same at intervals ever since they'd left the city—the county force had put men at each main junction along the route to Flanders Moss, feeding in progress reports with religious regularity.

'Shouldn't we speed things up a bit?' queried Kelso, leaning forward a little in his seat, eyes blinking earnestly through the thick spectacle lenses. In varying ways, he'd already asked the same question at least a dozen times since they had set off.

'They're in no hurry,' soothed Thane easily. 'We'll be in time, Kelso—in plenty of time.'

The radio crackled again with yet another message from

County H.Q. control. In the front seat of the car Phil Moss checked the map on his knee then gave a sour chuckle. 'Keep going,' he told their driver. 'Rendezvous point's as before—beyond the Ardmoor Hotel.' He turned round, an appreciative grin on his face. 'Somebody's playing it smart, Colin. Greenlaw goes in here'—one thin forefinger stabbed at the map—'but we go on to the next track, three miles along. Look.' He demonstrated with the same finger. 'If we go in on the second track it'll be like tackling the other arm of a horseshoe.'

Thane saw for himself and nodded. The Kelpie path where they'd found Dalziel's body lay distant and separate. But from close beside their rendezvous point with the county team the second of the two tracks snaked in to join with the first. There was no other way out for Greenlaw's truck, unless the men aboard it were prepared to take the almost impossible risk of attempting to turn their heavy vehicle on the narrow path to which they were committed. The county men, in fact, had set up what amounted to a collision course.

And Greenlaw? The man's confidence was clear from the truck's no-nonsense journey from Glasgow. The Glen Ault boss must be happily relaxed, convinced that he'd nothing to fear.

A warm glow of satisfaction invaded Thane's mind at the thought. All that was needed now was a little luck. . . .

. . . . .

They rendezvoused with the county party a few minutes later. Kennedy, the Stirlingshire inspector, was pretty much as his telephone voice had suggested—a bluff, stout Highlander whose blue uniform had little slack to spare and whose face was a weather-bronzed scowl. His trousers were tucked into calf-length rubber boots, and the scowl changed to a friendly enough welcome as they met.

'I've a sergeant and four men with me,' he reported. 'Two cars—and, of course, you know young MacSorn.'

Thane nodded to the red-haired trapper who was once again to be their guide. 'Glad you could come, Alistair.'

'After what I saw the last time . . .' MacSorn gave a grim

shrug. 'Well, it's the least I can do, Mr Thane.' He glanced at their feet. 'You've got boots with you?'

'This time, yes,' confirmed Thane. 'They're in the car. Phil——'

'I'll get them.' Moss beckoned to John Kelso. 'I shoved in a pair for you. Come on—and let's hope you've cop-sized feet.' They went off together.

'What young MacSorn and I have in mind is fairly simple,' declared Kennedy in his ponderous, methodical fashion. 'But then, maybe you've a thought or two of your own——'

'All I want is to give them time to start work in there,' Thane reassured him. 'And this is your territory, not mine.'

'Fine.' Kennedy was visibly relieved. 'No offence, Chief Inspector, but we can never be sure about you fellows from the city. Anyway, our idea is that they won't just be stopping on the track. It would be too risky, even in a place like this.'

'Have they any alternative?' Thane raised a puzzled eyebrow. 'I've seen the map.'

MacSorn chuckled. 'The map's got plenty of blank spaces around here, Mr Thane. From what Inspector Kennedy told me, these two will want somewhere they can keep their truck under cover. That means off the tracks—and there's only one place where it's possible. It's a bare suspicion o' a path, most of it overgrown. There's one or two like it in Flanders Moss—places where somebody once tried to build a new road but had to give up.' He slapped a flying beetle from his arm. 'This one goes off to the north for a little bit near where the two tracks join on your map. It's not wide—at best they'd have to drive in and reverse out, with no chance to turn. But at this time o' year the reeds and weed are thick and high enough around to make you imagine you're in a jungle.'

'They could hide a truck?'

'A truck?' The trapper snorted. 'Man, they could hide a railway train, and you'd never see it till winter.'

Thane considered for a moment. 'Alistair, could you get us there on foot? Could we leave the path and cut across the peat-bog?'

'Why?' demanded Inspector Kennedy, no enthusiasm in his voice. 'Surely all we've got to do is go up to where this path starts, put a car across the track, and go in and get them?'

MacSorn agreed. 'The only place they could go would be into the peat, Mr Thane—and only a dam' fool would try that.'

'A fool, or two men who know what's waiting for them if they're caught,' corrected Thane quietly. 'I don't want to risk a man-hunt through this type of nightmare.' He eyed the trapper thoughtfully. 'Can you do it?'

'Well . . .' MacSorn's face was far from happy. But, at last, he shrugged. 'I don't like it, but I'll take you.'

Walking clumsily in his over-sized rubber boots, another pair for Thane tucked under one arm, Phil Moss returned a moment later. He listened to the plan, blanched a little, and asked a question of his own. 'If—when we do this are we liable to bump into anything unfriendly on the way?'

'Maybe the odd serpent.' The old-fashioned term came naturally from Kennedy's lips. 'But they're only adders, Moss—and they'll be more frightened than you.'

That, decided Moss under his breath, was unlikely. He had the city man's distrust of any creature that didn't have a collar round its neck or wouldn't answer to a whistle.

Now that they were ready, Colin Thane was impatient to move. Two men and a car were despatched to block the first of the two tracks—he trusted Alistair MacSorn's opinions, but saw no sense in taking chances. Then the two remaining cars set off, travelling slowly, engines little more than a pulse-beat as they headed into the bog-land. Mac-Sorn was in the lead car with Inspector Kennedy and two of the county men. The two Millside detectives shared the back seat of their car with Kelso, leaving the front passenger seat to the county sergeant, who cheerfully offered their driver a cigarette then whistled tunelessly between his teeth as they jolted along.

Moss leaned forward. 'These snakes, Sergeant——'

'Ach, if you see one just boot it,' advised the man easily.

'Adders—yes, they're members of the viper family,' said Kelso, trying to be helpful. 'I remember——'

'And I'd rather not know.' Moss glared at him, and the exciseman closed his mouth and stayed in a hurt silence.

Thane watched their route. MacSorn had been right— this part of Flanders Moss had an even wilder aspect than the area around the Kelpie path. They were travelling between a head-high curtain of reeds and flowering myrtle, pressing so close that it brushed against both sides of the car as they passed. The brake-lights of the car ahead winked on for a moment, and a dapple-brown shape sped across the path and disappeared.

'Deer,' remarked the county sergeant absently. 'Nothing like a bit o' venison, eh?'

They crawled the best part of four miles before the lead car halted. Their car drew in at its tail, they got out, and joined the other men grouped around the trapper.

'We're near enough now,' said MacSorn quietly. 'We can stick to the track for a spell, but let's do it without noise.'

One constable was left by the cars. The rest of the party followed MacSorn, their rubber boots moving silently over the muddy surface. At last, he signalled them to stop again.

'About here, I think,' he murmured.

'You're sure?' Thane was worried. The cars had disappeared from view. All around was the same unchanging, featureless vegetation, vegetation which, in the failing light, seemed to press in on them in near claustrophobic fashion.

'Wait now. . . .' The trapper scowled around for silence and listened. He sniffed the wind like an animal. He listened again, though his audience could hear only the buzz of flies, the occasional rustle of some small four-legged wanderer and the sound of their own over-loud breathing.

He was satisfied.

'We're all right—and they're where I guessed, Mr Thane. You still want to cut across?'

'Yes. But we'll split up. Moss and I come with you.' The burly Millside detective beckoned Kennedy closer. 'Inspector, you take the others. Move on to where this path of Alistair's leads off the track and stop there until you hear trouble. Then come up—and fast.'

Kennedy grunted his understanding. He turned back, gathered the rest of the group round him with a sweep of his hands, and spoke to them for a moment. They padded off, John Kelso last in line.

'Which leaves us.' MacSorn rubbed his chin as he inspected the two detectives. 'All right, I go first. You next, Mr Thane—then Inspector Moss. We'll go single file. Stay quiet and keep your heads low. Stand in the wrong place

171

and'—grim humour glinted in his eyes for a moment—
'well, you'll make life difficult. Understood, gentlemen?'

They nodded.

The trapper's pace was slow and infinitely careful from
the moment they left the track. He moved through the
reeds in assured but respectful style, each step forward an
individual decision. Behind him, both sweating at the
nerve-racking pace, sometimes struggling as their feet were
gripped by the peat, Thane and Moss followed closely.
They skirted apparently solid carpets of green, close-woven
grass and crossed waterlogged stretches which seemed more
dangerous. All that mattered was to follow MacSorn's footsteps, and distance had lost any meaning.

A lizard dropped down from one tall, bent-over branch
of myrtle and vanished. A frog exploded out of the peat-
water almost under Thane's feet. He heard a splash, looked
back for a moment, saw Moss dragging his right leg back
out of a swamp-hole and read the silent curse framed on
his lips.

When MacSorn stopped them it was a relief. The trapper signalled them to wait, went on by himself, vanished
briefly, and then returned, triumph on his face.

'Just a little way now—and keep low,' he cautioned.

They followed him at a crouch, gradually conscious of a
faint, occasional rattle of metal coming from somewhere
ahead. It ended just as MacSorn waved them up alongside
him. He let them settle, then parted a last thin curtain of
reeds with his hands, forming a gap only an inch or so
wide.

Thane looked out across a fifty-yard stretch of thin,
straggling weed and bog. The truck was there, angled to
the limit of the rough path. Part of its canvas hood was
rolled back, the tailboard was down, and a gangway of
heavy planks bridged the gap from its platform to the mud
below. Greenlaw stood beside the tailboard and Ed Yuill
was a yard or two away, fastening the shackle of a block-
and-pulley chain to a mud-soaked loop of rope. The rope
snaked across the track and disappeared into the thick
scrub and weeds beyond.

'Alistair. . . .' Thane moved close to the younger man,
his voice a bare whisper. 'Could there be firm ground on
the other side?'

MacSorn scratched his head. 'Maybe—I don't know for sure,' he admitted. 'There's the odd wee stretch where things aren't too bad—especially near the paths. The surface might give a little but be thick enough underneath. Some of them are natural, others left over from the days when the old cattle-drove paths were being built. But I don't know this one.'

Phil Moss gripped Thane tightly by the arm. Greenlaw had jumped aboard the truck platform. At the same time, Yuill walked confidently across the apparently liquid peat on the far side of the path and disappeared into the scrub beyond. They heard him whistle—and Greenlaw set to work, winding away at the hand-winch end of the pulley chain. The sheaves of the pulley block rattled as the chain tightened. He kept turning, the rope shuddered off the ground, straightened, took the strain. Gradually, skidding and slithering, resting on its side on a crude sledge of wooden slats, a dark bulk of a whisky cask emerged from the scrub with Ed Yuill behind it, helping to steer it on its way. The cask was mud-covered, but the two men, working with a practised precision, manœuvred it to the bridge of planks. The pulley block rattled again, the cask groaned its way up into the truck and disappeared from view.

Thane watched for a moment longer until Yuill reappeared with the freed chain and its shackle. Then he let the reeds close together and looked at his two companions. 'If we wait until they're busy with that pulley contraption again——'

'In this light we could be almost on top of them,' agreed Moss softly. 'Alistair, can we take a chance on the stuff in between?'

MacSorn hesitated. 'Well—yes, if we have to.'

They got ready. In a matter of moments, the pulley chain rattled again. MacSorn parted the reeds, they saw the two men by the truck concentrating on their task as a second cask came into view—and they moved quietly out of cover, MacSorn in front, Thane and Moss close behind him.

The trapper moved at a fast walking pace, lightning judgement behind each step. The gap narrowed while the pulley rattled on and the second cask began mounting the plank bridge.

MacSorn's luck ran out when they were two-thirds of the way across. His foot hit an apparently solid tuft of marsh grass. The grass divided and he pitched forward, splashing down into the liquid peat.

The splash and the flurry of movement were enough. At the pulley-drum, Greenlaw slammed on the brake lever and spun round, a shout of warning on his lips as he saw the three figures so menacingly near. His right hand dived towards his hip pocket, while, below him, Yuill stared from behind the cask, momentarily frozen where he stood.

The peat-bog shuddered beneath Colin Thane's feet as he pounded across the gap, conscious of Phil Moss following in equally desperate style. Greenlaw's hand came up from his pocket, a stubby automatic pistol in his grip. The gun's muzzle swung towards them—and Thane's left foot hit unresisting peat. He stumbled and fell forward, caught himself on hands and knees, half-saw, half-sensed Yuill still watching as if hypnotized. He struggled to pull himself up, Greenlaw's twisted face staring down at him and the automatic's muzzle a sickening dark circle—then a small black object hurtled past from behind.

Phil Moss's baton, the short, lead-loaded non-regulation stick he always carried, had behind it every ounce of energy the wiry little Millside man possessed. It struck Greenlaw on the left temple with a stunning force, knocking him back, the automatic exploding in sheer reflex, the shot going high and wide. The Glen Ault boss collapsed, his shoulder smashing against the pulley-drum's brake lever as he fell.

Halfway to his feet, Thane tried to cry a warning as the frenzied rattle of the freed tackle chain spinning through its pulley blended with the grating screech of the whisky cask sliding back down the planks.

Half a ton of cask and whisky, tobogganing out of control, hit Ed Yuill as if he was a paper curtain and swept him away. If the man screamed, they did not hear. The heavy cask and its sledge slats jerked as they met the track, carried on then sank in a turbulence of mud and peat-water as it smashed through the thin crust of bog, Yuill still spread-eagled across it. Man and cask disappeared. Only the chain remained, its links vanishing into the peat.

Forcing himself forward, Thane scrambled and splashed

the last few feet, reached firm ground and the truck, and threw himself on to the platform. Greenlaw was trying to rise, his hand groping for the fallen automatic. Thane hit him once, cruelly and efficiently, where throat met jaw below the left ear. The man went down again, limp.

As Phil Moss and MacSorn reached the track after struggling across the bog, Thane was already winding furiously at the pulley-drum. They helped him, hearing the shouts and running feet which heralded the arrival of Kennedy's party.

The cask emerged at last, covered in dripping ooze. But Ed Yuill had vanished.

'Colin. . . .' Phil Moss shook his head. Breathing heavily, Thane stopped and leaned back against the truck's canvas hood as Kennedy and his men trotted up.

'You three all right?' demanded the panting, red-faced Stirlingshire man.

Thane nodded.

Kennedy looked past him to Greenlaw, then glanced around. 'And the other one?'

'We'll need a rope and grapnel again,' said Alistair Mac-Sorn quietly. 'The peat took him.'

'I see.' Kennedy's lips tightened. 'We'll take care of the tidying up—that included.'

Thane stooped as he heard Greenlaw groan, picked up the automatic from the truck's floor and shoved it in his pocket. Metal clinked as Moss squatted down beside him and he edged back to give his second-in-command room as the handcuffs snapped on the Glen Ault boss's wrists.

There was still the whisky. John Kelso was standing near the truck, inspecting the cask they'd hauled back from the bog. He beckoned him over.

'The rest of it's over in the scrub—but watch how you go.'

'Right.' Kelso looked unhappily around for a moment, then began to pick a delicate path towards the bushes.

Greenlaw groaned again and began to stir. Thane bent wearily over the man, and shook him by the shoulder. Slowly, Greenlaw's head turned and their eyes met.

'It's over,' said Thane, no emotion in his voice.

'Go to hell.' The man spoke painfully, yet still with a

175

dash of defiance. Then he stared down at the handcuffs on his wrists, as if refusing to believe they were there.

There were twenty-three casks of whisky hidden among the scrub. Along with the two dragged clear, they represented close on forty thousand pounds worth of the golden liquor—and yet that merely constituted the current stock of the Glen Ault operation. Thane hardly cared, even when Kelso brought him the news, a beaming delight on his broad face. He watched, too, as Ed Yuill's body was at last dragged up by the searching grapnel—but his mind was on what remained to be done. Kelso would stay with his whisky. The county men had their tasks. But the last act of the case must be at Millside, back where it had all begun.

The drying peat-mud crackled on his clothes as he crossed over and thanked Alistair MacSorn. The young trapper shook hands with the quiet, natural dignity of his kind.

'Phil. . . .' Thane nodded to his second-in-command. 'Time to go.'

'We're ready.' Detective Inspector Moss gripped Greenlaw by the elbow and pushed him forward. The tall, twisted-faced prisoner glanced briefly towards the tarpaulin which covered Yuill's body, shrugged, and let himself be led along the path towards their car.

.   .   .   .   .   .

They reached Glasgow by midnight, to be met by a thin drizzle of rain. From the car, they bustled Greenlaw across the pavement and into the brightly lit antiseptic atmosphere of the Millside Division station then up to the C.I.D. room and through to Thane's office.

Greta Rodell was there, a cold, withdrawn look on her face which changed little as she saw Greenlaw brought in by the two Millside men. Sergeant MacLeod stood behind her chair, and the rake of red claw-marks down his left cheek told their own story.

'Thought you'd be here, Greta,' said Greenlaw laconically.

She nodded, her eyes searching past him as Phil Moss shoved another chair beside her and thumbed Greenlaw into it.

176

'Looking for Yuill?' Thane paused in the act of hanging his hat on its peg by the door and shook his head. 'He's dead, Greta.' Her face registered what could have been pain for an instant, and he answered the question forming on her lips. 'Call it—well, an accident. A cask took him into the peat-bog.' He crossed to his desk, took his time about settling behind it, then glanced towards Sergeant MacLeod. 'Get everything, Mac?'

MacLeod pushed a bulky manila envelope across the desk. 'These for a start, sir—and some business ledgers. She had a safe built in behind the bathroom cabinet.' He stroked the claw-marks tenderly. 'She didn't like us opening it.'

Greenlaw gave a hoarse bray of laughter. The woman still said nothing, watching Thane open the envelope and tip out its contents. There were three bank-books in different names, a passport, a wad of banknotes which he didn't bother to count, and a number of folded papers.

'You'll get a receipt for all of these,' he said mildly, working his way through the collection. One of the papers made him raise his eyebrows in surprise. He whistled softly and glanced at the couple. 'This is something I didn't know.'

'That we're man and wife?' Greenlaw shrugged. 'It kept things in the family—Ed was her brother.'

'I'm sorry.' Thane said it absently. Greta Rodell showed no particular signs of mourning at the loss, only the same bitter, continued disgust at her situation. He ignored them again, finished the collection, and turned to the neat clip of report-sheets which were also waiting. The silence in the room was complete as he read them through, the rustle as he turned each page loud in its clarity. At last, finished, he pushed the clip aside.

'Three of you and Frank Humbie,' he said unemotionally. 'Well, you had a good run while it lasted.'

'While what lasted?' Greta Rodell spoke for the first time, her voice like ice.

'Theft, fraud, evasion of duty——'

She didn't bother to wait until he completed the catalogue. 'These are only words. Have you proof, Chief Inspector?'

'Greta . . .' Greenlaw gave a wry shake of his head. 'After tonight that sort of thing's pretty much a waste of time.'

He turned towards Thane. 'And then there was last night too, wasn't there? How are you going to explain away that little episode, Chief Inspector?'

Thane sat back in his chair, arms folded. 'Moss and I accompanied a Customs and Excise Department surveyor in an authorized entry and search. We acted as witnesses while he drew samples from whisky stock. Is that what you mean?'

'Is it hell!' Greenlaw's nerve was unshaken. 'You know what I'm talking about, Thane. We thought we'd been raided by kids—but it was you, wasn't it? You smashed up those whisky casks in the warehouse. Do you think you can get away with a rampage like that?'

'Smashed casks?' Thane blinked. 'Phil, do you know anything about this?'

Moss showed a solemn, wooden face. 'We entered with keys and I locked up afterwards. John Kelso can confirm it.'

'Which takes care of everything,' grimaced Greenlaw bitterly. He looked down at the handcuffs on his wrists. 'Do I need these now?'

'Mac . . .' Thane nodded, and MacLeod freed the man's wrists. Greta Rodell watched for a moment then crossed her legs, opened her handbag, and deliberately lit a cigarette.

'Thanks.' Greenlaw massaged each wrist in turn and gave a sigh of relief. 'What happens now?'

'Don't you know?' Colin Thane pursed his lips for a moment. 'We did something else last night—we got young Dalziel's body out of Flanders Moss.'

Greta Rodell shrugged. 'What was it? Suicide?'

'You know better than that—both of you.' Thane's voice held a hard and menacing persistence. 'He was murdered —in the same way as Jean Humbie.'

Greenlaw stirred and said carefully, 'We've a right to ask for a lawyer.'

'You have,' agreed Thane grimly. 'And you'll get one— but not yet.' He tore a sheet of paper from his desk pad, scribbled on it briefly, then nodded towards Moss. 'Phil, telephone MacMaster and check on this, will you?'

Moss took the note, glanced at it, and gave a nod of understanding. He went out of the room without a word.

'Trying to worry us, Chief Inspector?' Greta Rodell gave a cold mockery of a smile as the door closed. 'If you're so sure of your facts shouldn't you be getting round to cautioning and charging us?'

'That's coming.' Thane cut her short and leaned forward, hard-eyed. 'There were four in this at the start. But now there are only two—you and Greenlaw.' He saw the brief, startled glance that passed between the couple and nodded. 'Frank Humbie's dead. He hanged himself—he couldn't take any more, and you know why.'

'Do we?' Greta Rodell mashed out her cigarette on the desk ashtray and regarded him steadily. 'I don't know what this is about—even if I did, you'd better remember that husband and wife can't be forced to give evidence against one another.' Her mouth formed a thin, hard line for a moment. 'Maybe Humbie killed Dalziel. Supposing it happened that Ed killed Humbie's wife—just don't try to involve us. Remember, it was Humbie and Dalziel who broke into the office——'

'We proved that was a lie a while back,' rapped Thane. 'Hasn't it occurred to you that Humbie could have left a suicide note?'

'I don't think he did,' she said coolly. 'If you had one——'

'Greta!' Greenlaw jerked forward and started to get to his feet. Sergeant MacLeod pushed him down again.

Her blonde head shook disapprovingly. 'Don't be stupid, George. They're bumbling around the edges, nothing more.'

'Do you think so, Greenlaw?' Thane pointed a sudden forefinger at the man. 'How would you explain Frank Humbie getting home half an hour before your safe-raiders were seen making their getaway?'

'So he went off early,' answered Greenlaw sullenly. He shifted uneasily in his chair. 'I'd like a cigarette.'

Thane shrugged. 'Ask your wife.'

She gave Greenlaw both cigarette and light. Then she closed her handbag again and sat motionless as before.

'It's time for the truth,' Thane told them with a trace of weary anger. He tapped the report sheets on his desk. 'Greta, your brother lived in a boarding house. On the night of the robbery he came in around 1.30 a.m. But on Thursday night, when Jean Humbie was murdered, three

179

people saw him arrive back at ten o'clock. He'd been drinking heavily—but what matters is that, being at the boarding house, he couldn't get out to Jean Humbie's flat before she died.'

'We've got our own alibi,' said Greenlaw with almost desperate speed. 'Greta and I were together—at my place.'

'On both nights?' Thane grunted, then looked past them as the office door opened and Phil Moss returned.

'I contacted MacMaster,' reported his second-in-command briefly. 'He says he can do it.' Then, looking almost cheerful for once, he took up a position by the window.

Thane's voice changed to a soft, deadly purr. 'Greenlaw, empty your pockets.'

'Why?' protested the Glen Ault boss.

'Mac——'

Sergeant MacLeod did it for him with scant ceremony. Wallet and keys, handkerchief, a pair of driving glasses, a penknife—the pile grew. 'That's all, sir,' said MacLeod at last.

Thane picked up the penknife and pushed the rest to one side. The knife had one well-worn cutting blade and another shaped as a combination opener and screwdriver. He held it lightly between his fingers, turning it over.

'I'll tell you what I think happened,' he said quietly. 'Young Dalziel was going to contact the Excise Department. He'd stumbled across some evidence when he tried to help out while Greta was off sick . . . that was before he could be told to keep his nose out of her work. He tried to find out more, and he thought Humbie was a friend. But the moment he tried to quiz Humbie about whisky deliveries you were told. He had to be killed, with Humbie taking a housebreaking rap to cover things up.' Thane put down the knife. 'Somebody was hidden in the delivery van all right when Humbie brought it to the warehouse. But Dalziel was already dead by then—because when Humbie met Dalziel that evening it was easy enough to lure him out to where the rest of you were waiting.

'You gave Humbie the robbery alibi—because while that was going on he was dumping Dalziel's body out in Flanders Moss. But your timing was wrong. What happened? Did the safe take longer to force than you'd expected?'

180

Greenlaw was staring at him, his eyes showing the mounting strain. But he said nothing.

Thane shrugged. 'Anyway, Humbie stuck to the timetable you'd arranged and got home too soon. If he'd left it for another half-hour or so things might have been different. But he thought the robbery was over, that you'd already left Dalziel's penknife and the cashbox in that stolen car.' He looked down at his desk for a moment. 'And now we've got your penknife, Greenlaw. Strange, isn't it?' He nodded towards Moss. 'Let's see what's in that handbag, Phil.'

Greta Rodell clung to her bag for a moment then snarled and let Moss take it. He dumped the contents on the desk —lipstick and paper tissues, a money purse, compact, keys, the cigarettes and lighter.

'Nothing there.' Thane shook his head in mild disappointment. 'Now let's talk about Jean Humbie. She needed help'—a brief shadow crossed his face—'and she didn't get it here. We didn't believe her. So once she'd found out a little more she came to you, Greenlaw. Didn't she?'

'I don't have to answer.' The man switched his gaze to a spot a foot above Thane's head.

'Jean Humbie came to you or Greta, one or other. She said she had proof her husband hadn't been in the robbery—and that meant she had to be silenced or the whole set-up was ruined. She was told to go straight home and leave the rest to you. Only she didn't—she was still trying to find out who'd been with Frank in that car. She thought it was Barbara MacPhail. And while she was trying to locate Barbara, there were two people waiting at Gradient Terrace, waiting to kill her. That's how it was—wasn't it, Greta?'

'How would I know?' she countered harshly. 'I thought it was a brunette who was seen at the flats.'

'It was,' agreed Thane calmly. 'And it was a brunette who was with Humbie on the night before. But one of my d.c.s. spoke to a hairdresser named Ballini—your hairdresser. According to Ballini you bought a dark wig from him a couple of months back. A party wig, he called it. They're common enough—but the strange thing is that we couldn't find it in your house.'

'I threw it out weeks ago,' snapped the woman.

'Perhaps,' said Thane steadily, relentlessly. 'But there's some burnt ash in the rubbish bin in your backyard. The Scientific Bureau can do quite a lot with it. Just as they can do plenty with this . . .' He picked up the penknife again and swung his gaze towards Greenlaw. 'The blade used to loosen the back-plate on Humbie's TV set left a clear impression. If this knife matches up . . .' He didn't bother to finish. His smile was a mere stretching of muscles. 'Greenlaw, put your hands on the desk, palms down.'

The dead exhaustion of despair in his eyes, the man obeyed.

'You too, Greta.'

She glared at him then slammed them down on the wood.

'Keep them there, and listen. I saw Yuill's hands before I left Flanders Moss. Now I've seen yours. The post-mortem reports on both Dalziel and Jean Humbie spoke of small bruises around their faces—bruises caused by fingers gripping hard while they kept the mouth and nose from getting air.

'But there was something else. Almost every one of these little indentation bruises also showed a tiny, close to microscopic, skin haemorrhage at one edge. Somebody's nails caused them . . . sharp nails. Not Ed Yuill's. His were broken, and chewed, engrained with dirt. Yours are short, Greenlaw. They could have been cut since then, but fingernails are unusual things. They're called keratin tissues, they even grow for a spell after death—and they grow at almost exactly one eighth of an inch per month. I needed one more fact—that was why Moss went out. A forensic expert can look at your nails and tell me how long it is since they saw a file or scissors.

'But we don't need a professor to look at yours, Greta, do we?'

She drew her hands back from the desk and sat with her fists clenched in her lap.

'Prove it,' she invited bitterly.

Thane nodded. 'We will. There's the car, for instance—the car that took you and Humbie out to Flanders Moss. Dalziel's body was in the trunk—we've got hair and fibre traces to establish that. We've got little flecks of mud from the underside, mud from Flanders Moss. We've tyre tracks that match.'

Greenlaw took a long, shuddering breath. 'Greta, I told you——' he said hopelessly.

'Be quiet.' She took command, no hesitation in her manner, the words forcing out from between her teeth. 'We demand legal representation—and for the rest, I've told you. Prove it.'

'In court.' There was neither pity nor triumph on Thane's face, only a momentary disgust. 'You used Humbie to lure young Dalziel and dump his body. You left Greenlaw and Yuill to fake the break-in. You took Greenlaw with you to Gradient Terrace—but you're the one I really want, Greta. You killed two people, shut them off from life with your bare hands. What kind of woman does that make you?'

There were gaps between what he knew and what he could only guess. But that was the reality of murder investigation, the harsh contrast to the wishful ideal of neatly packaged evidence. But he had enough—and somehow, looking at Greenlaw, he knew he'd have more.

'Phil, take them down. Formal caution and charge for now.'

Moss steered the man and woman out, with MacLeod in close attendance. He was gone roughly quarter of an hour and when he returned he found Thane relaxed back in the big leather chair, a cigarette burning between his lips.

'Well, Phil?'

'It's over,' agreed Phil Moss. 'It's over and they know it.' He put a pill on the tip of his tongue and flipped it back. He swallowed, then, gradually, a grin crinkled across his face. 'There was a telephone message for you earlier on —I got it. Here.' The piece of paper he hauled from one pocket was badly crumpled. He smoothed it out and passed it over.

Thane glanced at the message, looked again, and sat bolt upright.

'You've seen this?'

'I spoke to him.' Moss chuckled.

John Kelso had been blandly formal. Her Majesty's

Customs and Excise would be grateful for an early statement of the quantity of dutiable spirit accidentally destroyed by Chief Inspector Colin Thane during a visit to the Glen Ault Whisky Liqueur Company's premises. Once received, a reckoning of responsibility could be made.

'What did you tell him?'

'Well . . .' Moss beamed cheerfully. 'I said that I didn't know what the devil he was blethering about and that neither did you.' He winked. 'Mind you, there's too much juvenile delinquency around here. It's time we did something about it.'

'We will,' promised Thane. 'Right now.'

He got up, reached for his hat, and thumbed towards the door. 'Come on. I phoned Mary. We're having steak and chips—and to hell with your ulcer for once.'

'No liqueurs?' queried Moss.

Thane shook his head—and shoved Moss on his way.